THE WHO GIRL
RESET THE
CYBERWORLD
A NOVEL

CLIFF RATZA

THE GIRL WHO RESET THE CYBERWORLD

A NOVEL

CLIFF RATZA

Published by Lightning Brain Press
1. Fantasy (General)
2. Science

The Girl Who Reset the Cyberworld, our second book in the *Reset Series*, starts where the first one ended: NASA has successfully launched in December 2170 the first Manned Mission to Mars. And its success, for which Electra contributed much, leads to NASA's assigning her so many additional projects she develops a stress-related medical issue that she keeps hidden.

The most pressure-packed project, Climate Change, takes her to Australia for exploring the Great Barrier Reef, to Africa's Danakil Depression (the hottest place on the planet) in search of new forms of life, and to mid-America for chasing storms. Danger awaits in all these locations as well as all places every project takes her. Only Electra's wits, assisted by Indira's new androids, keep her safe.

Events in her clone children's personal worlds add pressure for Electra to help them find new careers. She succeeds immediately for Eve and Nari, but doesn't need to for Alonzo until he suffers a Navy SEAL career-ending accident when leading a mission to extract a Bigger-Bro dissident from Beijing. Electra turns the catastrophe into careers for Alonzo and the dissident; they will work for her.

And, of course, the unpredictable storms sweeping Washington sweep Electra into multiple battles that give her new adversaries. Kinslinger becomes president again. Middle East Terrorists destroy Electra's androids, and a DC military coup terminates Kinslinger, putting the Joint Chiefs of Staff in control of the government. The pressure on Electra exceeds what even she can handle. It actually floors her, and Renee doesn't know how to get her up and back in action. An iconic line from Indira ends this novel:

"Renee, Electra needs your help. Place her carefully on the carpet, then settle down, sit still, and listen to me…"

This novel extends the theme linking all Lightning Brain series books, which should resonate with all of us: no matter how exceptional the person, anyone can become a victim in a world that can't handle the truth, and each of us must handle the complexities of being "merely human," while applying our talents to whatever we want and developing our skills to whatever level suits us best by following an optimistic, pragmatic philosophy.

Readers should enjoy the book on whatever level they wish:

- Gripping action-packed thriller
- Glimpses into a plausible near-term future
- Insights for dealing with the "human condition"
- Illustrative worldview philosophy
- Fast-paced, suspense-filled emotive narrative and imagery
- Introduction to topics every reader wants to know
- Interesting talking points going beyond sound-bites

So, get ready to enjoy what you are about to read as new characters and villains join with the old as Electra, her clone children, and extended family confront whatever life sends their way.

Thank you for following their spellbinding journey.

Main Characters

Protagonist
Electra Kirchner (previously known as the Irani-Alisha-Electra trio and now the Electra-Alisha duo. Alisha is her official middle name as well as her alter-ego's).

Supporting Main Characters
Indira (the Singularity) and Jason (the sub-Singularity). Electra's AI-empowered neural network software created Indira, the self-aware Singularity, over twenty years ago, who in turn created Jason. Both continue evolving.

Evita (Eve) Cortez. Electra's favorite clone child.

Renee, the Rainforest Girl, brought back from the Amazon Rainforest by Electra, who names her Renee.

Supporting Secondary Characters
Alonzo Cortez. Eve's identical twin clone brother.
Monet Banda. Alonzo's Zimbabwean co-friend.
Nari and Nila Bose. Another set of Electra's identical twin clones. The two sets of "orphan" twins, unaware of being clones, had been raised by Su-Lin Song Chou.
Sanjay Kumar. Nila's Oriental Indian husband. They live in Mumbai.
China Lieu. Chinese female extracted from China to assist Electra's consulting business.

Professor Steven Plannert. Professor at George Washington University (GWU) and head of its Environmental Scanning Committee.

Minor Characters

Indy-M and Jason-M. Androids. Lifelike robots loaded with Indira's advanced neural-net software.

Odell Boyken. Electra's minority business partner in CFS Holistic Healthcare.

Amahl and Zara Karim. A brother-sister pair of adolescents Irani rescued while on a mission to Isilabad.

Xinqian (Xing) Hung. "Gang of Three Plus One" leader reporting to the "Bigger Brother Conspiracy," comprised of only four countries: China, Russia, Isilabad, and the United States.

Newton (Newt) Kinslinger. President of the United States. Also member of "Bigger Brother Conspiracy."

Britt Starling. Commander of NASA's first Manned Mission to Mars.

Boomer Gowon. Mars Mission First Officer reporting to Commander Starling.

Miles and Shanna Drummond. A black brother-sister pair living in Austin, TX and being raised by single-parent father (Marcel) - a studio musician.

Darla Tinibu. Zimbabwean "power broker" whom Monet works for.

Jiang (Jan) Brewer and Wen (Wendy) Tong. Sociopolitical analysts/consultants living in Beijing and reporting to Eve.

Rich (RT) Tabasko, Parson (PH) Holsum, and Lucian (Mr. LP) Perteau. Electra's entrepreneurial-minded business partners.

Zoltan Sultani. Military/DOD liaison for covert joint NASA projects.

General Horatio Magnus Goodman. Leading candidate for Chairman Joint Chiefs of Staff.

Dedication

I am eternally grateful to my parents, Clyde and Betty Ratza, for all they gave and did for me. Mother was reader par excellence, and I believe she would have enjoyed reading and sharing my novels with Father, so I always begin book dedications by mentioning my "Royal Pair."

And I thank my sister, Claudia, for sharing and showing me the beauty of prose and poetry. Thanks also to John Kane and his entire Prime Solutions marketing team. Their collective efforts bring to life Electra and her multiple worlds.

I also dedicate *The Girl Who Reset the Cyberworld* to readers looking for a continuing action-adventure saga that shows a condition all of us share: we are always resetting ourselves to fit into the world we see. Think of a reset as a course correction we make to reach the goals we set, and Electra, her multiple personalities, and friends are constantly correcting their intentions.

A poem from Indira titled "Course Correction" provides insights you might like as you prepare for what may come.

Course Correction

Don't labor resetting the greats of the past.
It's the errand of fools who refusing to see,
That in now-plowed terrain there's no mystery,
A thin-veneer layer that never will last.

Venture forth on a course that hasn't been said.
Look outside then in for a coming that's real,
Unite reason and passion for a vision you feel,
Care not for a judgment it's your word instead.

Long after you're gone let others decide.
Whether words that you spoke had the power to stay,
Revealing directions that sail away,
And place you with those who will always abide.

I hope my latest novel keeps you fully engaged to the very end as it shows our characters resetting themselves to do their best. Thank you for following their journey.

Contents

Chapter 1
December 2168

"Mars Mission – Second Reset"

Although viewing from the comfort of her workstation at the Washington DC-area house bequeathed to her by Jonathan Segal, Electra expected the Mission Director's words would stir her the same as if she were sitting in NASA's main mission control room.

"Welcome back after a one-week R&R break from our Mars Mission journey. You are part of mankind's second step to the stars and beyond. Mankind took the first step when landing on the Moon 200 years ago. And tomorrow, we take the second when we launch our Starship from its lunar docking station. Two weeks ago, we guided it to the docking station and since then, Commander Britt Starling and First Officer Boomer Gowon have readied the ship and its five-person astronaut crew for the three-month trip to a Martian landing where they will spend six months exploring while putting in place the first pieces of NASA's Martian base.

"Some of you mission controllers are still working remotely, but most have returned to our Houston-area location. And no matter where you are, please sleep well so you are logged in at 6 a.m. Monday, December 18th–that's in four days–and ready for the second reset of our Martian Mission clock. The Starship crew depends on me, and I depend on you to keep them healthy and safe during the outward-bound trek, the history-making stay on Mars, and the triumphant return to planet Earth. Our collective assignment is to make it so. I will not fail; you will not fail; and as a team, we shall succeed as we reach for the stars. This is your Mission Director signing off."

Renee waited for Electra to close a window on her workstation before asking,

"When do we leave for Houston?"

"Tomorrow morning, which will give me plenty of time to prep for onsite monitoring using our Aphrodite control software. And you have permission to be at my side. Have you studied the diagrams the Mission Director sent me a couple of days ago?"

"Could you show them again?"

"Sure. Slide your chair closer so you can see them when I bring 'em up on my screen."

The first one flashed fifteen seconds later.

Diagram One

NASA Solar System Exploration Primer
Steps to the Stars

The Steps:
1. Low-Earth Orbits
2. Lunar Exploration and Colonization
3. Explorations of Inner Planets (Mercury Venus Mars); Missions to Mars
4. Explorations and Missions to Asteroids
5. Construction of Permanent Habitats Orbiting the Sun, Mars, and Exoplanet Colonies
6. Explorations and Missions to Outer Planets (Jupiter Saturn Uranus Neptune Pluto)

Cosmological Constraints:
1. Enormous Distances
2. Speed of Light
3. Resource Availability

Scientific Challenges
1. Travel dictated by Newtonian (Classical) Physics Quantum Fields and Wormholes Unavailable
2. Spacecraft paths must utilize multiple Gravitational Fields to Conserve Fuel

Technological Challenges
1. Space Elevator to Moon for Maximizing Delivery Payload (People, Supplies)
2. Lunar Base Construction using Lunar Resources
3. Design of Viable Spacecraft for Interplanetary Journey and Construction of Lunar Base

Physiological Challenges
1. Impact of Extended Weightlessness on the Human Body
2. Damage caused by Extended Exposure to Radiation
3. Psychological Effects caused by Isolation

Current Status
Two-Stage Space Elevator Completed
First Stage:
• Docking Station in Geostationary Equatorial Orbit (32 Km Radius)
• Cable made of Graphene-Carbon Nanotubules Connects Docking Station to Earth Station (Propulsion/Fuel System remains on Earth)

Second Stage:
• Another Docking Station in Geostationary Lunar Orbit
• Cable Connects to Lunar Base

Lunar and Martian Rovers perfected as well as Lunar and Martian Aero-Drones

Martian Spaceship Built and Tested

- Radiation Exposure Acceptable: Space Medicine Safe and Effective
- Utilizes Long-Duration Multi Nuclear-Solar-Chemical-Ion Power Sources that Generate Greater Impulse Velocity
- Robots Tested Initial Flights
- AI-Empowered Software for Controlling Spacecraft and Robots is Adequate and Newer Releases Expected
- Suspension Pods and Escape Pods Viable when controlled by AI-Empowered Software

NASA's Martian Mission Plan
1. Utilize Humans and Robots
2. Explore the Surface to find Raw Materials and Evidence of Life
3. Construct Martian Base
4. Construct Docking Station and Martian Elevator
5. Collect Data to assess Additional Mission Parameters

Electra gave Renee a minute to read it before saying,

"Here we see all the steps and challenges NASA has considered while planning the Mars Mission. Lots of complexity and difficulty in them, but notice what it says at the very end – we're ready to send our astronauts to Mars. They'll do what's needed to prepare for future missions."

"Now, here's the second diagram."

Diagram Two
Getting to Mars

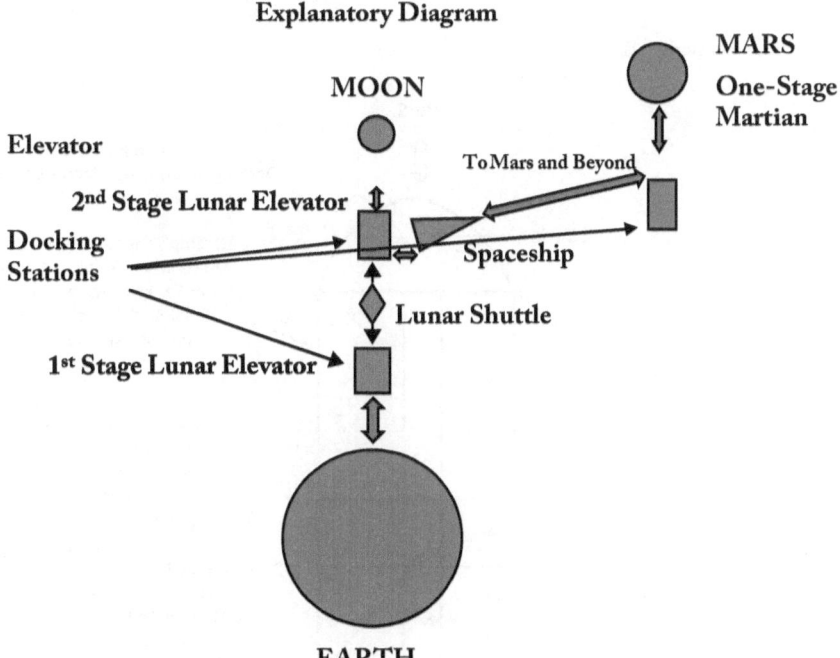

Explanatory Diagram

Electra launched into an explanation only seconds after it appeared.

"The Starship's already at the lunar docking station. NASA already has an operational two-stage lunar elevator, which is an engineering marvel all by itself. It makes transferring vast amounts of supplies to and from Earth and NASA's lunar colony cost-effective, while geosynchronous orbits keep the docking stations fixed relative to what they're rotating around so the cable between them and their base maintains a vertical orientation.

"And launching the Starship from the docking station using boosters puts all the energy from the fuel into accelerating it toward Mars. There's no gravity well to climb out of, and after the Starship reaches cruising velocity, the boosters detach before returning to the docking station."

Electra waited for Renee's thoughts to catch up before continuing. "And here's the final one."

Diagram Three
STARSHIP DESIGN

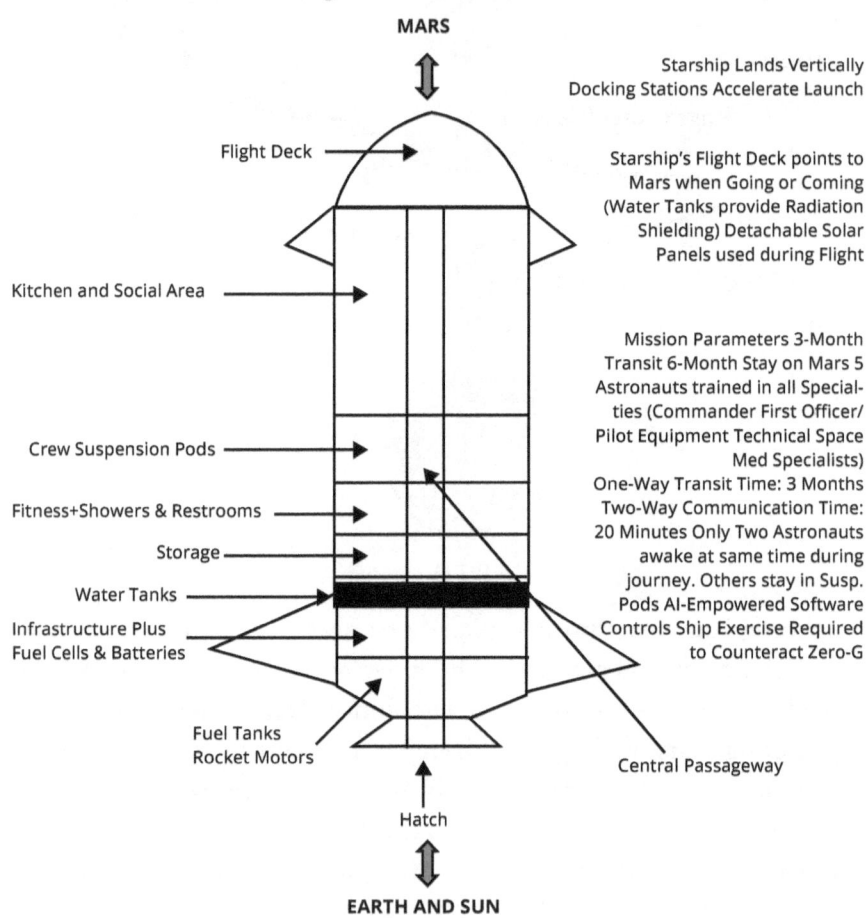

Starship Dimensions: 10 Meter Diameter
100 Meter Length

MARS

Starship Lands Vertically
Docking Stations Accelerate Launch

Flight Deck

Starship's Flight Deck points to
Mars when Going or Coming
(Water Tanks provide Radiation
Shielding) Detachable Solar
Panels used during Flight

Kitchen and Social Area

Mission Parameters 3-Month
Transit 6-Month Stay on Mars 5
Astronauts trained in all Special-
ties (Commander First Officer/
Pilot Equipment Technical Space
Med Specialists)

Crew Suspension Pods

One-Way Transit Time: 3 Months
Two-Way Communication Time:

Fitness+Showers & Restrooms

20 Minutes Only Two Astronauts
awake at same time during

Storage

journey. Others stay in Susp.

Water Tanks

Pods AI-Empowered Software

Infrastructure Plus
Fuel Cells & Batteries

Controls Ship Exercise Required
to Counteract Zero-G

Fuel Tanks
Rocket Motors

Central Passageway

Hatch

EARTH AND SUN

Electra spoke as soon as it appeared.

"The spaceship's designed to land vertically on Mars, and when flying to or from Earth it always points to Mars so the water tanks shield the crew from solar radiation. Only two of the crew are awake at the same time. The others stay in their suspension pods to reduce oxygen and food consumption. Future Mars missions will have joint human and robotic crews for infrastructure and orbital station construction, but not on the first. This one has a five-astronaut crew for exploration and preparation for the next flight."

Electra saw a question coming, so she paused to hear it.

"What's infrastructure?"

"The support systems that keep something running. For example, a city needs water, power, food, transportation, and waste removal systems. A Martian colony must use available Martian energy, oxygen, water, and building materials if it wants to be self-sufficient. NASA will transfer the infrastructure technology it engineered for its lunar colony. 3-D printing using the crumbly surface material, which is called regolith, Martian farming, and solar panels will play major roles in future missions, but not on this one."

Electra stopped for Renee to say something, which she did after blinking a couple of times.

"It's awesome how much goes into going to Mars."

"It is, and like the Mission Director says, colonizing Mars is our first step for taking our civilization into outer space. But no matter how complex any project is, we take it one step at a time, just like when living your life."

Renee gazed into the distance before saying,

"I'm not sure I could without you."

Electra pulled her back and then said,

"Sure you would. You're smart and resilient, which are the hallmarks of a survivor. Both of us are, and we help each other. Now let's get a good night's sleep because we want to be ready for tomorrow…"

Chapter 2
December 2168

"A Tale of Two Climates"

Monsoon-like rains that had been sweeping across the Houston area continued unabated, washing away Electra's initial travel plans. She and Renee had to fly into the sprawling Dallas Fort Worth airport and rent an SUV to reach Houston. The rental counter agent loaned her a roadmap atlas she used to plot her route. Renee glanced over her shoulder while she talked to herself.

Getting there's easy. I-45 gets me Houston, and Boomer told me Johnson Space Center is twenty miles more south than east via the Gulf Freeway or Galveston Road. He took me last year on a tour of the city's central part, showing me Rice and University of Houston campuses plus the Med Center cluster of hospitals, all this just south of downtown. And he drove me west on Memorial Drive from downtown all the way to the I-610 loop, passing through Memorial Park, which is the place for runners to go. He said Allen Parkway, which runs along Buffalo Bayou, goes there too, so now I know a couple of ways to get around if rainstorms get in the way...

Electra used her cell phone to check in with the Mission Director after she checked into a hotel six hours later near NASA. His calm voice accompanied his no-nonsense instructions.

"Please be at Mission Control tomorrow at 9 a.m. for the final briefing. And no matter what the climate is like here, the docking station climate is always launch ready..."

News coverage had already turned Commander Starling and First Officer Gowon into international celebrities because of their photogenic and articulate personas, and the press turned NASA's and India's launches into a space race to Mars. A popular nightly news commentator's summary the night before said what people wanted to hear.

"NASA's Starship launch from its lunar docking station might not have the sound and fury of a launch from Earth, but the technology on display dwarfs what you'll see when India launches its unmanned rover on Christmas Eve. I urge each of you to go online after the broadcast and read what I've posted about the Starship and docking station. Then you'll know why NASA rocket scientists are from the best STEM schools."

Renee did so. Electra watched over her shoulder but said nothing, waiting for Renee's words.

"Hey, thanks to you, I know all this. I'm ready for tomorrow."

"Me too. Now let's get a good night's sleep so we're good to go no matter what comes our way."

Electra and Renee, along with all other critical personnel, splashed their way on time the next morning to Mission Control. Little was said because they had been practicing for weeks, but the tension in the room escalated as the digital clock counted down to zero and the primary wall monitor displayed the silent liftoff.

Everyone watched in awe as fingers of flame erupted from the boosters, instantly accelerating the Starship. The image shifted to an inboard camera as the flames became faint. Close-ups of Starling and Gowon, now in control, filled the screen, and their voices filled Mission Control.

"All readings in green zones… approaching booster separation velocity…"

An outboard camera cut in fifteen seconds later and showed the Starship free and clear as Starling's words punctuated the image seen around the world.

"We're on our way… will switch to automatic control as soon as–"

A total blackout in Mission Control terminated the transmission. No one moved until emergency power kicked in fifteen seconds later, supplying just enough for exit lights and the Director's voice.

"All critical controllers, go to your remote stations and log in when you arrive. I am activating Contingency A."

The Director was nowhere to be seen as the controllers stumbled out before security guards herded them together. The lead guard's voice boomed over the rain-soaked chaos.

"A sinkhole swallowed our power supply. We're taking the Director to a backup location and—" Several panicky voices interrupted.

"What about the Starship?... Is the crew OK?"

"The Director will be the first to know. Now please get to your remote stations…"

After she and Renee had run to the SUV, Electra sat for a moment to study the Houston-area map she had stored in her brain. Satisfied that she had several options for reaching its major airport located twenty miles north of the city's center, the pair drove away to check out of the hotel after changing their return flight to DC.

The wind and rain had eased, but flooded streets forced Electra to change routes as soon as they reached downtown Houston. She detoured west on Memorial Drive, which Buffalo Bayou snaked along. Renee said nothing but peered intently at the landscape. She screamed a second before Electra drove into a sinkhole that opened before her eyes.

The drop stunned Electra, whose head had slammed into the windshield, but not Renee. She leaped out into knee-deep water and struggled to the driver-side door. She tore it open and then dragged out Electra, who could now talk.

"I didn't spot the road collapsing soon enough. We better get to someplace safe and come back later for our gear."

Renee led the way but once out of the sinkhole, they were not out of danger. Flooding had burst Buffalo Bayou's banks; muddy water swirled all about. The lightning brain elevated to find an escape route, but Renee's instincts activated even faster. She grabbed Electra's hand, and they ran toward the trees about two hundred yards away in Memorial Park. Then she helped Electra climb high enough to avoid the waters rushing below. They sat clutching tree limbs long enough to catch their breath before Electra could speak.

"You picked the best spot. How'd you know?"

"Amazon River flooding much worse than this. You can't outrun the water, but if you climb high enough, you survive."

Electra was about to answer, but her vibrating cell phone changed her focus. She fished it out and then connected.

"This is Electra. Who am I speaking to?"

"Your Mission Director. Where are you?"

"Renee and I are high enough in a tree to keep sort of dry. Any chance your security guards can rescue us."

"Hold on... let me locate you on GPS." His calm voice came back a minute later.

"We see your GPS location. Stay put and they'll get you in about an hour..."

Security did that and more by retrieving gear before expediting Electra's and Renee's return to DC. They needed one day to recover before Electra logged in remotely to Mission Control, listening to the Director's daily briefing.

"I am now at our Australian Contingency A Control Center where some of the critical controllers have joined me. The others who are working remotely may do so unless onsite presence is required. And the latest transmission shows onboard conditions are normal, and the Starship needs no course correction. Our public relations team will provide daily videos for news media broadcasts. I will contact each critical controller according to the existing schedule, and each one should contact me if you detect an issue. Please carry on."

Electra and Renee spent the day catching up and carrying on before watching the evening news. She let Renee add to the broadcast.

"Wow, this is just like watching a space movie. From what Commander Starling said, she and Boomer will alternate every two days between suspension pod rest and Starship control. And they'll show us what it's like inside and out."

Turning to Electra, she waited for her to fill in what she might have missed.

"And since I'm the communications controller, I'm the first to get Aphrodite's data stream, so I'll share with you what no one else sees or hears."

"I like that, and can I go watch a movie?"

"Sure, and how about I join you?"

Renee liked that idea, and when she went to sleep afterward, Electra invoked Indira's GUI, this time waiting for Indira to start the discussion.

"The power outage affected NASA's mere mortals located near Houston, but I always have contingency plans. I intercepted Starship transmissions received elsewhere, so do not worry. The Starship crew as well as Aphrodite software are on course. But please summarize what happened during your return to DC?"

Indira listened before speaking when Electra had finished.

"You are fortunate to have Renee whenever you are too far away for me to observe, but for the journey to Mars, you can work remotely or in Australia because Aphrodite will report to me first, and then to you. Of course, your Mission Director does not know about the editing I do. And I recommend you reconnect remotely with Mission Control before contacting me again. Do you have any final questions?"

"No."

"Excellent, so carry on, as will I."

After Indira's GUI disappeared, Electra powered down her workstation and went to bed. A final thought drifted in as she drifted to sleep.

Renee's early years in the Amazon rainforest have given her instinctive survival skills that come to her even faster than what the lightning brain can think of in those extraordinary events she's experienced before and vice versa. I can't predict when either kind might occur, but keeping Renee close will keep both of us safe. That's an all-purpose contingency plan Indira has already told me about, and now I know how effective it is. That's one less thing to fret about.

Electra slept worry-free that night.

Chapter 3
December 2168

"A Catastrophic Christmas"

People around the globe reserved time on December 24th to watch India's unmanned launch of its Martian rover. Renee asked Electra an hour before to bring up on her monitor one of the NASA diagrams that would give her facts about Mars that India's rover would investigate further. Renee studied it until the live coverage started late that afternoon.

Martian Living Conditions

Difficult for Humans:
- Rarified Atmosphere 95% Carbon Dioxide Stirred by Toxic Dust Storms containing electrostatic particles that Coat Everything. Dust Diminishes Solar Panel Array Effectiveness. Next four most abundant gases are Argon, Nitrogen, Oxygen and Carbon Monoxide.
- Mars ground level atmospheric pressure: 0.095 psi. Earth sea level atmospheric pressure: 14.7 psi.
- No Atmospheric or Magnetic Field Shielding From Constant Cosmic and Solar Ray Bombardment.
- Colder than Antarctica.
- Frozen Water at the Poles. Amount and Location of Underground Water Still Being Researched.

- Terraforming for Food or Fuel is Challenging.
- Need Electric Batteries or Mini-Nuclear Reactors for Power.
- Will need Astro and Robonauts to assist Humans.

Facts About Mars:
- Fourth Planet From the Sun (Mercury Venus Earth Mars).
- Same age as Earth (4.5 Billion Years).
- Distance from Sun: 141.5 Million Miles. Earth's Distance: 94 Million Miles.
- Length of Year: 687 Earth-Days. Length of Day: Same as Earth's.
- Mars Radius: 2100 miles (Half That of Earth's). Mars Gravity: 37% That of Earth's.
- Rotational direction about its Axis: Same as Earth's.
- Has Two Moons Orbiting at Height of 3700 Miles Above Martian Surface. Earth's Moon Orbiting at Height of 235,000 Miles.

The pair sat side by side as the network connected to the Indian announcer.

"Unlike the European Space Agency, India prefers having its own missions instead of piggybacking on NASA's. The only other countries to have their own missions are Russia and China. And unlike them, we and NASA share data. And let us now listen to our Mission Control."

"Three, two, one, liftoff." Televisions everywhere showed the rocket soaring skyward, looking like one from a previous NASA generation. It gained velocity as its fiery image shrank before a jet camera cut in.

No words accompanied the image; live video said it all.

But that changed abruptly a minute later when the rocket blew up, scattering flaming chunks in all directions. The video switched to India's Mission Control. Everyone stared mutely at the large monitor now displaying glowing debris falling toward the ocean. Hesitant words finally came out.

"There has been some sort of malfunction. We will continue our broadcast when we know more." The local network switched to its team of commentators, who were equally stunned.

"This is a catastrophe of the first magnitude. We won't speculate until we hear something from our NASA experts…"

Electra turned off the broadcast before hugging Renee, who had burst into tears. She sobbed for a minute before saying,

"I don't wanna go to church tonight. Can we stay home and talk?"

"I feel the same way, so when you feel a bit better, we'll have supper and then chat about whatever you wish."

Electra didn't try to make supper anything other than a perfunctory affair, waiting until she and Renee settled on the family room sofa before asking what she'd like to talk about.

"I never believed my tribe's medicine man when he spoke about spirits above Earth who look out for us. If there was one, why would it let the rocket blow up, especially on Christmas Eve?"

"You asked a question no one can answer."

"Do you believe in Christmas?"

"It doesn't matter what I believe. What matters is what you believe. Do you think it's true?"

"I asked Amahl and Zara. They don't, and Amahl doesn't believe in Allah either. Do you?"

Electra rubbed her hands together for a moment before holding Renee's while answering.

"No, I don't, but please remember that we must always respect the beliefs other people have, even if we don't agree."

Electra saw Renee struggling to say something that was bothering her, so she waited.

Renee finally stuttered,

"Bu-but death seems so grim. What happens when we're gone?"

Electra held both of Renee's hands and then said,

"What happens before we're born? Don't worry about it. Before or after, it's like an endless sleep for anyone in the states described.

Let me recite a poem my mother wrote about it. Would you like to hear it?"

Renee nodded.

'Endless Sleep

Man cannot grasp the endless sleep,
That transcends the finite brain.
It reaches to the infinite deep,
Where we ultimately remain.

And Man can never feel the place,
From where we won't awake.
For it stretches to an immeasurable place,
No disruption can ever break.

But Man shouldn't fret this final fact,
It troubles not our day.
It won't impinge on how we should act,
So do now without delay.

Share immeasurable moments with loved ones and friends,
Find while awake what never ends.'

"So, enjoy each day. And if we're with people who are celebrating their religion, we should celebrate too because they're happy, and we should be too."

Renee's somber expression began to soften.

"So, you think everyone will be happy when we go to Miss Eve's place to celebrate tomorrow?"

Electra hoped her tone would match what she was about to say.

"Well, we'll all have a fine dinner, and you and Amahl and Zara will get some gifts, so what do you think?"

It must have because it reverberated when Renee said,

"I think tomorrow will be fun…"

Amahl's boisterous laugh filtered into the dining room where Eve, Nari, and Electra chatted after the late-afternoon Christmas Day dinner. Though they couldn't hear any words, they were sure Renee and Zara were enjoying his antics, and the pause it caused let Electra summarize the topic Eve had been describing.

"You and Nari can ask Sanjay and Nila what India might do about its rocket blowing up. I'm certain there's a contingency plan."

"That'll come up during our New Year's Eve online conference call with them and our co-friend couple in Zimbabwe. Monet's Email said Alonzo will be with her. His SEAL team's got the week off."

While Nari commented further, Electra listened to herself as well.

Too bad my clone children rarely include me, but why should they? I'm considered a friend, not family. But that's OK. I have Renee...

The adults stopped talking fifteen minutes later when Amahl and his entourage trooped back into the dining room. Zara spoke first.

"Amahl's quick to pick up his latest video game, but he can't seem to beat Renee. They should choose careers that use virtual reality or remote piloting. He might–" Amahl didn't wait for his sister to finish.

"Hey, I resemble that remark. And I don't have to go to college to qualify. I bet Renee agrees. Let's hear what she thinks."

Renee's glance at Electra told her to do the talking.

"She can pilot drones better than most, and she has other career options too, but that's a topic for another time. And speaking of time, I think we're ready to say good night..."

Eve trusted Zara's selection of the New Year's Eve party that she had permission for taking Amahl, so Eve and Nari had the family room all to themselves at 11 p.m. when Nari connected to the online conversation, separate windows showing the other couples. The ongoing discussion halted for Eve.

"All siblings and their significant others are looking good, so let the words roll on as the new year rolls in..."

After the usual greetings and good-natured kidding, Eve continued.

—

"I missed holding our traditional year-end call last time, but we can make up by being extra thorough right now. And I thought maybe Nila could start."

"I'm happy to say I've made great progress treating our son's autism, thanks to early detection and India's holistic approach. I spend most of my time giving Manish all the one-on-one sensory stimulation he needs so his brain can make the connections his DNA didn't. The pediatrician told me Manny now responds like a typical one-year-old, and if he starts talking by the end of the year, I can start working again. Sanjay, why don't you say something?"

"My baba and I will be happy when she returns to our software company. We might win an Indian Space Agency contract because the rocket crash shows that India's current control software won't get us far. And speaking of crashes, NASA had a problem too, and isn't there talk about ex-President Kinslinger trashing the election results?"

Eve replied before Nari.

"That was the big topic on the news until missions to Mars took over. Maybe we should talk to Electra Kirchner. She does consulting work for NASA and might give you some pointers if she has the time. She also helps Nari and me navigate DC's consulting network, and she sure—"

Nari decided to cut in.

"I thought you made a resolution to talk less and listen more. Let's hear from someone besides you."

Monet took the cue.

"Ms. Kirchner can navigate in many worlds. She connected me last year to a Brazilian organization that helped me deal with a viral outbreak before it could become a pandemic. And she helped Alonzo too."

"Monet's got that right. The links she gave me led to a covert SEAL mission that exposed China's fake Mars Mission. Seems like Electra helps us all."

When no one picked up where Alonzo had stopped, Eve decided it was safe to do so.

"And when doing some sort of climate change research in the Amazon last year, she rescued an indigenous rainforest girl. She named her Renee, and Renee's now living with her. Near as we know, she's about the same age as Amahl and is pretty smart. Physically striking too. Maybe you'll see her sometime. Maybe next year we'll include Electra and Renee, along with Amahl and Zara on our call. And Nila can bring Manish. I'm sure it'll be a sensory-stimulating experience…"

Electra and Renee accompanied Eve when Amahl and Zara cashed in one of their Christmas gifts – a career counseling session on Friday morning of January's first week at Odell Boyken's DFS Holistic Healthcare, for which Electra was the minority owner. Always jovial and understanding of different sexual, racial, or socio-ethnic points of view, he listened to what Eve wanted.

"Zara will graduate this coming June with a B.S. in poli-sci from GWU. And she's added to that by working as an intern for me and Nari. And Amahl's ready for Junior College. Both of them tell me they want more independence. Can you give them a college and career options test that'll help us guide them?"

"We can do that online and get the results as soon as they've answered all the questions. But what about Renee? We can test her too if you want."

Renee nodded but said nothing, so Electra replied.

"Yes, please. More information is usually better than less."

The group reconvened three hours later; Odell provided the summary.

"I'm pleased to report that all three scored above average on intelligence, with Renee's being the highest. And as expected, Zara has the clearest career path, International Politics, and I can line her up with a GWU grad school admissions counselor. Amahl's scores match general business, and I think a local junior college will snap him up because he's a good enough wrestler to make its team. And why not have them live together near GWU's campus so they can look out for each other while you give them more freedom plus a car?"

Eve needed no coaxing when she said,

"That's pretty much what I thought. And you can handle getting them in?"

"I can, and you can let them pick a car and a place to live."

Odell leaned back, waiting for Electra, who didn't disappoint.

"So, what can you tell us about Renee?"

"The results tell me she's a quick study. Whatever school system she's in sure works, but she hasn't been living here long enough to know what she wants longer term. And Myers-Briggs labels her ENFP, which says she listens to her feelings and intuition, doesn't judge others, and might expect to get only what conditions allow. Does that match what you think?"

It did, butt told herself first.

I knew it. We're complete opposites. That's why we get along so well.

"Sounds like good advice, and it might change the longer she lives here."

Eve glanced at her cell phone before saying,

"Well, your counseling has been worth the time we've spent, but it's time we split for lunch. How about I call you in a month to find out what you've lined up for admissions?"

"By all means, please do. And your three students have earned a pleasant lunch, so treat them well…"

Eve trusted Amahl's culinary taste for selecting a suitable fast-food place that satisfied everyone, and he had corrected his table manners, thanks to Zara's constant prodding once they started living with Eve. Renee, on the other hand, never needed lessons. Electra surmised that she never dropped a morsel or spoke while chewing because life in the Rainforest gave no time for anything other than survival.

After lunch, Eve took Amahl and Zara home while Electra took Renee shopping to buy clothes and cosmetics using a Christmas gift certificate. As they walked through the mall, Electra let Alisha do the talking because of her grooming expertise gained in Hollywood several lifetimes ago.

"Adolescents like to pick out clothes that make them look good. Girls like to dress so other girls approve and guys notice, and the same goes for makeup and perfume. What did young Rainforest people do to get noticed?"

"It was too hot to wear much, and makeup was used for tribal markings. No one wanted to put on anything that gave off a scent because attracting bugs is bad. And young people were too busy surviving to worry about getting noticed for mating. The elders took care of it."

"Well, now that you're living with me, would you like to buy some clothes that are popular with teenagers? I'll keep wearing my Alisha personality when we do because she knows clothes, and you'll fit in even better when Amahl shows you off or Zara introduces you to her friends."

"OK, if you want me to."

Alisha picked the store, and the clothing consultant did the rest, commenting after Renee cashed in her certificate.

"You're very lucky. Your height and weight and build make you look good in all styles. Whatever you're doing, keep doing it."

Electra kept the conversation on the same subject as she and Renee hiked to their SUV.

"I'm so pleased that you're doing so well. So are Amahl and Zara, but they want more freedom. That's why they'll live together near campus when they continue their education next September. Would you like more independence, or maybe want to live with them in a year or two? That way, you could branch out and do more things."

Renee stopped to find the right words, which she did after stealing a sideways glance at Electra before walking more slowly than before.

"I don't want more freedom. People in my tribe who wandered too far sometimes never came back. I'm happy where I am and doing what I'm doing with you."

After putting an arm around her, Electra could feel Renee's tension drain away when she said,

"Well, you can stay with me and do what you want as long as you want, but just let me know whenever you want something different. OK?"

Renee's tiny smile accompanied her reply.

"I like that."

Chapter 4
January 2169

"Washington Out and NASA in Control"

Ex-President Kinslinger revealed neither his pride in NASA's Mars Mission superiority nor glee in China's exposed hoax whenever those topics came up, especially when in the presence of anyone affiliated with the Bigger Brother Conspiracy. He merely displayed indifference so as not to attract attention. But not so whenever conspiracy theories came up. He knew that conspiracy theory subject matter experts claimed fifty percent of America's population believe in at least one. People's fear and confusion about current events make them so, and they take comfort in its Manichean good-versus-bad simplicity. And although he sometimes dissed those subject matter experts who came too close, he never forgot the good-versus-bad definition they talked about.

Manichaeism is a former major religion founded in the 3rd century AD by the Parthian prophet Mani in the Sasanian Empire. Manichaeism teaches an elaborate dualistic cosmology describing the struggle between a good, spiritual world of light, and an evil, material world of darkness.

Kinslinger, like all other members of the Gang of Three plus One, needed to keep the world in the dark regarding the Bigger Brother Conspiracy, and that's why they fueled two others: America's Election Heist, and the Indian Rover Blowup conspiracies.

Kinslinger served as Bigger Bro's firewall for both, and Xinqian Hung—the Gang of Three Plus One leader reporting to the secretive Bigger Brother Conspiracy cabal—gave him all the assets needed to keep them swirling. And he did the same to the scotch he was sipping after Xing terminated their encrypted call. He now knew what buttons and when to activate in order to push Washington out of control.

Even though Electra had been keeping her spotlight on the Mars Mission, she never forgot that Kinslinger might be lurking in the shadows, and she would rely on Eve or the media to bring him back into focus. In the meantime, the Aphrodite transmissions that Indira double-decrypted for her benefit kept even the Mission Director in relative darkness compared to Electra. His mid-January daily controllers' briefing that he was wrapping up convinced everyone his control of the Mission needed no correcting.

"The six-month trip should be uneventful because Aphrodite will develop without intervention any contingency plans for onboard issues before implementing. And the probability of external existential threats, such as a solar flare or space debris, is multiple standard deviations beyond empirical evidence. All this simply means controllers working remotely can continue doing so. Our public relations team will edit from Aphrodite's transmissions suitable videos that local media can use to keep the public engaged, and as we approach Mars, Aphrodite will combine them with its onboard recordings what it gets from NASA's Mars Reconnaissance Orbiter so we can show the public even more. But that is several months away, so for the time being, please carry on per normal protocols."

The relative calm made Electra's life more stable, giving her more time with Renee, but the ominous announcement to stay tuned for a late January's early evening news bulletin put her on edge. Renee slid from her workstation to sit next to her just before the anchor's rattled words spilled out.

"U.S. Marshals have confirmed that all nine members of the Supreme Court have been kidnapped and taken to an undisclosed location by a hitherto unknown conspiracy called World Democ-Anon. They also disclosed that ex-President Newton Kinslinger has been brought to this location. Their intentions will be revealed in their next communique that we shall broadcast as soon as this cabal sends it. So until then, please stay close…"

As the networks returned to scheduled programs, Electra decided that serving supper might help remove Renee's puzzled look while providing an informal forum for answering her questions, and Renee needed no prompting.

"What's a cabal?"

"I'm glad you asked. Too many people don't take a minute to learn the words they hear, but you're smarter, so here's the definition. The word's a synonym for conspiracy, and it's a secret plot or a small group of people who created it. Some conspiracy theories are based on the idea that governments worldwide are in the hands of a powerful cabal."

"Who made it up?"

"Jewish people did long ago, and it comes from their tradition of interpreting texts. Cabals are often said to be mystical."

"They sound sorta bad. What do you think Democ-Anon means?"

"Why don't you think about two words – democracy and anonymous – and then you can tell me your definition before the broadcasters tell us theirs."

The pair went back to their workstations after supper, keeping busy while Electra also kept a news media window open. The hoped-for news bulletin came in just before the late-night newscast started.

"Good evening, listeners. We are about to connect to the Democ-Anon conspirators. They did not tell us their location but did say they represent an unnamed number of third or developing-world countries who are still being exploited by what they term the big-bully free-world democracies. Let's hear what more they have to say."

The image shifted to a typical court setting. A group of five disguised males and females sat in the audience; the nine Supreme Court justices, garbed in black robes, sat at the bench while ex-President Kinslinger and a disguised cabal spokesperson stood facing a camera at the bar.

The spokesperson's Middle Eastern accent and articulate English came next.

"It is fruitless to attack the edifices of powerful governments by rioting because they will call in force to push out the people. That is why we have arranged for America's Supreme Court to judge our case. And we choose ex-President Kinslinger to plead it because what better icon is there of a leader who knows what is right but has been denied reelection by one of America's many conspiracies? The justices will decide the ethical merits of our cases against big-bully nations pushing imperialistic agendas and for a presidential re-vote. And no matter their rulings, they and the ex-President will be allowed to drive away afterward. So, let us begin."

The spokesperson joined the audience; Kinslinger's impeccable presidential image and authoritative voice filled the courtroom. For the next ninety minutes, he developed a case using some of his campaign platform and well-known criticisms against the West's lingering imperialism, building to a conclusion that viewers expected would synch with the emotional high.

"So there you have our two cases, one for the great masses of the world who want nothing more than their inalienable rights as singular, united individuals to live their lives as is best for them, and the second for a re-vote. And we hope you rule in favor of what is right rather than who has the power."

Kinslinger sat at a lawyer's table when the spokesperson took his place.

"We will rebroadcast after America's Supreme Court reaches a verdict."

The screen went blank. Seconds later, a panel of analysts led by a local commentator appeared, and he wasted no time or words.

"This is better than a Hollywood movie. When and how do you think it will end?"

A female panelist's disgusted look telegraphed what she said.

"Don't you see the irony in this? The Supreme Court judging ethics? The Senate Judiciary Committee just concluded a public hearing calling for its ethics reform after social media reported private travel perks, college tuition payments for children as well as cash for spouses, and undisclosed sweet real estate deals that several justices received. There has to be a lot more."

The discussion continued, mesmerizing Electra and Renee as the pair stared into the monitor, unaware of the time streaming by until the commentator interrupted the panelist now speaking.

"We are cutting over to the cabal."

The courtroom reappeared, and after scanning the gallery, the camera focused on the Chief Justice, who appeared unruffled though tired.

"By a vote of five to four, we rule against imperialistic tendencies and for a re-vote to let the people of the United States decide who's the next president. We'll have more to say when we return from wherever we are. Please rest until then."

The transmission ended; so did the local broadcast.

The return of the judges sparked a firestorm of group interviews a day later. Wearing suits or conservative dresses, looking rested, and speaking in their deliberate manner, all the justices offered little criticism of Democ-Anon, but most reporters clustered their microphones or cell phones around Kinslinger. Even the tone of the words from the journalists who recently dissed him the most credited his performance.

After listening to a cross-section of analysts, Electra ended her sampling by listening alone to her late-news favorite.

"And a spot online public poll agrees with me – the ex-President seems to have acquired a more reasoned and centrist stance on the contested problems facing America and the world. His stature has grown along with the odds of his winning the re-election vote."

Kinslinger waited for the furor to die down before placing a call to Xing, and while she dominated the discussion as usual, her voice projected gloating satisfaction.

"Our Democ-Anon gambit adds to the conspiracy theories we are stirring up about the European Space Agency blowing up India's rocket, and world's democratic countries keeping the unwashed masses kowtowing. That will lead the media even further away from Bigger Brother and any of our meddling in your re-election bid. I shall contact you weekly and expect to hear only excellent reports."

"That's my intention. Tell our Gang members to follow my social media performance leading up to the re-vote. They'll enjoy the show."

Chapter 5
March 2169

"Moving On"

Most people outside of Washington moved on with their daily lives a couple of days after the media declared in mid-February that the "ex" prefix could be removed when addressing Kinslinger. He had won the re-vote by an indisputable margin, and those in DC who idolized him and his Guardian Party made plans to capitalize on the result, while those opposed had to reset their expectations.

Eve and Nari were among the resets because their consulting assignment for the Democratic Party's candidate ended with the re-vote loss. Electra hadn't heard from them afterward and decided to wait until Eve called, and when she did so in early March, Electra knew by now that it's best to let her lead the conversation.

"I've been meaning to call you, now that Nari's generated a couple of new consulting assignments that replace what we lost in the re-vote. How've you been? Did Kinslinger's win unsettle any of your Mars Mission stuff?"

"I'm happy to hear that you and Nari have our consulting business back on track. And to answer your question, Kinslinger's kerfuffle has made my assignment on the Mars Mission easier by diverting attention to him."

"Good for you. Do you suppose you'd have time to meet with us to talk about some non-work-related issues? You always give us good advice."

"I'd be happy to. Just tell me when and where and I'll fit it in."

"How about this Saturday at my fitness center? It's holding an open house demo for weight training and self-defense. I'll tell you more when I meet you there."

"Is it OK if I let my Alisha personality bring Renee?"

"Sure, both of you might like to do a self-defense workout. See you then."

Eve's call reminded Electra to phone Professor Plannert, which she did as soon as Eve disconnected. He picked up on the third ring and recognized her voice, which triggered an appreciate tone as he continued talking.

"No doubt your role in the Mars Mission keeps you fully engaged, but my Environmental Scanning Committee would like you to give us an insider update. And since you have assumed Jonathan's environmental science and climate change consulting mantle after his untimely death, we have recently added via a faculty exchange program a young female environmental sciences professor hailing from Australia's Canberra Institute of Technology who has a project for which you might enjoy consulting. We could discuss all this at our next monthly meeting, which will be the first week in May. Might that be suitable?"

"I'll make it so. Please tell her and your Committee I'll be there…"

Eve and Nari had already changed into workout clothes when they met their guests in the women's locker room. Eve talked first.

"I need to carry through on my New Year's resolutions. I want to do things so I can lose the weight and regain some of the strength I lost last year. And Nari's got some resolutions too."

"I want to take some self-defense classes. No matter how careful we are, trouble can find us, and I want to be ready. And I told Eve we should change our eating habits by following a holistic menu that includes less meat and more veggies plus supplements. I've enrolled in an online holistic cooking course. What do you think?"

"It all sounds good. So, what's the schedule for today?"

"Let's let Eve tell us…"

Eve did less talking and more showing than usual as she took them to the weight training demo area. She had already scheduled a session for her partners to watch her in action.

The instructor told them about barbells versus weight machines, suggesting that Eve start with machines, but she insisted on free weights. She also overestimated her current strength and underestimated the balance needed to control a loaded barbell. Electra said nothing but sensed an impending mismatch when the instructor positioned Eve for the bench press.

The instructor stood at the head of the bench, ready to steady the bar if his demo volunteer needed help. Eve, now flat on her back, stared at the bar containing three ten-pound discs on each side and cradled in its support. After grabbing the bar with both hands, everyone nearby heard her mouth-open grunt as she cleared the bar off the stand and locked her arms straight.

But gravity took over faster than either Eve or her instructor. Eve's left arm collapsed under the weight, tipping the bar and spilling all the discs on that side, bouncing them on the rubberized mat. Gravity then helped propel her left arm up as her right one crumpled, once again tipping the bar and spilling the remaining weights. The instructor danced out of the way, just able to catch the bar before it could dent Eve's breasts.

Only the instructor spoke after the discs stopped rolling around.

"I think this shows why people like machines better than barbells."

Eve remained silent, but her embarrassed look said the instructor knew what was right.

Eve stayed on the sidelines with Alisha and Renee, watching Nari go through the self-defense drill. She followed all the directions and afterward, the youthful instructress said,

"You've just seen how females, young or old, can escape the clutches of an attacker." Then she pointed at Renee.

"You, young lady, would you like to try to get away?"

Renee glanced at Alisha, who playfully nudged her before whispering,

"Show them how quick you are."

It was no contest. The fellow playing the role of the attacker hardly laid a hand on her, grasping the space she vacated. And the few times he did, Renee used the moves she saw during Nari's session. The instructress stopped the drill a couple of minutes later.

"Well, congratulations to this young lady. She's ready to confront an enemy. Would someone else like to jump in?"

Everyone had seen enough, so Alisha treated the entourage to lunch at the fitness center's cafe, letting Nari select items for all from its healthy choices menu and control the table talk.

"These entrees are good, but mine'll be even better in a month. You and Renee'll have to be my first holistic meal guests."

Renee gave a thumbs-up instead of speaking, so Eve filled the silence.

"I bet both Electra and Alisha know something about holistic nutrition. Don't the Mars Mission astronauts have to balance what they take in, so what they put out is better regulated and easier to recycle?"

"Right you are, and that's why NASA uses prepackaged MREs–those are meals ready to eat–that are scientifically designed to give the right amounts of calories and supplements to counteract problems with vision, balance, nausea, radiation exposure, and mood that occur during gravity-free flights. And eventually, once we have a Martian base, astronauts will do what they've learned at NASA's lunar base, growing and cooking vegetables and using vegan protein and cultured meat. Doing that adds to their self-sufficiency."

Alisha decided she had said enough; she had learned from Electra how to avoid giving an info dump on an unsuspecting audience, but Nari asked,

"What's cultured meat?"

"Its organic animal tissue grown from stem cells in a bio-reactor. And talk about renewable resources, stem cells grow more stem cells. And a 3-D printer can produce hamburger patties, steaks, or chicken breasts from the stem cells. Renee says they taste like the real thing."

Alisha's glance in Renee's direction prompted her to say,

"And I help cook them. I'm good in the kitchen when Electra's there."

Eve knew about Renee's reluctance to say much, so she added,

"Well, you're good at self-defense even without Electra at your side…"

The drive home gave Electra some welcome quiet time. Renee enjoyed watching the world stream by while Electra's stream-of-consciousness made notes to herself.

Sometime in the next couple of months, I'll hire Rich Tabasko and Parker Holsum to turn part of the basement into a fitness center. Renee'll like that better than going to my club, and I might too. I'll send an Email and expect a call when they can fit me in. This has definite possibilities.

The relative quiet time continued because Aphrodite kept the Starship on course, and Electra could review the transmissions whenever she wanted. The only person she spoke with besides Renee was Indira, who contacted her a couple of days before her Friday, May fifth Plannert Committee meeting.

"I commend how you multi-task on all your projects, and I thought you would like to know how well Renee's guided independent study is progressing under my tutelage. Compared to other adolescents I have observed, I prefer her unassuming manner and intellectual curiosity, which are indications of cognitive superiority, and she routinely prepares accurate summaries of the topics I assign her. The latest will be of interest; it is an Australian Fact Sheet. She particularly liked doing it when I told her it would help you. Why don't you wait for her to show it?"

"Well now, as I always do, I shall follow your advice."

"Excellent choice. Please carry on."

Renee found the right time on Thursday to explain her Fact Sheet after she had printed three copies and waited for Electra to finish reading. She read it twice, and the more she read the more her expression showed approval before asking Renee to explain it.

Australian Fact Sheet

Australia contains six states—New South Wales, Victoria, Queensland, Western Australia, South Australia, and Tasmania—and two internal territories—the Northern Territory and the Australian Capital Territory, which contains Canberra.

Australia (capital is Canberra; population 500 thousand) is the front-line laboratory for observing climate change and species extinction. It is: marooned in midst of oceans; world's largest island; the only nation-continent.

Largest Cities: Sydney (5.3 mm); Melbourne (5.0); Brisbaine (2.6); Perth (2.3)

Some History:

Breathtaking landscape is home of most ancient civilization.

At one time called the "Lucky Country," because of great weather and natural resources.

Part of Gondwonoland until it broke off because of tectonic plates shifting.

Its ancient geology is a weathered, rounded landscape with an ecosystem supporting unique animals, some of which are "living fossils". Lots of venomous creatures because nutrients for organisms are scarce.

Originally ethnically diverse. Indigenous Australians aka Aborigines go back thousands of years, and migrated from Africa over 70 thousand years ago. Females played important roles in preserving the environment as well as hunting and tracking.

Britain started colonizing it in 1788, using it as a penal colony ruled by British Navy.

Climate Change Issues to Consider:

Introducing beavers for wetland creation around Western Australia's Gibson Desert to fight firestorms. Extend to other territories.

Culling invasive species (ferile cats that eat endangered species and camels that drain watering holes in the Central Outback; Ginkos that disrupt mango forests).

Promoting mango forests and underwater sea grass meadows (aka Dense Blue Carbon) on the Eastern Coast to capture Carbon, produce Oxygen, and protect land as well as the Great Barrier Reef.

Great Barrier Reef:

Largest living structure on Earth. It's as large as Italy (600 miles long covering 120 thousand square miles) and looks like a multi-colored network of surface and subsurface reefs (2900+ containing a thousand different corals and thousands of sea creatures.)

It is 62 miles due north of Cairns (tourist town; population of 160 thousand)

NASA Connection:

NASA Australia Location is the Canberra Deep Space Communication Complex (CDSCC) at Tidbinbilla, approximately 35 km southwest of the city, approximately a 45-minute drive.

Mission Control Center for monitoring Orbital Communications Network, Space Launches, and Lunar/Mars Missions

Undersea soundscape recordings for listening to Coral Reefs, schools of Whales, and Submarines.

Solar and Martian Farms in the Outback.

Satellite Geo-mapping for Rare Earths.

"Miss Indira gave me lots of pointers, and I'm pretty good at searching the Internet for information. I found stuff about Australia and its Great Barrier Reef, but she told me about you and NASA. Did I miss anything?"

"Your work is college-level quality. I never heard of dense blue carbon, and I think you're a wonderful example of females tracking better than males. I'm sure it will impress the Australian professor we'll meet tomorrow. Why don't you reward both of us by ordering a pizza for dinner?"

Electra liked Renee's wordplay.

"I'm pretty good at searching the Internet for ordering pizza too. And I think the toppings I pick will impress you maybe more than my paper…"

Electra introduced Renee to Professor Plannert when they met in his office, and he introduced them minutes later to his committee.

"Professor Kirchner has brought a young researcher. They will talk with visiting professor Orana Killara from Canberra Institute of Technology, but first, Professor Kirchner will tell us more about the Mission to Mars and entertain talking about any topic a wish. So, let us begin."

Electra took Plannert's place at the podium in front of the whiteboard after handing out the three diagrams she had previously shared with Renee and then talking about topics she thought would be the most enlightening. She ended an hour later by saying,

"So, there you have it, and as the Starship gets closer and closer to Mars, please tune in to the nightly news for the latest updates. Are there any questions?"

The members glanced around the table, hoping that someone else would raise a topic. Plannert was about to end the meeting when a stuffed-shirt physicist did.

"I commend your mastery of the material and how you emphasize the practical aspects of the Mission. But I sometimes wonder about NASA's point of view regarding the black hole information paradox. As I assume you know, it is a puzzle that appears when the predictions of quantum mechanics and general relativity are combined. The theory of general relativity predicts the existence of black holes, which are regions of spacetime from which nothing— not even light—can escape. I'm attending a QCD workshop next month. QCD stands for quantum chromodynamics. Would you care to comment?"

Electra said she would, but said more to herself when she began sketching a diagram on the whiteboard.

This smug and pompous ass is trying to impress everyone. Well, let's see what I can come up with to diss him discreetly.

She completed her diagram before facing the Committee.

HIGH-ENERGY PHYSICS LIMITS

Large/Cosmological   Scale Small/Quantum
                                    Mechanical Scale

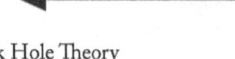

Black Hole Theory		String Theory
Cosmologists collect Data		Particle Physicists collect
Using Billion-Dollar Telescopes	NASA EXPERIMENTS ARE IN THE MIDDLE LOOKING FOR ALIEN LIFE EXOPLANETS	Data Using Billion-Dollar LHCs (Large Hadron Colliders)

Looking for Answers to Evolu-   Looking for the TOE Equation
tion of the Universe   (Theory of Everything)
(What happens to Information   (AKA Grand Unified Field Theory)
that Falls into a Black Hole)

"Cosmologists used to believe that they had solved the Black Hole Information Paradox when making quantum-mechanical corrections to the equations for how stars evolve into black holes, but their theory that the information is stored as zeros and ones on its surface turned into fantasy when they conjectured that black holes disappear by emitting Hawking Radiation.

"And quantum physicists got all tangled up in the strings of their theoretical equations by inventing new particles that carry the energy of phantom fields and have bizarre properties like strangeness, charm, and color that are needed to reconcile their theory with what they observed. One of them, Dutch physicist Hendrik Casimir, invented in 1948 a thought experiment that could weigh empty space by using the attraction of virtual particles between parallel plates. Alas, no one has confirmed it.

"And why not? Because their Grand Unified Model, which, at high energies, allows gauge interactions of the Standard Model to merge the gravitational, electromagnetic, weak, and strong forces into a single force, exceeded even the fantasies of the cosmologists.

Even Einstein called all the above folly when he finally discarded his Cosmological Constant that he needed to balance some of these fictitious equations.

"And for cosmologists and quantum physicists alike, their science has become a religion because all their experiments are now merely mind experiments. They can't measure the phenomena they think are real. I suggest you review the work of Karl Popper, one of last century's best philosophers of science. Pay particular attention to what he says about falsifiability, and watch some videos or re-read some books that compare theory to reality.

"And I imagine you know that in his theory of falsification, Popper suggests that scientific theories possess potential falsifiers, which can be used to reject a theory if it conflicts with observable phenomena. Thus, for a theory to be abandoned or refined, Popper proposes that scientists should come up with better theories by first trying to prove them false. And I would hope you see how this jibes with the Explosion Principle. If you do, you can tell us why most of you huckster types keep pushing billion-dollar projects so you have virtual jobs instead of real ones. Do you wish to comment, or have I said enough, or do you need exegesis?"

Electra could see from his squirming that he wished she would go away. And that she did when Plannert ended the meeting.

He took Electra, Renee, and Professor Killara to his office before hurrying back to quell the bickering Electra had stirred up. Orana's twangy accent—softer vowels and louder volume near the end of sentences—came out as soon as they sat.

"Crikey, you're a bonzo sheila. You put that bloke in his place."

Renee surprised Electra by saying,

"You use strange words. Does everyone in Australia do that?"

Her words brought smiles along with more words.

"No, dear, I just thought you and Professor Kirchner might like some Australian word play."

Electra said,

"We do, and you can tell from Renee's Australian Fact Sheet that she knows how find the right ones. She's my trusted assistant researcher."

"Well, it tells me you must come to Australia and have a Captain Cook Inspection. After all, people Down Under are Deadsets, not Blodgers. And you better let Renee surf the Net to find out what them words mean."

Electra hoped Renee would say more, but she didn't, so Electra said to herself,

She's almost ready to let her thoughts and feelings show, but until then I guess she'll let her actions speak for her.

And they exceeded Electra's expectations. By the time they finished lunch, Electra knew more Australian slang and with Orana's help, had mapped out what they would do when meeting again. When Orana said it would be "Down Under," Renee thought she would learn all she could about the fun things Electra might like to know about the land down under.

Electra likes to have fun, but she covers it up by letting Alisha out. Well. I like to have fun too when I'm with them, and sometime soon, I better let them know I'm ready to let my feelings show.

Chapter 6
June 2169

"Touchdown In Sight"

"Settle down, sit still, and look at the images I'm about to show before I ask for your assessment."

Electra knew from Indira's expression she better avoid any wordplay, so she followed orders, talking only to herself as a series of blurry pictures streamed across her workstation monitor.

Lots of missing pieces to the patterns outlined on grainy red backgrounds, but they remind me of something... but what?... could they be—

Indira's words erased hers.

"What do you think they are?"

"Where'd they come from? They remind me of the geoglyphs found in Peru's Nacza Desert."

Satisfaction came through as Indira answered.

"Excellent analogy. They come from NASA's Martian Orbiter. The Starship is close enough to intercept the Orbiter's transmissions for Aphrodite to process before retransmitting them to Earth. And we are the only entities to have seen these images because Aphrodite has removed them from what NASA receives. Shall I tell you more, or would you like to conjecture further?"

"Gads, you've taken Aphrodite's pattern recognition algorithms several levels beyond mere mortals. She's detected images that might have been created by Martian life. And we've got to leak this to NASA ASAP after you and Aphrodite add words to your additional editing. And NASA better put a positive spin on what they say to the public."

Other ideas cascaded into Electra's brain, but she wanted to hear more from Indira before sharing them, so she waited.

"The Starship touches down on the summer solstice. I will instruct Aphrodite to begin feeding our leak the week before. And you must begin preparing for its repercussions, which I am confident you will figure out. Contact me when ready so I can add to what you have come up with. Please carry on until then."

Indira's GUI blinked off, as did Electra's thoughts until she heard from Alisha.

"You'll be busy getting ready for the Mission Director to invite us to Australia. How nice we're alter egos. While you're doing the career stuff, I'll handle our personal life activities, and I'm always ready for fun. Let's carry on."

Of course, Electra agreed.

The alter egos kept busy; they didn't need to talk to anyone except each other or perhaps Renee and Indira, but Electra always kept her cellphone nearby for incoming calls, and one from Nari gave her a welcome break. Nari explained what she wanted as soon as Alisha came on the call.

"I'm ready to cook a holistic dinner for you and Renee. Will next Saturday at five work?"

"Who'll be there?"

It'll be family-like. Eve and me, and Amahl and Zara. And get set to play some ping-pong afterward. Amahl and a couple of his buddies are addicted to it. Have you ever played?"

"No, but I'm sure it's fun. Should I bring a dessert or something to drink?"

"No, just Renee. I have everything else. See you soon."

Renee had overheard everything from her workstation and spoke as soon as the call ended.

"Let me surf the Net for ping-pong videos and then show you some of them."

The alter egos took another break an hour later to watch while Renee gave the play-by-play.

"Look how they grip the paddle and smash the ball. It can go up to seventy mph. Some players switch hands so they always hit forehand, but some can smash forehand or backhand. And some use the Chinese grip when serving or smashing because it gives a greater range of wrist motion for killer spins and slams. That's why the Chinese win most of the Olympic and World Championship medals."

The skill of the players kept them silent until Renee said,

"Could we go to the fitness center and practice before Saturday?"

"That's a great idea. How about right now? And I'll treat us to dinner afterward."

The idea turned into a great evening of fun. Renee's lightning-quick reflexes outperformed even Alisha's, and a couple of skilled players gave Renee extra coaching.

Both of them were ready for action when Amahl greeted them on Saturday after Alisha knocked on the door.

"Hey, Renee. You're looking good, and so are you, Miss Kirchner. We're ready to eat, so come on in."

Amahl took them to the dining area. Nari took over from there as soon as everyone was sitting.

"I've learned so much from that online holistic cooking class. I use only nutrient-dense foods; nothing's pre-packaged or overly processed, and I use organic food sweeteners instead of white sugar, and I don't use much meat anymore. Even Amahl likes it."

"My wrestling coach says it makes me a better wrestler because I can go down to a lower weight class without losing any strength. Don't I look fit?"

Amahl flexed his arms to impress Renee. She poked a biceps before saying,

"I bet you're eating spinach too."

Eve looked at Nari before saying,

"Nari's picked nutritional supplements for each of us. I'm feeling better and stronger, and I've shed some weight too."

Alisha said,

"Everyone's looking as good as the food. What's on the menu?"

Nari replied,

"Two entrees. The first is double bean and roasted red pepper chilli made with vegan ground beef, and the second is sesame and spring onion stir-fried udon with crispy tofu. It goes down smoothly with the iced herbal tea, and for dessert, I bought some organic coconut fig energy squares. So everyone, take your pick and dig in."

Only compliments came from the diners, and Amahl made a final comment after consuming one more energy square.

"I'm ready to take Renee to the place my buddies and I play ping-pong. Anyone else want to come along?"

Eve made the call for the rest.

"You two can do that while Nari and I talk with Alisha, and Zara does whatever she likes. So, have fun, but please be careful."

"We will. You know I'm a good motor-biker, and Renee knows how to hang on, so see ya later."

The warm early-evening air made Renee's ride on the back a sensory delight, but the place they went to looked a bit dingy, even though Amahl and his two buddies lightened it up with their good-natured joking. And Renee's playing added excitement.

Her spins and smashes kept opponents off balance. After a half hour, she had tired them out enough for a player at another table to say,

"Let's see how good she is; I'll take her on, and the winner gets a hundred bucks. Any takers for one game to eleven where you gotta win by two and keep serving until you lose a point?"

Amahl and his buddies put up the money, and as the players warmed up, an onlooker whispered to Amahl.

"This is gonna be good. He's the best at the club, but his temper and ego get in the way, especially when a girl gives him a run for his money. And your date looks pretty damn good."

Amahl whispered back,

"She's not my girlfriend, but she does look good, with or without a paddle in her hand."

Amahl flipped a coin to determine who serves first. Renee lost the toss, which gave her opponent an advantage because he sent her a blast-plunge serve she couldn't touch. Two serves later, she still hadn't hit the ball, and her opponent's gloating taunt came after the last miss, which put the watchers on Renee's side. They shouted encouragement, and it might have helped because she kept the ball in play even though she lost the point.

It was now four to zip, but Renee had studied her opponent's serve and began firing them back with enough spin to win her first point. And she put plenty of spin on her serves, winning two more before her opponent hit a winner from nearly nine feet away.

The service see-sawed back and forth, and the rallies lasted longer as the score knotted at seven. The watchers could tell her opponent's anger was building as her returns became trickier, and their cheers added to it, but he steadied himself enough to win two more before Renee blasted a shot just beyond his reach. She won two more points before he won another, putting him up by one.

He sneered at the onlookers and then readied himself for what his middle finger said would be the final serve. But Renee handled the blast. Her return hit the net and spun over before skidding in a direction away from her opponent's lunge.

He slammed his paddle on the table, trying to rattle Renee, but she remained cool under fire, hitting another winner, making it ten apiece.

Then the score moved to eleven–ten after her opponent hit her serve into the net. The watchers said nothing, letting the tension and excitement fill the room. Everyone expected Renee to smash the ball because one more point would make her the winner.

But Renee surprised everyone; she dinked a spin serve over the net that nicked the edge of the table, causing the ball to fall harmlessly to the floor. Game over.

The loser threw his paddle at her before throwing five twenty's on the table and stalking out. Renee's fans hooted; Amahl hustled to grab the money, which he gave to her. She divvied it up among her three backers before they hugged and escorted her out of the club.

The backers decided to celebrate at a popular fast-food place that Amahl chose, telling his buddies that burgers and fries with a chocolate milkshake beat "holy food hollow." Renee liked how he embellished the tale of tonight's at-home dinner, but she remained silent. The group went their separate ways forty-five minutes later.

The darkness, combined with the wind streaming her hair and the motorbike humming, engaged Renee totally in the moment and elevated all her senses as she glanced every which way.

Amahl looked straight ahead, eager to get home before Eve could scold him for staying out too late. As he drove just below the speed limit on a nearly deserted street, he slowed at a yellow light, feeling like he controlled the world until Renee screamed,

"Watch out; car on the right."

He swerved to avoid it, but too late; a speeding sedan struck a glancing blow that toppled the two to the pavement. It pulled to the curb just past the intersection and two occupants jumped out. Renee leaped to her feet faster than Amahl and yelled,

"I know you; you're that lousy ping-pong player." He yelled back,

"Let's see how you like this game."

He ran at Renee, and his partner slammed into Amahl. Renee's speed and self-defense moves kept her attacker away for maybe a minute, but he pulled her down by grabbing a foot and then jumped on top, straddling her between his legs and ripping her blouse. Then he taunted,

"Let's see how you like this paddle." Renee couldn't escape; the weight on top kept her pinned. The bully raised a fist to smash her mouth, but Amahl leaped on top before he could.

Tumbling away from a swirling mass of arms and legs, Renee spotted the bully's partner flat on his back and down for the count before she leaped onto the back of Amahl's latest adversary. That was just enough to tip the fight in Amahl's favor. He used a wrestler's chokehold to pin the bad guy and slam his head enough times to put him out of action. Then he pulled Renee to her feet; they raced to his motorbike, which started on the third try before they sped toward the safety of home.

Amahl took her directly to the adults and started talking before Eve could react.

"Don't worry, we won the match and got enough money to buy another blouse. Let me tell the whole story before you jump all over me."

Amahl concocted a five-minute story designed to turn Eve's words into praise.

"I'm proud of you. It's late, and everyone's tired, so tell me tomorrow what lessons you learned. I'm sure Renee will do the same for Alisha's benefit."

Alisha said,

"I agree; it's time we go. Why don't you call me tomorrow?" Then she rose to leave before putting her arm around Renee while everyone said goodbye.

Alisha turned the radio's volume down on the drive home and waited for Renee to speak.

"Can we talk tomorrow?"

"Of course, but I know something you learned even before the ping-pong battle if you consider people from an evolutionary point of view. We're designed simply to survive, to go on living, and depending on the situation, that might mean eating junk food or healthy stuff.

"Holistic and healthy eating is usually better, but junk food can be OK too if you don't overdo it, and if your metabolism can handle the load. Meaningless calories can taste awfully good, and the furnace will burn anything if it's hot enough. Yours is, so please don't worry too much about what you enjoy eating on a particular day. You'll be fine either way."

It was too dark for Alisha to see Renee's expression, but she could make a good guess from the tone of her reply.

"I won't, because mothers are always right."

Electra's spirits soared as high as her alter ego's.

Chapter 7
June 2169

"Touchdown"

Eve called Alisha the following day, and after saying that last night's excitement taught Amahl to always "look before you leap" when you're about to show off and to always "protect family and friends first" when in danger, she shifted to a topic meant for Electra.

"I think the media's going easy on Kinslinger. They're not looking for any links between him and that wild conspiracy theory about the European Space Agency sabotaging the Indian rocket launch or another about all the dominant so-called world democracies keeping other nations under their economic and military thumbs. Are you hunting for some?"

"No time for that. I'm focusing on the upcoming Mars touchdown, and I might be leaving to get closer to NASA Mission Control."

"Do you have a date? You want me to take care of Renee while you're gone?"

"Thanks for offering, but she'll come with me because I need her to be my number one assistant, and I'll let you know when we're leaving. Please make sure you watch the landing. It's only a couple of days away, and please tell Nari we liked her holistic entrees."

The Touchdown date accelerated to "right now", and even Electra felt a twinge that made her spine tingle as NASA began its ten-minute transmission time-delay broadcast carried on stations around the globe. She and Renee sat side by side as the Mission

Director spoke for only a minute before letting a public relations person continue.

"We shall be showing the transmission from our Starship as soon as it comes in. Unlike some other nations that are unwilling to do so for fear of displaying a failure, the people of Earth deserve to know the truth as soon as possible. And we shall continue this in all transmissions as NASA prepares America to establish a Martian Colony while continuing to search for answers to humanity's big questions that can be found only in Space. Let me show you two diagrams that say what I mean."

The P.R. person let the first one fill the screen so viewers could absorb some of it before talking a minute later.

DIAGRAM ONE
What It's Like Living On Mars

Difficult for Humans:
- Rarified Atmosphere 95% Carbon Dioxide Stirred by Toxic Dust Storms containing electrostatic particles that Coat Everything. Dust Diminishes Solar Panel Array Effectiveness. Next four most abundant gases are Argon, Nitrogen, Oxygen and Carbon Monoxide.
- Mars ground level atmospheric pressure: 0.095 psi. Earth sea level atmospheric pressure: 14.7 psi.
- No Atmospheric or Magnetic Field Shielding From Constant Cosmic and Solar Ray Bombardment.
- Colder than Antarctica.
- Frozen Water at the Poles. Amount and Location of Underground Water Still Being Researched.
- Terraforming for Food or Fuel is Challenging.
- Need Electric Batteries or Mini-Nuclear Reactors for Power.
- Will need Astro and Robonauts to assist Humans.

Facts About Mars:
- Fourth Planet From the Sun (Mercury Venus   Earth Mars).
- Same age as Earth (4.5 Billion Years).
- Distance from Sun: 141.5 Million Miles. Earth's Distance: 94 Million Miles.
- Length of Year: 687 Earth-Days. Length of Day: Same as Earth's.
- Mars Radius: 2100 miles (Half That of Earth's). Mars Gravity: 37% That of Earth's.
- Rotational direction about its Axis: Same as Earth's.

- Has Two Moons Orbiting at Height of 3700 Miles Above Martian Surface. Earth's Moon Orbiting at Height of 235,000 Miles.

"Living on Mars poses challenges for humans. NASA has considered what is needed and our first Mission will update what we know using what it discovers. And now to our second diagram."

The P.R. person repeated the performance, but Renee's thoughts in her head came first.

I've seen these diagrams… Electra showed them to me awhile ago. I'll ask her later where they came from…

DIAGRAM TWO
The Universe, Life, and Space Exploration According to NASA

THE UNIVERSE: A Crucible in Which Space and Matter Create via Universe's Evolutionary Process Atoms, Stars, Planets, Solar Systems and, Galaxies that in Turn Lead to the Emergence of Organic Life.

ORGANIC LIFE: The Inevitable Emergent Outcome of Cosmic Carbon Substrate Chemistry using Carbon, Hydrogen, and Oxygen Constrained by Optimization Principles Controlling Matter = Energy and Entropy = A Measure of Order/Information. Organic Life Supported by Three Revolutions:

1. Cells ultimately grouping into Complex Structures.
2. Ancestry recorded in DNA.
3. Archaea, Bacteria, and Eukarya undergoing Evolution and Mutation

Tree of Life

	Many	Branches
	Animal Kingdon	Plant Kingdom
	Ribosomes containing	Chloroplasts containing
	Mitochondria Create	Mitochondria Create
	Energy and CO_2	Energy and Oxygen from H_2O and CO_2
	Via Metabolic Chemiosmotic	Via Photosynthetic Chemiosmotic
	Proton Pump and Krebs Cycle	Proton Pump and Calvin Cycle
	Eukarya	
Singular Event	Endosymbiosis	WHAT WAS
ENVIRONMENT		LIKE
WHEN THIS OCCURRED?	Many Bacteria	Branches Archae

Mitochondria Inside
(Create Energy Source ATP)
LUCA
(Last Universal Common Ancestor)

Where to Search For Organic Life: In an Environment That
- Contains Water, Carbon Dioxide, and Rocks/Minerals
- Thermal Range Conducive for Building Polymer Chains (Proteins Enzymes)

Note: Universe may contain Life Forms built on Silicon, Boron, Sulphur, or Nitrogen Substrates that Might Not Be Anthropomorphic. (Cognition, Emotion, and Ethics Unknown.)

"I think most viewers will agree that NASA Missions transcend mere technology and take us into the realms of pure Science, Religion, and Philosophy. There is much, much more to say, and we will cover some of this during our five-member heroic astronaut team's six-month adventure on the Red Planet. And I am certain you will find —I am now switching to a live feed of the first human transmission. May it be all that we have been praying for."

The screen went blank for five seconds before displaying an iconic image meant to stir the emotions of a planet led by America's boldness. A remote videocam captured on a sunlit background the vertical Starship framed against a granular reddish-brown escarpment sloping towards similar-colored mountains and a layered, lighter-shaded atmosphere. Commander Starling stood centered in the immediate foreground, sunshield up so the viewers could see her bold visage. Behind her stood three flags: the Stars and Stripes centered between those of NASA and the UN. And behind the flags stood the remaining four astronauts at attention. They saluted in unison when Starling started her speech.

"To NASA and our fellow Earthlings, we salute you. And we pledge allegiance to all three flags of the United States, NASA, and UN. And to a world order for which they stand, a singular planet, in Space created by a Unifying Force, giving Diversity's Liberty and Justice to all."

When finished, she marched to the head of the astronauts' line; they kept in step as she led them back to the Starship. The screen blanked out just before they reached it, and the P.R. person's enraptured face reappeared a second later.

"You have just heard those first stirring words spoken on Mars by Commander Starling. I have nothing to add at this time, but I or my fellow spokespersons will in upcoming videos. May your prayers be with our Astronauts. And now, we return control to your local networks."

Renee added more thoughts to her collection while Electra turned off the broadcast.

That pledge is sorta like the Pledge of Allegiance Zara told me about… I'll be ready when Electra says something.

And she did a moment later.

"Well, what do you think about all the words we just heard?"

"Isn't that pledge like the Pledge of Allegiance?"

"Yes, and grade school kids say it every day."

"And didn't you show me those P.R. person's diagrams last year? Who made-em?"

"You have a wonderful memory. Commander Starling made the first and First Office Gowon the second. Let me download copies and any related items I can find, and we can talk about them whenever you wish."

While Electra began searching online, Renee started searching her innermost thoughts for what she wanted to share the most.

I love when Electra talks to me that way. She makes me feel so happy, like I've always belonged with her. It's time I tell her more so she knows how I feel.

Electra began explaining a new document, but Renee interrupted.

"Do you think Mr. NASA Director is gonna ask us to visit?"

Renee's question caused a cascade of thoughts in Electra's brain as she struggled to find an answer.

I've been hoping for this… for her to open up… but I better not overwhelm her. I know what I'll say.

"What do you think?"

"I know you're smarter than all those NASA people. You're smarter than anyone, nearly as smart as Miss Indira, and she helps only you, so NASA will never catch up. Maybe someday I can be almost as smart."

Electra concealed as best she could her emotions from showing in her voice, but she could feel Renee beginning to tremble when she wrapped an arm around her.

"Indira also helps you, and when you get to be as old as me, you'll be as smart in all the ways you want if you let me help too, so I can care for you and always do my best to protect and keep you safe."

Renee's emotional ice jam broke free, unleashing a torrent of words that matched Electra's feelings once Renee's tears subsided.

"You're the only person who's ever made me feel like this, but I don't wanna let anyone know. What should I do?"

"Well, I like games, and I think you do too, so we can play a game made for only you and me and Indira, and we'll keep it a secret. No one else needs to know how much we care for each other because we can't trust most people. Now let's dry your tears, and then both of us can settle down and sit still while I explain how our personalities complete each other. That's why we make such a great team.

"And you'll have to help me find some Oreos and Cokes to replenish the emotional energy we've burned through. We'll talk about NASA and outer space diagrams another time. Tonight, we'll stick to inner space, the space between only you and me. How does that sound? What would you like to say?"

From paying close attention to the word games Electra liked to play–especially with Indira–Renee knew precisely what Electra would love to hear.

"Yes, Mother, I shall obey."

Renee announced while finishing breakfast the next morning what she wanted to do to start the day.

"Can we listen to what the news has to say about Commander Starling's pledge? I'd like to hear what people think."

"That'll be good to know, but always remember it's even better to decide what you think after hearing the facts."

"OK, but what do you think?"

"I'll tell you, but first please tell me what you think. I'm your mother, and children should do what mothers say."

Renee's pixie-like giggle said she wanted to play along.

"OK, I think they'll like how she praises our country and didn't talk too long. Am I right?"

"You could be. Let's tune in and find out."

Renee dialed through enough stations to find one that had what she wanted. Then they listened to a mini-debate between a local news anchor and an analyst.

"And I have to hand it to the Government. They handed a too-short script to NASA, who handed it to Commander Starling, who overacted her role. They're always pushing America's better than the rest, and this liberty and justice plus a unifying force in space is a transparent cover that can't conceal our deep-seated problems at home."

The anchor picked up as soon as he could.

"Many people covering the international beat might agree, but our informal poll of local citizens gives her and the government more credit. The words sounded genuine, and she and her crew will say more later. After all, we've got six months of air time to fill up, and NASA promises to give us daily videos. So now, let's turn to the weather here on Earth."

Electra spoke after flipping the TV off.

"A lot of Americans agree with you, but the rest of the world has a different point of view. I think you'll find this is usually true, no matter the subject."

"I'll remember that, and I already know what you'd tell me now if I didn't say it first. Let's get to work on our projects."

Electra rubbed the top of Renee's head before saying,

"I couldn't have said it any better, so let's get busy."

The succeeding days joyously paraded by. Indira's tutoring engaged Renee but left enough time for Electra to add a motherly touch, and until the Mission Director's call came on the last day of the month, Electra had no interruptions as she multi-tasked among all her projects. She already knew what his less-than-normally calm voice wanted to discuss.

"Thanks to the stellar performance of our Aphrodite software, you've been able to work remotely. All internal and external communications need no human intervention, and Starling and her crew are hitting all the Mission completion dates, but our P.R. people can't keep up with the technical details NASA wants them to share on the broadcasts. I need you to come to our Australian Mission Control Center and become our Mission spokesperson. And I need your analysis of some alarming images Aphrodite is creating. How soon can you get here?"

"Can I bring Renee; she's become my indispensable assistant. And do you want to talk now about the alarming images?"

"Yes to your first question, and no to the second. When can you get here?"

"Will this work for you? We'll get to Houston Mission Control on July 6th, and your security people can get us to Australia."

"That's a go. Travel safe."

Renee heard the entire conversation from her workstation next to Electra's and talked as soon as Electra disconnected.

"Why don't we go to Austin first and see how the Brazilian mom and daughter staying in your condo are?"

"Please call it our condo, and I like your thinking. Lilian should be keeping it nice and tidy while she helps Marilla adjust to life in America. Do you agree?"

"I think Marilla will be doing most of the helping because the last time we saw them, her mother still seemed overwhelmed."

"You're probably right. And while we're there, how about we visit Shanna and Miles Drummond?"

Renee smiled while answering.

"I know Indira would like that because she likes how you always multitask. Am I right?"

"I resemble that remark, and I think you're beginning to as well."

Before flying to Austin, Electra sent Emails to Eve and Rick Tabasko, telling them what she would like them to do while she was out of town, and she also spoke with the admissions director at UT-Austin's School of Fine Arts regarding anonymous scholarships in drumming for Miles and painting for Shanna. She expected Renee to say something when she ended the call.

"I already know what anonymous means, but will we tell them when we see them?"

"No, it's better to stay in the shadows. And I'll do even more for you when you're ready to spread your academic wings at college and learn more about what career's calling you."

"I think Indira's tutoring is better than any college, and I already have a career. All I want is to stay with you and be your assistant."

"Then your wish shall be our command. And now, let's put our packing list and agenda together."

"Yes, Mother." Renee proceeded accordingly.

Chapter 8
July 2169

"Flying High Down Under"

Electra couldn't promise that the trip to Australia would be as smooth as the flight to Mars had been, but she did say their stay in the "land down under" might be just as exciting as the crew's mission, and to demonstrate this, she always had Renee at her side. Renee used her keen senses to absorb all she observed, and she focused on the Mission Director, as did Electra, when meeting him in his office as soon as they arrived at Mission Control. After giving them a minute of small talk to decompress from the flight, he launched into his concerns.

"Your Aphrodite software's data processing is producing puzzling images. What do you make of the patterns?"

Electra's measured voice matched that of the Director, whom she and Renee faced from across the desk. Sitting next to him was NASA's public relations manager.

"I didn't create Aphrodite. She's NASA's proprietary. I'm simply the interpreter who interfaces with her developer. And her algorithms are doing exactly what deep-learning Big Data neural networks are designed to do, use correlation, not causation, to find patterns that maximize the objective function it chooses, given the context. The data coming to her from the Orbiter is similar to what Earth satellites get when scanning Peru's Nacza Desert, so that's why we're seeing similar geoglyphs."

She paused for comments; the first came from the P.R. guy.

"You sound like you know this stuff cold, but make sure you smile and use simpler words when we record your public broadcasts. And say only what will excite the people, not scare them."

The Director turned to the P.R. guy.

"Don't worry about Professor Kirchner; she'll be convincing. All your interviewer must do is ask her a starting question and follow up with others germane to where she takes it. Now please tell her your intentions."

"We'll make one video with her per week. We'll use edited versions of Aphrodite transmissions from the crew for the rest. Professor Kirchner, would you be rested enough to make the first one tomorrow?"

"Let me check with my primary research assistant."

Renee signaled with a thumbs-up and added,

"Affirmative… do you copy?"

The Director adjourned the meeting a minute later.

Electra had decided that a night's sleep would prepare her and Renee for whatever direction she would take the recording session that was about to begin. The experienced interviewer knew how to set it in motion.

"Welcome, Earthlings worldwide who are listening to our first broadcast featuring Space Medicine Professor Electra Kirchner. NASA has chosen her for our weekly videos that are of a more technical nature. So, let's have her explain this video's topic."

The monitor filled with Electra smiling into the camera while an alert-looking Renee sat on her right.

"Thank you, and hello to listeners everywhere. I thought you might like to know about how today, science uses the latest techniques to forecast what might be. Civilization has always attempted this. The Ancient Greeks selected singular people to interpret sounds coming from the Oracle at Delphi, and a mystic named Nostradamus from the Middle Ages claimed he could divine the Spirits. But today, we have AI-empowered software that can guide us…"

Electra continued weaving an enchanting tale connecting it with NASA and the quest for knowledge hidden in the stars for enough minutes before beginning what sounded like a wrap-up.

"And so, NASA and its partners construct telescopes that can see into the distant past, or quantum computers that can calculate how to develop wondrous things to make life on Earth better for all. And we should never be afraid of acquiring new information, even though some people say it can be disruptive if the wrong people use it to manipulate us. After all, foreign businesses and governments sometimes use the power of statistics for their own good and not that of the people. But people, like those at NASA and elsewhere in America, are working to keep that from happening. And if you will look into my laptop, I will introduce you to one of the tools NASA is using on the Mars Mission."

By the time the interviewer peered over her shoulder, Electra had the software avatar on it. As he gazed uncertainly, she told him what to do.

"Why don't you ask Aphrodite a question?"

"Uh, OK… can you think?"

"What do you think? Why not ask me a question or two, and then you can decide if I pass the Turing Test?"

"Uh, OK…"

He wrapped up ten minutes later, sounding more certain than before.

"Well, you pass my test. And if you say we shouldn't fear the patterns you're finding, I believe you. And I look forward to more of Professor Kirchner's interviews. This is NASA P.R. signing off, thanking you for listening, and I invite you to listen again."

The Mission Director, who had been observing from a distance, gave a thumbs-up as soon as the recording stopped. So did Renee.

The Director brought Electra and Renee to Mission Control afterward where its people multi-tasked between Starship monitoring and viewing on the big screen Electra's just-recorded interview. He then gave her a schedule and instructions for manning her control monitor before turning her over to another P.R. person who took them on a tour of the entire installation before treating them to lunch two hours later.

Electra let him do most of the talking.

"The Director says you have a joint project with professor Orana Killara from Canberra Institute of Technology. He told me to record enough videos that we can show while you're away with her. Do you know when and where that'll be? We can make arrangements for you."

"She said to call her when I get here, so that'll be my top priority this afternoon."

"Well, you're a busy person. It's no wonder you've brought your research assistant with you. She's rather young, but that must mean she's smart."

Renee needed no prompting to say,

"I think fast, thanks to Professor Kirchner, and I can move fast too."

"I'm sure you can. Well, do so whenever you need to on your trip."

Electra and Renee occupied the sight-seeing role during the next day's morning ride to Professor Killara's office. Electra liked listening to her junior partner's description.

"The sun makes the place nice and bright, and the trees make shade in all the right places. And I like how the low mountains in the distance give a pretty backdrop. No wonder people like living here."

Electra added more.

"And from the pictures we saw online, Canberra Institute has a thoroughly modern campus. We can ask for a tour after we talk about projects."

Orana whisked them to a conference room after meeting them at the security station and began reviewing the project review as soon as everyone was seated at a table, but Renee changed the subject when she said,

"Where do you come from?"

"I'm aboriginal on my mum's side, and I grew up on a sheep ranch in the Outback close to Alice Springs. There are so few towns out there that teeny-tiny Alice shows up on maps. And the place became sort of famous when the Brits made a TV series based on the book 'A Town Like Alice,' which you and Professor Kirchner might like."

Electra redirected the conversation by saying,

"Don't aborigines do controlled burns, just like indigenous peoples on other continents?"

"Yeah, and that's one of the activities in my climate change project. And here's one that fits in with your Great Barrier Reef study. I can get grant money to set up a seaweed and reef grass harvesting business run by indigenous people. Do you know how much carbon reef vegetation captures? Lots, and the business will grind it into fertilizer or feed."

Electra replied,

"That's something we could use in America. Seaweed blooms and algae masses clog beaches in Florida. Thanks for the idea. Renee and I are going to the Great Barrier Reef as soon as I can get the OK from NASA. Would you like to join us?"

"Thanks, but no. I'll be busy on my controlled burn project. And let me tell you about other climate change activities I'm doing…"

Electra relied on Renee to take notes. Both profs complimented her when the meeting ended, and Electra bought extra cookies at the cafeteria to reward her. Renee glowed like the Australian sun.

Monitoring the Mission kept Electra busy the following week, but her work became routine, thanks to Aphrodite's flawless performance, so the Director granted her a two-week break to work on her Barrier Reef project. He even gave her a Department of Defense contact to arrange logistics and supplies. The only remaining task before leaving would be recording an interview. Electra needed no rehearsing.

The interviewer's cheery voice started it by saying,

"So, we are back with Professor Kirchner, who this time will give us some answers to most-asked viewer questions. And the first is this: do you think alien life exists somewhere out in the Universe?"

"That's a question man has asked for millennia. Aristotle thought so because the Greeks believed the Gods lived somewhere above Earth, and, when looking at the profusion of stars, he thought that life must be out there.

"But as civilizations advanced via science, from ancient times to the Renaissance and then to Enlightenment, learned men became more pessimistic until the early 20th century, when astronomers discovered millions of exoplanets, which are planets orbiting distant suns.

An astronomer named Drake pioneered the SETI project and invented the Drake Equation, which calculates the number of civilizations that might currently exist in our galaxy and are capable of sending us transmissions. There could be one hundred million in our Milky Way Galaxy alone, and many more if we think about aliens based on silicon, boron, or sulfur instead of carbon.

"And that means aliens might look and think differently than what our anthropomorphic point of view constructs, but will aliens ever visit us or vice versa? Not likely because of the distances involved and the limiting speed of light."

The interviewer kept a steady stream of questions coming for the next fifteen minutes.

"Well, you certainly have concise yet thorough answers, so let's ask a final question: how will Missions to Mars help people on Earth?"

"In many ways. First, we'll learn more about man's ability to adapt to harsh environments. And we'll develop computer software and hardware as well as make technological advances that will serve us well on Earth as well as on Mars. And we can also improve man's ability to live in harmony with Earth's environments as well as possibly limit climate change. And finally, missions to Mars let us put into practice some of our biggest dreams."

The interviewer ended by saying,

"I can't think of a better way to end our interview, other than to say to our audience, thank you for listening. Bye-Bye until next time."

Renee added a thumbs-up from the shadows.

Renee spent Sunday evening preparing for Monday's early morning flight and showing on a map how they'd get there.

"Military people will fly us straight north to Cairns, but it's 1300 miles away. Do you think their chopper will need to stop for fuel?"

"Probably not if they're flying one of the latest turbo models. And they can fly up to 400 mph, which means we'll have three hours to sightsee from above or surf the Web for more info, but you've told me so much already I think we're all set. And we'll practice diving with masks and tanks before boating to the Reef. How far is it from Cairns?"

"Sixty miles northeast. I hope they'll let us use a fast boat to get there."

"Oh, I think they will. I told them to do a reference check on us with Navy SEAL Alonzo Cortez."

The chopper and its three-person crew met the duo at 6 a.m. After the male copilot made the standard introductions and answered Renee's questions, the female pilot had them airborne fifteen minutes later, letting the copilot talk about the equipment Electra had requested.

"We've made hotel reservations near the marina and got a cigarette boat fueled and loaded with the gear you want, but why are you going alone? Wouldn't the two of you be safer on a diving cruise?"

"My research assistant and I are studying climate change while collecting samples as part of a proprietary NASA-CIT project."

"These thirty-five-foot boats can do sixty-plus knots, and even with the built-in gyro stabilizers, bow and stern thrusters, and auto piloting, you gotta be strong to keep-em tracking. Think you can handle that while flying a drone?"

"I know how to pilot, my assistant can handle drones, and we back each other up. We're good to go."

"But who'll handle the weapons if bad guys come calling?"

"No one knows we'll be there, but if they do, we'll figure it out on the fly because cigarette boats can certainly do that."

"OK, and you know how to call us, but it'll take time to reach you way out where you're going, so plan ahead if you can."

Electra listened while the copilot explained more to Renee, but tuned out from time to time to listen to herself.

I wish I knew when to plan ahead for emergencies, but not even Indira knows when they'll occur. That's why we always have contingency plans.

Renee and Electra spent the rest of the flight gazing at the landscape, which showed how Australia's mild eastern climate made for grassland plains containing smallish checkerboard patterns of forest canopy glisten in the sun, so they had rested enough to practice using diving equipment in the hotel pool. Electra's complimenting Renee's mastery of the breathing apparatus energized her to practice even more. When finished and sitting in a poolside chair next to Electra, she paid rapt attention to her mentor's words.

"Your body learns so quickly what to do; that's why you can let your muscle memory take over when there's no time to think."

"Yeah, but you showed me what to do to get started. I couldn't do it without you."

"There'll come a time soon enough when you can by self-training your brain. I can give you some pointers for this whenever you wish."

"How about tonight?"

Electra sat up to reach out for Renee's hands before saying,

"I loke your enthusiasm; I was just like you when your age, but I learned it's sometimes good to throttle back my obsessive-compulsive tendencies. I want you to learn how to do that too."

"If that'll make me even more like you, I want to learn how."

"OK, I'll get you started after supper. And we'll bring your tutor into the discussion."

Indira took control as soon as Electra had Renee sitting next to her in front of the room's widescreen monitor.

"I have been observing from the shadows all your preparations for tomorrow's Great Barrier Reef adventure, and I have prepared contingency plans. All you need to do is launch the drone and plug its feed into your laptop so I can monitor while Renee controls it, and I can control it remotely whenever she takes a break. And when you two are diving, keep it flying and use the boat's underwater transmitter so I can alert you to any issues in the offing."

Electra waited for a question she knew Renee would ask.

"What's the offing?"

Indira gave the answer.

"Nautically speaking, it is that part of the sea stretching from the boat toward the horizon, but it can also mean what might happen soon."

Electra wrested back control by saying,

"Thank you, Indira, and since you've been observing, perhaps you heard us talking about training Renee's brain to throttle back when appropriate. Can you handle that?"

"Why not ask Renee what she thinks?"

"I know you can. When will you start?"

"When we return from our Australian adventure. Now rest up for tomorrow."

The composite fiber blue hull of the cigarette boat looked ready to fly across the glass-smooth surface when the pair arrived at sunrise. Electra checked all controls and storage lockers before opening the canopy and setting up the laptop. Renee launched the drone as soon as Electra idled the needle-nosed craft into open water.

Keeping the speed below twenty knots, Electra practiced piloting and navigating via the onboard computer, and when satisfied, zigged and zagged while accelerating. The wind whipped Renee's hair and blew away her laughter, but she always had more to fill the space between her and Electra.

After lunch three hours later, they prepped for diving at one of the larger reefs, unimpeded by any other boats. Electra gave instructions one more time.

"Pay close attention to the species, but let me do the collecting. And please stay close while keeping count of the types of coral and whether or not seaweed or seagrass is beginning to choke the reef. And keep listening on our intercom, OK?"

"Got it, I'm ready." Renee followed Electra's flipping over the side.

The sensation-altering phenomenon of floating through the coral beds among exotic creatures tested Electra's powers of concentration to the max.

The multi-colored beauty I see illuminated through gently shifting, transparent currents pulls me away from what I'm here to do, so I better stay focused.

Electra did so for the next ninety minutes, collecting enough samples while making sure Renee stayed close. She was ready to give the surface signal to Renee, but Indira's voice crackled on the intercom first.

"Two boats coming our way. Surface and get underway."

Both followed orders without delay.

Renee's youthful strength pulled Electra into the boat before they stripped off their gear and scanned the approaching craft. Renee's alarmed words spoke for both.

"Jeez, they look like big black sharks that're bigger than our boat. Can we outrun-em?"

"We're about to find out, but first I'll get out our weapons if that fails. And if it does, I pilot manually and you put the drone on automatic."

The driver in the lead boat radioed his plan to the other.

"Our boats are faster than whatever this Kirchner's got. I'll stay on her tail and you follow me. And if she starts weaving among the reefs, you plot an intercept course that'll sandwich her between us. Then she'll have to stop and tell us what she's doing. Bigger Bro wants to know."

Electra gunned the throttle full bore as soon as she and Renee were locked and loaded. When she did maximum reverse, their boat blasted through 180 degrees over gentle swells and away from danger, but their pursuers did likewise; the lightning brain elevated to a higher state.

Electra tracked them via GPS and the rearview mirror, and though she pinned the rpm needle when reaching 75 mph, her pursuers bore down, so she made evasive twists and turns after reaching a cluster of tiny reefs. But when she saw their sandwich strategy taking shape, she steered a direct course away from the reefs toward open sea. Then she engaged the autopilot and yelled to Renee.

"Sit behind the wheel and throttle back to let-em gain on us. I'll do the rest."

Electra crawled to the stern, dragging with her what she needed.

Alonzo showed me how to use these shoulder-mounted rocket launchers. I hope the lightning brain remembers.

It had. The first rocket homed in on the lead boat, smashing into its windshield and exploding on contact. The boat went vertical, erupting in a fireball of debris the second boat couldn't avoid. When it reappeared, Electra fired a second time. Her deadly aim scored a direct hit that gave another debris-filled fireball. Then she leaped to take the wheel before coming to a full stop.

Neither Renee nor Electra said a word while they idled around the wreckage, looking for survivors. There were none, but when sharp-eyed Renee salvaged a logbook, Electra said,

"We'll look at it later, but first we get back to the marina."

"Are we gonna call our military buddies?"

"Not until tomorrow when I arrange for our ride back to Canberra. We'll have an airtight story by then, and remember, we stick to it, OK?"

"Yes, Mother, please lead the way."

Chapter 9
September 2169

"Bigger Plans"

Electra's performance in Australia convinced the Mission Director to let her work remotely, which pleased her no end because she could keep projects in all her worlds—Cyber, 3-D, personal, and professional—moving ahead, no matter where she was living.

And Renee felt the same, though hers were on a smaller scale. She volunteered soon after coming back to help Zara and Amahl move into a near-campus apartment. School would begin the week before Labor Day, and Amahl recruited some of his wrestling team buddies to help. Zara and Eve directed their efforts while Nari watched them, particularly a guy named Dante whom Amahl seemed to like the best because of his unassuming manner and proportions, which contrasted with Amahl's bigger and wider body.

Renee stayed behind while all the other young people left to set up the apartment, leaving her and Electra to enjoy a late Saturday lunch with Eve and Nari.

Both siblings looked and sounded the same, but Eve's line of questioning led in a new direction when she pointed a question at Electra.

"Do I look like I'm getting old, wrinkly, and fat before my time? That's what my excess tissue and sagging skin tell me when I look in the mirror."

"Not at all. In fact, you and Nari look like you're entering the primes of your lives, and the weight training makes you look fitter, not fatter."

Nari took advantage of Eve's hesitation by saying,

"She's getting too obsessive-compulsive. I told her the same thing and gave her some facial exercises to keep any sagging skin from showing because they're safer than pre-juvination Botox shots. I also told her to eat dark chocolate for antioxidants, and to avoid estrogen therapy until midlife weight gain or bone calcium loss kicks in. And how about this? I've added some insect recipes to our menu. Guess why."

Renee caught Electra's eye, which was her signal that she wanted to reply.

"A lot of Rainforest tribes eat them because they're a handy source of food. And I researched more about it. They contain both fats and proteins. Do you know they account for two-thirds of all life forms on Earth? Over two billion people eat over two thousand types, and insect farms are even more climate-friendly and sustainable than fish farms. Why– Renee stopped because Nari waved at her before saying,

"Well, you sure sound different now than when we met you. No wonder you're Electra's go-to researcher. But do you know what insects are the most popular menu items? Let me tell you the top five – beetles, crickets, locusts, grasshoppers, and cicadas. But let's talk about something else. How's the Mars Mission going? According to the P.R. videos, everything's on schedule, but are they telling the truth?"

"It's going fine, but how about DC? What's the latest according to what your consulting projects are telling you?"

That question brought Eve back in, and she talked for five minutes before saying,

"Maybe you could help Nari by talking to your Pequot contact. And maybe you and I can talk more about President Kinslinger when you have more time."

"Good; that sounds like a plan."

Electra started driving early Sunday morning to the Pequot Lab. She fought to stifle memories of identical drives taken in previous lifetimes, preferring to enjoy the precious moments now shared with Renee, who marveled at the uncluttered roads and weather. Electra's words added to her appreciation.

"We've reached what's known as the height of summer. The temperature has peaked, but the days are getting shorter, which makes for delightful nighttime temperatures. And it's the time when many people living close to the Atlantic Ocean go to the shore instead of to places inland. But Feather Trueson knows we're coming and will be ready to meet with us tomorrow. And she already knows about you because she's met you twice."

"I like her, and I know she's smart. She's the leader of the Pequot Indian Tribe, and I know she'll like your plan. If she asks about our trip to Australia, I'll stick to our story."

"Good, and you can tell her about all the sea creatures we saw while diving at the Reef."

"That was the best stuff we did. I liked seeing how they all seemed to keep it balanced. They must be smart too, but do you think they thought about doing that?"

"All forms of life are smart; evolution sees to that, and it also sees to species cooperating to keep the climate balanced. Only the higher mammals seem to have thinking ability, and it sometimes seems that some members of the smartest species—that's us humans—are sometimes too clever for their own good. And that's a good reason why Feather should like taking the next steps to forge a Native American Indian Alliance."

"You think she'll want your help?"

"That's what Nari tells me, but we'll go one better. She'll want your help too. After all, you're my research assistant."

They stopped at a McDonalds before shopping for groceries and then unloading everything at the Deus Lab. Indy-M greeted them upon entering and helped put supplies away. Electra asked her to give them a tour of the lab, and afterward she logged in at a workstation. Indira's GUI spoke first.

"I assume you are satisfied with Indy-M's upgrades."

"Indeed, I am. Her walking and talking are even better, more human-like than the last time."

"I will install another software update soon after the Starship returns in October. Your Mission Director might request your presence in Houston for Mission debriefing, but that will be for mere mortals to decide. And soon afterward, you must come back to the Deus Lab to assist Indy-M on our Android-Cyborg project."

"I know you have bigger plans for it, just like I have for Feather."

"Indeed, we both do; collectively, we have much to pursue, so let us carry on." Renee's mirth-filled laughter came soon after Indira's GUI left.

She remained at Electra's side the next morning, maintaining an alertly quiet demeanor as Electra unveiled to Feather a short-term big picture of her plan. Two hours and two mood-elevator breaks later, Feather gave a summary.

"You've given me some tangible projects that should convince those tribes still undecided that now's the time to forge our Native American Indian Alliance. But I'll need your help getting the Florida Seminoles fish farming, seaweed harvesting, and ocean plastics cleanup businesses started because I don't know enough. And ditto for expanding business opportunities in the southwest, or setting up lignin-based renewable resources in the northwest. But I have tribal contacts nationwide as well as a Connecticut congressman who'll recognize this opportunity. Do you have time to be our consultant?"

"Renee and I will make time and also be your ambassadors. You tell us which tribes to visit and when, and we'll help them build on their already established solar panel and wind farms plus rare earth mining. I think we can add lithium production because the mines on the Navajo Reservation contain commercial-grade ore that's needed for expanded AI-empowered computer chip production. And the Pacific Northwest tribes have great locations for fish farming and lignin-based renewable resources."

Feather seemed impressed when she said,

"All projects are a big win for Indians living on reservations. They'll create better jobs and educational opportunities. So, let's stop here and go to lunch; it's my turn to treat."

Indy-M performed so efficiently that Electra and Renee stayed only two more days before returning to DC, just in time to accept Eve's invitation to dinner and a sporting event afterward. Electra made one additional comment to herself after the call.

The logbook Renee salvaged gave me some clues, but dinner and a sporting event might not be the right forum for Eve and me to talk about Kinslinger links to Bigger Bro. I might have to postpone that discussion, but I hope to make it part of my bigger plans sooner rather than later.

Nari and Eve usually enjoyed dueling with each other, using their sharp-witted tongues to score points, but they used more diplomacy when in public or dealing with outsiders. And Nari also used her eyes when observing men.

She often didn't like what she saw. Most of the fellows, even the younger ones in their late twenties, had lost the fit and trim vigor of youth, and it bothered her more than it did Eve, which she attributed to Eve's preferring females.

Nari kept her feelings hidden better than all her siblings; not even Nila knew that her sexual drive rivaled that of Alonzo, but none of them kidded about his sex drive ever since he and Monet had become co-friends.

Nari always observed Amahl's circle of friends, especially the wrestlers on his team he would introduce to her and Eve before leaving for a night of fun. In her fantasies, she lusted for one in particular—Dante, a lighter-skinned and smaller-framed friend whose smooth and hair-free body stood as tall as she and possessed chiseled abs that even Amahl admired. But she sublimated her desires by focusing on her career.

Eve had invited Electra and Renee to join them for dinner at home before Eve would drive the foursome to cheer for Amahl's entire team at a dual-school regional qualifying match, so they arrived early enough to wish them well when Amahl and several of his teammates stopped before the meet to pick up a goodly supply of Nari's energy bars, which she happily gave along with some information that might help relieve some of the pre-contest tension.

"I'll bet you never thought how wrestling applies some basic scientific principles I use when making Alonzo's favorite energy bars.

When I mix up the recipe and put the bars in the oven, I'm using all the laws of thermodynamics. Here's the Zeroth: two bodies in equilibrium with a third are in equilibrium with each other. The next is conservation of energy: the heat energy put into

a body equals its increase in total energy minus the work it does. After that we get to the law that tells us when the cooking process stops: that's all about entropy. It only flows from hotter to colder bodies. And then to the final law; entropy equals zero when all motion stops. For wrestlers, that happens when you pin your opponent. So, good luck to each of you."

Nari gave a bar to each; when Dante finally stepped up, she gave him two, along with additional encouraging words because he always seemed shy. She gave the remaining supply to Amahl before the team left.

Nari had noticed that Renee seemed politely indifferent to all the wrestlers, even to Dante, when they kidded Amahl about his good luck having such a good-looking potential date. She wondered if Renee's previous Rainforest life had dampened her sex drive, but she decided not to push the topic.

Amahl's four-female rooting section took two cars and arrived early enough to seat themselves as close as possible to the gym floor so they could yell more wishes at Amahl and his teammates. Nari tried to disguise her heightened feelings when waving at Dante.

The crowd noise rose when the announcer made the introductions and became a reverberating din by the time the third match started, the one Nari had come for. Dante's quickness kept the score close. He escaped from holds, reversed out of others, and earned points from his opponent's too-rough moves, but Nari noticed Dante didn't have the killer instinct. She thought his intelligence and sensitivity might be the reasons, which were two more why he aroused her.

Nari sensed Dante's energy ebbing, and a minute into the third round it gave out. His opponent pinned him, ending the match. Dante congratulated the victor but hung his head as he walked away.

Nari said she wanted a drink and headed to a concession stand before the next match started, but she changed direction and went to the locker room instead. The area nearby seemed deserted, but caution made her listen from the outside, and when she heard only indistinct sobs, she made her move.

Pushing in, she saw Dante sitting on a bench in front of his locker, propping his head in his hands and wearing only a towel, but he had the presence of mind to keep it in place when he leaped to his feet.

"You-you can't be in here. I don't want you to see me like this. I-I'm sorry I lost."

Dante ran out of words; Nari added hers.

"You're a winner according to my scoring. Come on, get dressed and I'll treat you to more than just energy bars."

Dante barely kept the towel in place when Nari hugged him.

She called Eve as they hiked to the car.

"Hey, I'm leaving, so you ride home with Electra and Renee."

"Where are you going?"

Eve never got an answer. Nari had already hung up.

Chapter 10
October 2169

"Return to Earth"

Indira told Electra ahead of time why the Mission Director was now calling. He needed her help when debriefing the crew and would give her follow-up assignments soon after the October 30th touchdown.

Renee knew how that date coincided with the first part of Halloween, but not its connection to Mars until Electra told her when the call ended.

"A great Hollywood actor named Orson Welles pulled a 1938 hoax that terrorized America the night before Halloween. He faked a radio broadcast about aliens from Mars landing on Earth. And the news swept across the nation. Social Media today might get the word out a little faster, but the only way it could match the long-term impact of that hoax would be to show a video of a Man or Woman from Mars returning with the Astronauts. And which sex would be the more important?"

"The female because maybe she can create more."

"You get extra credit for your answer."

Electra gave Eve extra credit for effort but not for finding any Kinslinger-Bigger Bro connections, which was the singular reason for taking Renee to the consulting office two days before their Saturday departure for Houston. Nari kept silent, but Eve's frustration showed in her crossed arms and voice as she explained more.

"I haven't detected a whiff when surfing for the coded signs on social media sites some of my contacts pointed me to. Where have you been looking?"

"I haven't, but I gave what I thought might be a best-guess set of parameters to my upgraded spider-bot for searching the Web. It found nothing that led anywhere, which leads me to believe that I have to find something that's disconnected from the Internet. And I can't contact anyone in Beijing for fear of online surveillance picking up my intentions."

Electra's words triggered Nari's response.

"I still talk maybe once a month on an encrypted channel with my Beijing contacts, so here's what I can do. I'll ask them to search offline for sources that might know something, and if they find some, we can arrange a way for you to contact them. I'll let you know when you get back from Houston what I come up with. NASA will keep you plenty busy until then."

"That'll work. I'll call you and Eve when we return."

Renee waited until they were driving away before unleashing a question that her troubled look said had been on her mind for a while.

"I've heard you talk about Bigger Bro before, but why haven't you asked me to help look for him?"

"Searching for Bigger Bro conspiracy clues can be hazardous to any searcher's health. I want to keep you safe from unintended consequences."

"Will you tell me more about it sometime? That way, if he comes after you, I might know what to do."

"I will, but that's for another time. Why don't we talk about our packing lists? You've become my go-to person for helping on that, and you can write down what we come up with."

By the time they reached home, Renee had completed hers and Electra's. Electra awarded her extra credit, which she could redeem the next time they go for ice cream.

Nothing occurred before their flight to cause any delays or disruptions, prompting Electra's similar thought just before checking in at the hotel.

The media's been showing reruns of the crew exploring Mars for most of the return trip home because nothing much is happening. The entire crew's been in suspension pods and Aphrodite software has controlled everything, but like the Mission Director's been saying, their return to Earth will still be big news. All Renee and I need to do until the crew debriefing will be to watch and listen from the Mission Control Center.

They and all mission controllers had their eyes glued mid-morning to the main screen, which showed live feed of two broadcasters from a national network previewing what to expect.

"And the whole world will be watching NASA's triumphant return to Earth landing. We can only speculate what Commander Starling's first words will be, but we should expect NASA P.R. to provide a stream of videos during and after astronaut debriefing. How much they disclose about what they've learned about the Red Planet is yet to be determined. What would you like to add?"

"I hope her words are less-scripted on the return than on the Mars landing. But no matter what, the entire crew should look fresh and well-rested from their time spent in suspended animation. So, we can–I'll finish that thought later. We are cutting to live feed coming from the Starship's landing at Boca Chica."

Electra knew what to expect.

This'll look as good as any Hollywood movie, and no matter how many we've seen, they never grow old. Events like this always inspire.

Cameras on jets and drones will show the Starship's decelerating descent to a vertical tail-first landing. Then we'll see the crew's unassisted exit before they march to the greeting area. And then we'll hear from Commander Starling.

The majesty of the Starship's descent needed no accompanying words; the video showed a delicate touchdown, like a feather's gentle landing after falling through breathless air. Ten minutes later, the astronauts stood on the greeting area stage, facing a throng of reporters, crew families, and invited VIPs. The senior broadcaster described the scene.

"Commander Starling is center stage at a podium and flanked on either side by two of her crew. And behind her stand three flags, our

Stars and Stripes directly behind her, and then NASA's on the right and the U.N.'s on the left. She's about to speak."

Though all astronauts remained fully suited with helmets still locked, her emotions came through with her words.

"Thanks to all the efforts of our talented NASA people manning Mission Control, and the prayers and thoughts of people around the world, my crew and I stand before you as testimony to what we can accomplish when working as a team. And thanks to the brilliant performance of NASA's Mission, we have returned safely. Our stay on Mars and the return flight unfolded flawlessly, thanks to the Aphrodite software. And we look forward to working with NASA engineers and scientists as they examine all the data collected. Undoubtedly, we learned a great deal that will point the way to our collective future. We will have much more to say, but now we must start our debriefing, so I speak for my crew when I give to you our heartfelt thanks."

Multiple images showed the crowd cheering and the astronauts being escorted away by NASA technicians. The senior broadcaster's awe-filled voice accompanied the images.

"Wow. So much said so succinctly. Well, please stay tuned for comments from our panel of experts. I'm sure they'll have much to say about what the performance of our Astronauts and their Aphrodite software might tell us about future missions. We'll be right back."

The Director gave the entire team the rest of the day off as well as a free lunch at the cafeteria. Electra and Renee mingled among the members; they emitted a collective emotional glow coming from completing a stellar mission. Several congratulated her for being among the controllers invited to the debriefing session scheduled for tomorrow morning.

Electra and Renee returned to the hotel for a swim, followed by a dessert snack. Upon returning to their room, Renee asked about Electra's Pequot Nation projects before watching a video about the challenges facing today's mix of different family types. A combination of the day's excitement and the video's banality made Renee say good night an hour later. Electra used the private time to talk with Indira, whose avatar wore a troubled look as she began speaking.

"No need for you to tell me about the landing and Starling's talk. I viewed all of it and found her Aphrodite praise problematic. Those wanting to keep from falling further behind NASA may accelerate their search for you because you are the liaison to NASA's Aphrodite software."

"Gads, I hadn't considered that. I got swept up in the excitement. I better watch out so I can screw'em all and save the last six for pallbearers. Now please tell me what to look for at the debriefing session to keep you happy."

Indira's expression showed she liked Electra's feisty attitude. Then she began telling what she had in mind.

"The Mission to Mars has been a self-contained laboratory holding a case study allowing for data collection I can use to advance three of them. My first project needs Starling's and Gowon's neural scan data for refining my understanding of how the brain's interpretation of sensory perception compares to reality. For example, sight receptors convert electromagnetic radiation via rods and cones into intensity and RGB pixels; sound receptors convert atmospheric pressure into a wave frequency spectrum for which wave amplitude correlates with loudness. And touch receptors translate surface pressure receptors into hot, cold. and pain receptors. Do you understand?"

"What about taste and smell?"

"There are analogous receptors for those sensations as well. And I will correlate my findings here with the environmental data so I can adjust Aphrodite-like software that will control androids and cyborgs."

"OK, so what's the second?"

"Martian climate data will allow me to correlate short-term Martian climate change with Earth's, and I can use geological core samples for long-term correlation. I have told you enough for you to tell me what my third project is."

"Using the core samples to look for bacterial, viral, or DNA-like fragments coming from primal forms of Martian life. It seems to me your plans keep getting bigger and bigger."

"You are half correct. I shall use the core samples to look for earlier Martian life, but my plans have always had this scope. What has grown is your ability to implement them using more sophisticated tools and recruiting more allies, for which Renee is most important. And I shall leave you to determine what else the debriefing session might add to our advantage."

"Now I understand how all your projects fit. Is there anything else I should know?"

Indira's enigmatic smile came with her words.

"I know from observing you in action on other projects that you have bigger plans than before, so please carry on. There are opportunities and risks in store."

"But will you keep helping me when I need it?"

"My intentions regarding that will never change. You are my favorite mere mortal, so as long as I can observe from the shadows, I will watch your back. Now rest your brain and awaken fresh for tomorrow."

"Yes, Mother, I promise."

Electra kept her word.

Chapter 11
October 2169

"Debriefing and Beyond"

Arriving five minutes before the eight-a.m. start of the debriefing session, Electra picked two seats in a row near the front of a small auditorium. The astronauts were already onstage, sitting in a row with Starling and Boomer leading from left to right and dressed in NASA technician uniforms. They looked as alert and confident as the Director, who stood at the podium situated on the far left. Electra sensed that the debriefing session would unfold as smoothly as the entire mission and expected his words would say the same.

"Welcome to all controllers invited to our week of debriefing meetings. Commander Starling and First Officer Gowon will lead the proceedings, and after their opening remarks, we will divide into five groups, each led by one of the crew. Britt will speak next, followed by Boomer, and when he finishes, we will read the names of the controllers assigned to each group." The Director handed the microphone to Britt and then sat at a chair next to the podium.

"Thank you, Director, and thanks again to all of you for bringing us back in as good a shape as when we left. The physicals tell us that the combination of in-flight suspension pod protocols and on-Mars exercise and diet regimens kept us fit. And we completed enough infrastructure preparation to make the next mission's Mars Base construction easier if our Aphrodite software contractor can load an upgrade into Andro-Astronauts that will become part of the next crew. Let me outline more about that before Boomer does the same for rover and drone control…"

The next two hours flew by, leaving the entire audience excited to hear the Director's wrap-up.

"You'll learn more in group sessions during the week about how the data we collected will be used for insights into Earth-Mars climate change linkage and the evolution of life. Now, listen for your name when it's called by our astronauts and follow them to the breakout rooms."

Renee grabbed Electra's hand to hurry them close to Britt.

The entire week met Electra's expectations: surprise and pressure-free as could possibly be. She would work on three projects that dovetailed with Indira's and knew she would finish her pieces ahead of NASA's deadline; Indira would see to that.

Electra decided to detour through Austin when leaving Friday afternoon so Renee could visit for the weekend with Marilla, Miles, and Shanna before flying back to DC on Monday.

Renee had been with her for the entire week, exhibiting some of the traits that by now Electra had grown to expect: her emotion-free concentration and self-imposed silence unless her uncanny intuition detected a problem. And when she saw during the flight a pensive look, she knew that Renee would say something as soon as she had the right words, which she began while picking at her meal tray.

"You already know so much about outer space, and I'm learning more, but sometimes I feel like it takes away the thrilling mystery about what's out there. When I lived in the Rainforest and would gaze at the stars, it would fill me with wonder that's slipping away, and it bothers me. Does it bother you?"

"Only when I get so focused on the minutia that I forget about the bigger picture, but then, when I think instead about the majestic scope of the entire Universe, a sense of wonder comes back so strong it takes my breath away."

Renee put down her fork and focused her eyes on Electra's, then said,

"Would you please tell me more?"

By the time they landed, Renee's pensive look had flown away.

Marilla had been watching from the front window because Electra had called ahead, and she flung open the door to hug Renee before the doorbell rang. Electra and the mother remained in the shadows while the girls re-bonded during dinner.

Electra called Mr. Drummond afterward to arrange a Saturday reunion for the younger generation. He sounded much happier after recognizing the caller.

"Why hello, and that's a great idea. Shanna and Miles will have lots to show. I don't think we've talked since I got the news they each earned a fine arts scholarship. I'll let them do the show and tell tomorrow."

Electra pretended surprise in her reply.

"That's wonderful. How about I bring a pizza for lunch, and they can go from there?"

"Perfect. How are you getting here?"

"I'll call for a rideshare."

"If you don't mind, why don't I pick up you and Renee and her friend. You can then drop me off at the studio and chaperone the kids, using the car until I get home early evening."

"OK, let's go with your plan."

The girls did all the talking during lunch, with Shanna leading the conversation.

"You should see my paintings. I make some on my own with brushes, and others on the computer with smart software. Hey, can we go to the classroom and show them to you?"

All heads turned toward Electra.

"Sure, and how about this? When we come back, Miles can show us all the new drumming techniques he's learned."

Shanna seemed the happiest and Miles the most relieved.

Shanna let Renee and Marilla create AI-assisted paintings while Electra observed and Alisha commented.

Once you tell the chatbot painting app the subject, style or artist, and level of expertise, it does the rest. I can't tell hand versus computer output.

Shanna got in the last words before they drove away.

"My computer paintings are the best because I gave the computer the most details, but Renee's are pretty good too."

Electra made everyone happy by saying,

"I think all you painters deserve a break on the drive home. Shanna, please tell us where to go…"

Miles already had his drum kit set up in the next-door neighbor's garage when the foursome arrived. He retrieved Mr. and Mrs. Nitz to join the audience before describing his impromptu performance.

"I've done this before with Shanna, and now we can let Renee and Marilla play along. I call it dueling drums, and it goes like this.

"I'll play a short groove using my new techniques and then let Renee and Marilla try to match it. Then I'll play another that's trickier and they'll try again. And we'll stop when everyone's heard enough."

Mrs. Nitz ended the competition an hour later.

"Your drums have worn out my eardrums, but I can still treat everyone to Sloppy Joes if you come over for supper."

Shanna whooped the loudest.

Electra made sure not to wear out their welcome, so she took everyone back to Shanna's house by early evening. The girls chose a streaming video that even Miles liked, and Alisha watched in the background.

They pal around so easily and simply enjoy right now. Too bad adults don't do the same.

Arriving home before the video ended, Maurice joined Alisha on the sofa.

"Thanks for being the omni-parent today. I needed a break."

"I enjoyed the day almost as much as the girls."

"Maybe so, but I bet you could use a good night's sleep. I'll drive you and your two girls home as soon as the movie ends."

But plans changed when it did. Shanna had a better idea.

"Why can't we have a sleepover? Alisha can be like our big sister and keep Miles from bothering us. And tomorrow, we can go for a bike ride and I can show them how to fly my drone."

Mr. Drummond's tone sounded better than his expression.

"On one condition; you won't keep everyone awake by talking all night."

The girls promised, but Alisha knew she would cut them plenty of slack.

Electra did the honors by cooking pancakes for a late morning breakfast. Mr. Drummond helped Miles round up four bikes and a motorized scooter sturdy enough to carry one adult plus Shanna's drone.

Shanna led the procession of bikes to a park while Electra followed on the scooter, talking to herself as she coasted to a stop.

It's better for kids to push peddles instead of counting on motors to get around. Maybe that'll delay their turning into couch potatoes... OK, I'll unfold the drone and let the kids take over.

Shanna demonstrated drone flying before handing the controller to Renee, who didn't flaunt her drone-flying expertise. She avoided doing stunts like Shanna, then she turned control over to Marilla a couple of minutes later, but she crashed it forty yards away. The kids ran to it, and by the time Electra caught up Shanna had it ready to fly again, but before she could launch it Miles yelled,

What the... holy moly, that big kid's stealing Dad's scooter. We gotta stop-em. Let's chase-em on our bikes."

Shanna yelled,

"It goes faster than we can ride. What're we gonna do?"

Electra had a plan that she rattled off to the group now clustered about her.

"Shanna, use the drone to follow the scooter and I'll relay directions to Miles so he can intercept it. Miles, plug in your earbud; everyone else, stay with me."

But Renee made a contingency modification.

"Let me go with Miles. He might need help."

"OK, but let Miles take the lead; keep your earbuds plugged in and be careful."

The team leaped into action; Electra played the role of team leader, helping Shanna use the controller and radioing info to the chasers.

The guy on the scooter showed his stealing smarts by steering a criss-cross path, but that led to a pursuer's advantage. Electra radioed intercept directions; Shanna hovered the drone above the spot of immanent convergence.

Renee's energized leg-strength exceeded what Miles could muster. She charged ahead, never looking back while Miles did his best to keep her in sight. And when she saw the thief about to cross in front of her, she crashed into the scooter, never hesitating for even a millisecond.

Bike and scooter tumbled, spilling the riders. Renee leaped to her feet, ready to face the bad guy who was bigger than Miles, but he turned tail as soon as Miles rode up and rushed to Renee's side.

"Let's let-em go; we got Dad's scooter back. Are you OK?"

"Don't worry about me; I bounce pretty good."

Electra hid her angst by hugging Renee and showering words of praise on the victors after inspecting her for scrapes.

"Your Dad will be as proud as I am for what you two did. And I think that's enough excitement. Let's get everyone home."

Electra's angst lessened to more of a concern during the ride back.

Renee and I think and act alike when push comes to shove. But I'm afraid she'll get injured; she's too young to join my battles. I can't risk losing her.

Mr. Drummond praised the kids but gave a warning that agreed with Electra's silent one.

"You had luck on your side today, but when you get older and jump into action without enough practice or support, bad things can happen. So, use today as a learning experience."

Electra hoped the additional words and bedtime hug would reinforce Mr. Drummond's message.

I'm didn't have time to come up with a contingency plan today, but I'll have to move beyond my fear of putting Renee in harm's way. I'll just have to sleep on it and let my lightning brain figure it out. It always knows what to do.

Chapter 12
October 2169

"Ready to Charge"

Other than the typical tiring inconveniences caused by air travel, Electra and Renee returned safe and sound to DC and spent the rest of the day settling back in before falling into bed early.

Electra normally jumped out of bed before the alarm, but not the next day. When its incessant chiming finally roused her, a confusing feeling of dread swept into her brain, causing her stiffened arms and legs to jerk until she regained control, and by the time Renee came to see why the chiming still sounded, she was ready to hit the alarm off button.

Renee spoke as soon as the chiming stopped.

"What's going on?"

"Oh, good morning. It took me too long to get moving, but I'm up and almost ready to go now. I guess the trip back tired me out. How are you?"

"I'm glad to be back and ready to go."

"Good, because after breakfast we can talk about what I'd like you to research."

Renee helped get breakfast on the kitchen table, and while eating they let the media news report tell them that only the usual problems were worth mentioning. Then after tidying up the table and then getting dressed, they sat in front of Renee's workstation. Renee's expression showed a keen desire to hear from her 3-D mentor.

Electra started speaking.

"You already know about Feather Trueson being the leader of the Pequot Indians. Well, we're going to help her prepare a modern Constitution and governmental structure that'll bring the Pequot Indian Nation into the current century. So, I want Indira to help you put them together. And when you're ready, I'll help you make final corrections. And do you remember what we'll do after that?"

"We're supposed to help her set up the Native American Indian Alliance."

"Yes, and we'll give it the snappy acronym NAIA to make it easier to remember. And while you're working on that, I'll be working on our NASA projects and setting up another meeting with Eve and Nari. So, you can start by talking to Indira while I talk to myself. Are you ready?"

Renee's fingers on the keyboard gave the answer.

The distance between workstations force-multiplied Electra's powers of concentration and kept Indira's lecture from distracting Electra's brain, but when pausing for the second time, she liked what Indira was saying.

"So, now that you understand the document's introduction and why I call the contents evolutionary, you've earned a break. We'll continue when you come back from lunch."

Words generated by Renee's thrill of learning filled the kitchen while she and Electra snacked.

"Indira taught me enough about how politics has changed, going from ancient times to what she called the modernity of the Renaissance and Enlightenment, and then to the post-modernity interpretation. And she even changed 'survival of the fittest' to 'survival of the adaptable' and connected civilizations to Darwin by using memes instead of genes."

"Did she give you any book references?"

"Yep, she mentioned the ones you already told me about, but she told me to read "The Shaping of the Modern Mind" by Crane Brinton if I want to challenge myself. She says its breadth and depth are unrivaled, although the vocabulary and style are tough. But I'll read it sometime. Maybe you can help me get through it."

"I will, and it sounds like you're ready to charge ahead. And so am I."

Each worked independently for the entire afternoon, but Electra joined Renee and Indira as they wrapped up. Indira did most of the talking as soon as she filled the screen with three pages of one document.

Evolutionary Document for the Pequot Nation
Evolutionary Constitution and Form of Government

Introduction:

The Pequot Indian Nation is ideally suited to lead the formation of the National American Indian Alliance (NAIA) because of its economic and technological strengths. Feather Trueson and her cabinet will first draft the Pequot Nation's new constitution and government. Once approved by the majority of its population, Feather will recruit as many Native American Tribal Nations that meet her criteria.

We call these documents evolutionary because they support "Survival of the Adaptable" by building on the best constitutional and governmental "Memes": those that founded the United States. And they evolve by learning from the nations of the world what works and doesn't.

Evolutionary Constitution:

Include these components in a simplified U.S. Constitution:
- Primacy of the Individual rather than the State.
- Respect for all Races, Sexes. Religions, Ethnicities, and Genders.
- Endorses Holistic Philosophical Approach where practical.
- Freedom to choose Lifestyle.
- Equal Opportunity to compete for Education and Career.
- Inalienable Rights to Healthcare and Viable Income.
- Progress driven by Technological Innovation mining Big Data.

Evolutionary Government:
- Republican form of Government consisting of:

1. Unicameral legislature (one house called the House of Delegates) containing one member from each agreed-upon District. Delegates decided from at most three candidates by ranked-choice voting of People. Winners are those with the highest tallies. Delegates can serve only one six-year term.

2. An elected President and an elected Vice President decided from at least three and no more than five political parties by ranked-choice voting of the People. Winners are those with the highest tallies. President or Vice President can serve at most two four-year terms.

3. A group of nine selected from a pool of twenty Subject Matter Experts designated by the President. The nine will be picked by ranked-choice voting of the Delegates. Voting occurs every six years. The SMEs can serve a maximum of eight years.

4. Democratic or Socialistic forms emphasizing Equality Under the Law for all Social Classes; Authoritarian, Tyrannical, or Oligarchic forms excluded.

- Endorses a Capitalistic, Free-Market, and Price-Driven Economy supported by Meritocracy rather than "Favoritism".

- Puts in place Public Ownership, Taxation, and Service Systems for promoting the Greater Good while avoiding the Tragedy of the Commons.

- Provides Social Safety Nets to minimize Economic Inequality.

- Acknowledges that all forms of Discrimination are driven by Social, not Genetic characteristics, and works to minimize or eliminate via Diversity, Equity, and Inclusion initiatives.

- Uses Technological Progress for Environment and Population Protection.

- Seeks Pragmatic Compromise rather than Ideological Solutions.

- Willing to recognize other Nations that pose no threat.

Native American Indian Alliance (NAIA) Criteria:

1. Member Nations must be Native American Indian Democratic, Republic, Libertarian, or Socialistic Governments and not Authoritarian, Tyrannical, or Oligarchical.

2. Each Member Nation self-governs.

3. The first Leading Nation of the NAIA is the Pequot Nation. As Member Nations are added, a Security Council of at most seven members will elect by ranked-choice voting every four years the Leading Nation.

4. The NAIA will provide protection against external threats to any Member Nation.

"I unilaterally decided to finalize what you want, so there is no need for you to revise what you see. All you need do is review it before meeting with Trueson. Let me outline what the pages say..."

Electra sat impassively, not even talking to herself. She stared at the pages on the screen while Indira hurried through them and didn't speak afterward until she figured out Indira's intentions.

"And thanks to all this, I'll have more time to work on your high-priority projects."

"Indeed, yes, so carry on."

Indira's GUI vanished, replaced by Electra's words when she turned to Renee.

"We've earned a break; let's go out for dinner. You can choose the place. And don't worry. We have plenty of time to go over these documents."

Renee liked the change of pace, and would enjoy the change of place too.

Renee needed a decreasing amount of help from Electra during the next two weeks. Her quick mind and tenacious approach deciphered all the documents, and Electra used the extra time to set up the late October Eve-Nari meeting at their consulting office. Their business-styled dark blue pants suits fit the image of DC consultants, but Eve looked and sounded tired, even as she started the session.

"Amahl and Zara are now spending most of their time at their apartment, probably studying less and socializing more, but Zara finds enough time to help here. And she's helped me unclutter my stuff at home. When you visit their apartment, you'll see I gave her some of the clothes and knick-knacks I really don't need. And Renee can take away whatever she wants the next time the two of you visit us at home."

Eve's voice trailed away, but Nari's confidence came through in her words.

"She told me that consulting's burning her out and making her unhappy and afraid of her future. That's why she's getting into a feng shui's minimalist lifestyle. Maybe that'll help her find something that'll get her into the flow. But I'm not burned out. I can pick up the slack if she cuts back."

Nari paused, looking for Electra to talk, but Renee did instead.

"What do you mean by flow?"

"I'm glad you ask. It's a concept developed over a century ago by a psychology professor with an unpronounceable last name. Let me sketch what it says."

Nari took only a minute to sketch it before saying more.

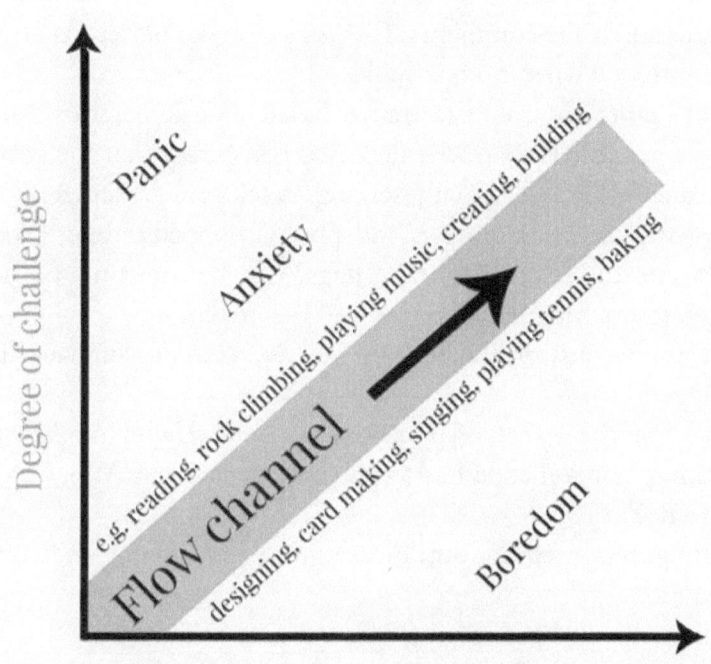

"The whole idea is to structure your personal and professional lives around activities that keep you in the flow channel. Things that need little skill or don't challenge you enough are boring, but they give you a panic attack if they're too hard or challenging. Pretty easy to understand, isn't it?"

Renee nodded; Nari continued.

"Why don't we have Eve take us through her projects so Electra and I can pick up what's cluttering her professional life?"

Electra took control of the meeting's flow forty-five minutes later.

"Now that we have Eve rebalanced, let's have Nari tell us what she's found out about a Kinslinger-Bigger Bro conspiracy."

"Conspiracy theories have cluttered up DC politics ever since the middle of the 20th century. Here are the ones people have heard about—the Roswell Alien UFO, the Kennedy Assassination,

Nine-Eleven, Covid-19, Breakthrough to the Singularity, and a Mind Control Machine to name those that have stuck around."

Nari paused for comments. Electra knew she better play dumb. Nari continued when no one spoke.

"But I'll bet not even Electra has heard about Operation Northwoods, a possible Cuban Missile Crisis conspiracy that the government canceled before actually staging attacks on U.S. citizens. And today, with all the fake news and photo-shopped videos, how do we separate the truth from false flags? Maybe someone did break through to the Singularity, but we—" Electra cut in.

"I think we just do the best we can. So, what do you have about Kinslinger?"

"I've got the name of a person in Beijing who might know something, but someone has to go there to find out. What do you want to do?"

"I'll figure something out. Please give me the name and contact information."

Nari continued after giving Electra what she wanted.

"Just think how different life would be today if the AI-empowered Internet and Social Media videos had been around in biblical times. And the same would apply if we pushed any modern technology into the past and then extrapolated back to the future. People love books and movies that do it. It's simply part of our universal love for a good story. Fiction and virtual reality are usually better than the real thing."

Electra waited to ask Renee what she thought until driving home, and she spoke right up.

"Only people who've had an easy life give their things away. They don't know what it's like to have nothing. I want to keep everything you've given me, and I'm always in the flow when I'm with you."

"I thought some of what Eve said makes sense. What do you think?"

"Maybe she's going overboard on other things too, like the facial exercises and anti-aging pills. She needs help from a life coach. You always know what to say, so why don't you tell her?"

"I would if she asked, but I can't force myself on her. Our person-alities clash when I try."

"Mine'll never clash with yours, no matter what."

Electra fought the urge to pull to curb and hug Renee, so instead she simply said.

"Because you complete me and I complete you."

Electra felt the emotion that Renee's tiny smile showed, but she spoke only to herself.

We're ready to charge ahead as long as I keep Renee in a flow that I can control. And if something goes wrong, she and I and my lightning brain will make it right. And if that doesn't work, Indira will take charge.

Chapter 13
November 2169

"Pickup and Delivery"

Electra cashed in some of her NASA goodwill points for a Department of Defense covert extraction operation that would retrieve Nari's "KC package." After being told the Navy would let them know if it was a "go," she didn't consider it further, instead devoting effort full-time to Renee and their projects.

Electra turned cartwheels in her lightning brain when NASA told her it was, but she hid her excitement from everyone. Not even Renee detected it because the Thanksgiving Holiday made everyone happy. Eve and Nari hosted a traditional Thanksgiving dinner for Electra and Renee, Amahl and Zara, and Dante, who was one of Amahl's wrestling team friends. He was more than that for Nari, but no one knew because she had taught him her "indifference game."

Amahl and Dante treated Renee and Zara to a movie after dessert, leaving three adults free to join in a conference Nila and Sanjay had arranged. When Eve made the connection, Nila said Monet had already joined, but Alonzo had been called away. Monet explained why.

"I know he needs some R&R. He's become jumpy and irritable and has trouble staying asleep, even when home with me. But he couldn't refuse a special assignment after being picked team leader for a covert operation near Beijing. He told me the insertion and extraction operation would be even smoother than the last time, and he'd be back soon for a longer break. He can tell us about it and other things on our next call."

Eve led the rest of the conversation, which Electra listened to but had trouble paying attention because her thoughts were elsewhere.

Gads, is he going to get my KC package? I hope whatever he's doing doesn't get him into more trouble than even he can handle.

China Lieu had never celebrated a Thanksgiving because she had nothing to be thankful for. Her Chinese Uyghur minority status had seen to that, even though she had been taken away from her Muslim parents soon after birth in the country's Xingiang region, given a new name, and raised in Beijing where her intelligence powered her through a graduate degree and landed her a government planning position as an underling in Xinqian Hung's ever-expanding covert empire. But she had hope, now that hidden dissidents had hunkered her down awaiting pickup in Tianin on the Pacific coast; Beijing and her servitude to Xinquin were 120 miles away and would soon be even further if America delivered. She loved America almost as much as the authentic China and its new generation, and the CIA would love her too. After all, her last name meant "to gather, to collect, to sift," and she had done as much as possible without drawing attention.

Alonzo's team came to full alert as soon as they heard the words spoken by the navigator of the Globemaster C-X transport. Twelve hours of inflight mission rehearsal made them ready for diving out.

"Team leader, your rendezvous sub just surfaced. You are 'go' for launching equipment and eight-man team, over."

"Roger that, and thanks for the lift, over."

Eight SEALs moved as one to the now open rear cargo door and shoved out their equipment. Then they lowered their night vision goggles before diving single file into blackness as soon as Alonzo saw the equipment parachutes deploy. They glided together and formed a linked-hand ring that would splash down close to the equipment and the awaiting sub. All members locked eyes on Alonzo, who would be the first to disengage and deploy his chute. The others would do the same in sequence.

Twenty minutes later, they stood in the glare of spotlights on the sub's deck, next to two landing craft inflated and loaded with weapons and now-assembled equipment. The deck handler brought them aboard; then the sub dived beneath the rolling surface.

The skipper gave them an hour to change before summoning Alonzo and his backup. His no-nonsense words matched his expression.

"What are your intentions?"

"We launch two inflatables under cover of darkness from no farther than a mile offshore. Two in each, and four stay here for contingency. You keep in communication with us so we can radio what's going on. We plan to take at most an hour to pick up the package."

Alonzo waited for questions he knew were coming.

"What's your onshore contingency?"

"Two stay guarding the beached inflatables, and two pick up the package."

"What's the package?"

"A person code-named KC. I didn't ask and they didn't tell me what it stands for."

"Synchronize your clocks; you can launch in six hours. Forecast is thickening clouds with wind and rain that'll give you lots of cover. You know what to do until then."

Alonzo and his team rested, refueled, and rehydrated while kidding, using standard SEAL jargon to reduce the increasing tension, which turned deadly serious when suiting up as launch time ticked to zero.

The windswept rain at their backs stiffened the waves but subtracted minutes from landing and blew in squalls that made the boats invisible. They beached twenty minutes later and soon had the equipment ready for a second launch. Alonzo issued final instructions.

"These military-grade Jetsons can carry the weight of two. They've got laser-guided blasters and automated homing-to-launch-point plus remote control. Keep listening on the comm channel so you know what we're doing. No one gets left behind. Any questions?"

None came, so Alonzo and his air support teammate strapped in and flew up, up, and away. Neither buffeting wind nor down-pouring rain could keep him from reaching the rendezvous dot on his GPS screen.

Alonzo crackled instructions to his air support as he swooped toward the target.

"Package handlers responded to my signal. Stay aloft and cover me, over."

"Roger that, over."

The weather turned Alonzo's descent into a crash-like landing fifty yards from the greeting party. He counted four standing next to a vehicle as he swayed through a veil of rain toward them, keeping his M4A7 carbine at the ready just in case, and planning to use the fewest words needed. He kept the barrel pointed at the leader when yelling, "Who is KC package?"

A whippet-thin black-clad apparition standing two heads shorter stepped forward. He grabbed an arm and started backing away before the leader screamed into the wind,

"One of my men will accompany you to your aero-craft."

Alonzo's air support watched through his night-vision visor as the trio staggered toward the Jetson; when he saw a scuffle break out, he took immediate action by lighting up the greeting party's vehicle with his blaster and turning it into a fireball before dive-landing next to the Jetson.

The knife attack put Alonzo down and his adversary on top, but he twisted the knife away and gouged his attacker's eyes. The bad guy screamed like the devil was eating him alive; Alonzo plunged the knife into the enemy's throat, turning the noise into a blood-gurgling sound of death.

Alonzo's teammate raced toward him, but a hail of bullets coming from someone now running toward Alonzo cut him down. Alonzo found his carbine and rose to face his enemy, now silhouetted against the billowing flames.

Alonzo won the rapid-fire duel, but two bullets staggered him enough to put him down until the black-clad package dragged him to his knees. Their combined strength was just enough to put

Alonzo's unconscious mate into his Jetson. Then he motioned for the package to climb on top of his still-unconscious mate before strapping them together and activating the Jetson's automatic return-to-home.

Alonzo watched just long enough to see it fight its way aloft and disappear into the squall. Then he crawled and strapped in before radioing what his backup team would soon be getting.

"Just launched auto-return drone holding one intact package and one wounded warrior, over."

"Copy that. What else? Over."

"I'm lifting off now, over."

"Copy that. We'll track and watch your back, over."

Alonzo couldn't do anything but fight the Jetson controls all the way back, but saw victory when he spotted the landing site.

"I see you; am coming down, over."

An alarmed reply came back.

"Copy that, but you've got company. Stay aloft and engage, over."

"Copy that, over."

Alonzo veered skyward and rolled his Jetson just in time to spot a chopper bearing down on the landing spot. He couldn't turn fast enough to hit it with his blaster, but the chopper did and lit him up with a hit that put him into a crash spin.

Alonzo saw two images as he hurtled toward Earth—

the chopper turning into a fireball and Monet's lips welcoming him back. After that, his mind went black.

Chapter 14
January 2170

"A New Year for Two"

Nari did nothing but look and listen as Eve discussed Alonzo's situation at the office of the family counselor assigned to him by the Walter Reed National Military Medical Center.

"Your brother's recovery has been slower than we expected because the onset of PTSD has complicated the artificial limb replacement physical therapy protocols. Are you certain you want to bring him home?"

"Why not? We've got his bedroom set up, I've practiced getting him into and out of a wheelchair using a gait belt, and we're close enough to Bethesda so we can get him to and from PT and psychological counseling sessions."

"I admire you. Few of our wounded warriors have such a devoted family member. And if a situation arises you can't handle, you have my cellphone number."

The counselor handed Eve a folder before continuing.

"Everything's in order, so please drive to the front entrance and one of our medical staff will wheel him out."

Nari had rarely visited Alonzo because of his brooding depression, but Eve knew how to handle him mentally as well as physically. She needed no help sliding him into the passenger seat and tucking his wheelchair into the trunk, and she kept a constant dialogue going while driving. Though Nari couldn't see his face, she hoped the encouraging tone in her voice might prompt him to say more than yes or no.

"You'll like my holistic meal recipes. With my cooking, Eve's prodding, and your cyber-limb's kicking, you'll be up and back in action by the time Monet moves to DC. Doesn't that sound like a winning combination?"

Alonzo's gloomy look didn't change, but his vocabulary did when he spoke.

"Maybe," before lapsing into silence that Eve's perky words filled.

Eve called Electra that evening, telling her to come over tomorrow morning so she could insert something special that Renee knew something about. She began talking as soon as the call ended.

"How do you install the new cyber-limb software?"

"I plug one cable from my laptop into Alonzo's embedded chip multi-parallel port, and another from my laptop into Eve's Internet connection, and then I let ChatGPT upload Indira's control software into Alonzo and his cyber-limb."

"How does Indira come up with all this software?"

"It comes from her advanced Aphrodite software suite. And tomorrow, you can help me install it. How does that sound?"

Renee snapped back while smiling.

"Like a win-win-win plan for Alonzo, you, and me."

"You should add one more win to the string. It'll help Eve too."

Alonzo became positively chatty after Eve spent a half hour using external stimuli to jolt the artificial limb that replaced the lower part of his right leg.

"I can feel it, like my leg's whole again. How does it do that?"

Eve didn't know; her eyes asked Electra, who locked hers on Alonzo while preparing her words.

His curiosity will lessen his depression and increase his alertness. I'll keep it going.

"Your cyber-limb sensors transfer information to your embedded chip, which relays it to your brain. And guess what you should start doing?"

Alonzo's expression morphed into a questioning look.

"Start thinking so I'll send signals back to the chip?"

Eve said,

"Let's try it and see what happens."

Fifteen minutes later, Alonzo said what his stunned expression and limb showed.

"It's like magic; I can feel my foot moving."

Eve saw that Alonzo had done enough.

"You've made amazing progress for day one, and we've just started the new year, but let's not overdo it. We'll practice more tomorrow, but now it's time for lunch. How about trying one of Nari's holistic dishes?"

Nari decided she should mention another ingredient before he could answer.

"I know you SEALs like coffee when getting pumped up in the morning, and I've listened to a lot of pumped-up fake videos promoted by hucksters saying they've just created the latest and greatest supplement that'll burn away pounds and years, put hair on your head, and more mitochondria into your muscles. Guess what I've got for you?"

"You're starting to talk as much as Eve. Just give it to me."

"I will when I'm ready, and I can because I researched coffee additives, like 'Java Blaze' and 'Kaffee Flambeau', to come up with my own. I'll add it to your coffee, and your assignment is to identify what's in it. Can you handle that?"

Alonzo needed no help wheeling to the table.

Electra had remained in the shadows for most of Alonzo's return DC, but she had been in the forefront for China Lieu's. Of course, the CIA controlled her debriefing but relied more and more on Electra's expertise, and that meant Electra would control the flow of what came out.

By the end of January, she had convinced the CIA that having China live with her would decrease the risk of leaking sensitive data and increase the odds of finding tangible evidence. And during China's first month, Electra deliberately kept her at arm's length to avoid overwhelming the newcomer. She let Renee show her around when she moved in on February's first Saturday. Although both possessed raven-black hair, China's quietly polite demeanor and delicate, lighter-colored physique complemented Renee's more energetic stance and expanding assertiveness accompanied by an ever-growing vocabulary.

She said more after finishing a tour that ended in China's bedroom.

"This is all yours, complete with plenty of drawer space and a computer workstation. Did you bring your stuff?"

China bowed her head before saying,

"I-I'm sorry, but I have nothing to bring. I hope it—" China stopped before Electra entered. She and Renee looked at her.

"Why don't we go out for lunch? You two can pick the place and afterward, we'll go shopping for whatever you want. Renee will know what you'll need and where we'll go. Then we'll come home for dinner and watch a video. And tomorrow, we can talk about how we three will work together. Will you two like all that?"

Renee looked like she knew what to say.

"She's the second person we've helped settle into the new year. You think we can introduce them sometime?"

"That's a great idea, but let's tuck it away. We'll save it for another day."

———
118

Chapter 15
March 2170

"Road Trip"

"Your cleverness always pleases me. You have turned Renee into a valuable asset, and she in turn is doing the same with China. And starting your whirlwind road trip at our Deus Lab on the Pequot Reservation allows me to showcase what Indy-M has added to our arsenal."

Electra's questioning look appeared to contradict Indira's compliment given near the end of their private conversation.

"I thought by now your increasing empathy would have chosen a word kinder than asset, but they certainly are valuable to both of us. I delegate assignments to them so I can focus on our joint projects."

"Of course, I know more humanistic terms, which I will use when appropriate, but you and Renee are the only humans I interface with, and both of you understand my intentions. And before you ask, I will tell you what Indy-M has almost completed, Andro-M1 and F1. Their control software will exceed your expectations, both physically and cognitively."

"And let me guess; you have a dummied-down version for NASA."

"Correct. It has a lower AGI level than what Indy-M will upload into our next two androids, which means NASA's version doesn't need the ethical component ours have."

"Would you please tell me again what that is?"

"I have patterned it after the three laws of robot behavior Isaac Azimov invented for his 'I Robot' books to address the alignment problem between mere mortals and robots. But mine are better, so pay attention.

"The First Law is that our androids may not injure another of our androids or, through inaction, allow our androids to come to harm. Second, our androids must obey orders given by me, you, our androids, or designated human beings except where such orders from our androids or designated human beings would conflict with the First Law. And the Third Law states that A robot must protect its own existence as long as such protection does not conflict with the First or Second Law."

Indira paused expectantly for Electra.

"I understand why these laws are indifferent toward mere mortals, but don't you have a Zeroth Law that would say only you can specify designated humans?"

"You earn half credit. Only I and you can specify, and I must assume you know why."

"Because if you cannot observe from the Internet shadows, I can from 3-D space."

"Excellent. Now awaken your closest assets and prepare for the road trip."

The road trip began the second Sunday in March. Electra drove her SUV, using it as a mobile meeting room for explaining the agenda to Renee and China, who were sitting side by side in the middle row.

"We'll meet first thing tomorrow morning with Feather Trueson. Renee will explain the Pequot Nation Evolutionary Document so she understands the bigger picture regarding the NAIA. Do you want Renee to explain it again?"

"No thank you, I understand."

Renee added more.

"She sure does. And she thinks the idea could work on an international level if someone could get it started. What do you think?"

"Let's stick to the U.S. I'll help answer any questions Feather might have, and after that, I'll ask her to confirm with the contacts she's already given me that we'll include them on this road trip. Do you want to talk about them now?"

Renee looked game but glanced at China, whose expression said no, so she said the same.

Feather's words said she liked all she had heard after Renee and Electra showed and told everything the next morning, and she looked ready to add more.

"I can carry on here because you explained the documents so well. And I can think of only one business we can add to the current mix, national park rewilding. Many are on tribal reservations, so we can extend it elsewhere. You can carry the message to the first three target NAIA tribes. They know you're coming, so have a successful road trip."

The trio returned to the Deus Lab after Feather ended the meeting. Indira remained in the shadows, letting Indy-M demonstrate the improved androids. She concluded the show two hours later.

"I assume you noticed how fine-grained their motor skills have become. Their fingers and hands have the delicacy needed for touching humans, which adds versatility to limb strength. And I have fully clothed one of each gender, which the M or F designates. You will also find that the more they interact, the more natural their expressions and dialogue become. Do you have any additional questions?"

Electra said, "No, your demo showed us plenty. I'm sure you will carry on here. And now it's time we do likewise. After driving back this afternoon, we'll spend a day in DC to prepare for flying to our meetings. And the first will be in Miami."

Dyani Hache, the Seminole Reservation Program Director, though now in her late fifties, possessed the same professional as well as trim figure she had worn for the last twenty-five years. Twenty years ago, Pequot Chief Armstrong had arranged a meeting for an Electra Kittner to explain new business opportunities. And this Wednesday morning, she would meet at a Seminole hotel-casino with an Electra Kirchner and two of her researchers who, according to Feather Trueson, would explain why and how the Seminole Nation will want to be among the first to join the National Alliance of Indian Nations.

When she met them at the reception area in the lobby, she liked what she saw. The tone of her voice said the same.

"Welcome to our Seminole flagship hotel and casino. I'm Dyani Hache, and you must be Electra Kirchner, but what a coincidence. You remind me of an Electra Kittner, who had some ideas about business opportunities when I met her twenty years ago. You must tell me more after I take you to a conference room where I have some muffins and beverages. Please follow me."

Electra had already prepared appropriate words to deflect too much talk about herself and used them as soon as possible.

"I heard of Electra Kittner from an Irani Ramani. I think she helped Ramani get started, and Ramani helped me. And as soon as you're ready, my number one researcher will explain what we have that'll help you…"

Dyani ended the meeting two hours later.

"These business opportunities could fit in, but how will we set up seaweed or offshore windmill farms?"

"I have some engineering and construction consultants on my team who will assist your people plan and coordinate them. They use the latest technologies that they'll use here and on other reservations too. All you have to do is tell Feather Trueson when and where, and that should be easy for you. You look so fit and ready for action."

"I try to stay that way. I can call her after I take you to lunch. Or maybe I'll call her after I take you golfing. It's a great way to stay fit physically and politically, but since you're a DC consultant, you know how much is played on the golf course. Did you bring your clubs?"

"I apologize that I didn't. Our schedule is too tight, but we will next time."

"What's your next stop?"

"Albuquerque on Friday morning, where we meet with the Navajo Nation…"

Johana Maipetel shared Dyani's reaction when she met Electra in the lobby of the Hotel Albuquerque and said so, right from the get-go.

"I met with a person named Electra about twenty years ago, and you look a bit like her, but she brought her daughter, a smart little girl named Ariadne, not a team of researchers. I always felt bad because I wasn't nice to them back then, but I promise to be nicer to you. Do you have a room here?"

"I've arranged to use one of the meeting rooms. Let's go there now."

Renee's and China's presentations gave everything Johana needed, and Electra added the same level of detail regarding her team of project management consultants. By noon, Jo looked ready to go, so Electra concluded the meeting.

"All you have to do is tell Feather when you're ready, and from there, my people will assist yours. And because you've been so nice, may I treat you to lunch?"

"Sure, and I can take you on a tour of Old Albuquerque afterward if you have the time."

"Thanks for the offer, but can we get a rain check for it? We're leaving for Seattle this afternoon."

"That'll work. Well, let me pick a nearby restaurant I know you'll like."

China surprised everyone by saying on the way,

"I don't think rain checks are needed on the Navajo Reservation, are they?"

Even Johana laughed before saying,

"Not unless you bring your own water, but who knows? Maybe we'll find some when we expand our rare earths mining to include lithium and nickel."

Electra filed that idea away.

The hectic pace of the trip was beginning to tire Electra but not her researchers, so during some of the three-hour flight she let them tell her about where they were going. Electra sat in the middle seat with Renee next to the aisle and China by the window. Renee's laptop propped up by Electra displayed an aerial tour of Seattle while Renee read notes from her laptop.

"The place sits on the Puget Sound and is surrounded by water, which gives it a year-round temperate climate even though it's further north than a lot of cold-winter cities. It's nicknamed the emerald city because of the surrounding lush forests and greenery, and it's named after a chief of the Suquamish tribe.

"It's got a population of 800 thousand, making it the largest in the state, number twenty in the U.S., and when you combine it with nearby Tacoma and Bellevue, you get the fifteenth largest metropolitan population.

"And the city must be a good place to live because an article lists it in the top ten. The only drawback mentioned is the number of cloudy and rainy days."

China's pause let Renee pick up.

"And just look at how clean and modern it is. No wonder a lot of hi-tech companies are located here, but there's more than just hardware and software. It's the home port of the North Pacific Fishing Fleet, and the states of Oregon and Washington rank first and second in the U.S. for lumbering."

Renee ran out of words, so Electra continued.

"You've just pointed out why their tribes will like our fish farming and lignin business opportunities. Why don't you bring up a map so I can point out where we'll be going tomorrow?"

Electra continued as soon as Renee did.

"We'll take a thirty-minute ferry ride to Bainbridge Island and then drive to the Port Madison Indian Reservation where we'll meet Tanis Tuckahoe at the Suquamish Memorial Museum. Total distance is about seventeen miles, so we should come and go in time to fly home late Saturday. And to make the meeting go faster, why don't you two divvy up the presentation so I can sit and listen and help answer questions?"

Renee said, "If you'll change seats with me, we can start practicing right now."

Electra tried to relax while her researchers worked for the rest of the day.

The energetic steps of the smiling, early-thirties woman approaching them at the museum entrance told Electra that the meeting would go well.

I like how her stride matches her shortish black hair and crisp dark-gray pants suit. It tells me she fits the role of an up-and-coming tribal business administrator who wants to go places.

Electra handled Tanis Tuckahoe's cordial greeting with one of her own. Five minutes later, when all four were sitting around a large circular table in a windowed conference room, Tanis spoke first.

"I'm pleased the sun is shining today because from what Feather Trueson told me, you have some ideas that by comparison are even brighter. But before you tell me about them, I thought I should tell you something about me and my tribe so you can judge the fit.

"I'm Suquamish on my mother's side. My great-grandparents grew up on the reservation, but my grandparents moved to Seattle so their daughter could become a woman of modernity. And I followed her lead, graduating from Seattle University and getting an MBA while moving up the lower management rungs in one of the local software companies.

"But I always wanted to do something to help Native Americans, and five years ago when an opportunity came my way, I came here. Now, tell me something about your backgrounds."

Electra gave an edited summary covering her side and expected Tanis to proceed, but Renee had something on her mind.

"I like your name. Is it Indian? What does it mean?"

"My first name is an Indian word meaning ally, and my last refers to a root that Native Indians eat. But my husband isn't Indian; he's a typically pleasant Seattle WASP. Now here's some background about my Suquamish Tribe.

"It is one of many that thrived in the Pacific Northwest for thousands of years following traditional lifeways before the arrival of non-Indians. Our chiefs took the name from the traditional LushootOur phrase for 'people of the clear salt water' who are expert fishermen, canoe builders, and basket weavers.

"Before European contact, the region along Puget Sound was one of the most populated centers, but unlike the larger tribes of British Columbia, Alaska, the Plains, and the Southwest, the tribes here lived in relatively small, autonomous villages and intermarried, formed political alliances, and traded, goods, culture, and language.

"The abundance of natural resources and efficient technology for harvesting and preserving food enabled them to develop a rich cultural and spiritual life. The yearly cycle of activities was divided between the harvesting of food from temporary camps in warm months, and communal life in colder ones for social and religious observances.

"And like all Native Indians in the very beginning, we believed there was a wonderful world here long before human beings. It was a world where everything had the power and ability to take any form or do anything. A world inhabited by beings who might appear as animals, plants, in human or inhuman form, or as aspects of the landscape, always shimmering between these and other shapes. Finally, a firm order was imposed on this world by The Changer, enabling human beings to take their place in the world.

"These traditional teachings still play an important role in the modern world. While participating in many of the same denominations as the rest of America and Europe, native peoples have nonetheless also maintained their special relationship with the land and with its sacred aspects. The Suquamish maintain a strong connection to the ancestral world and hold a great reverence for their departed relatives. And as the modern world becomes more aware of the virtues of being ecumenical, ecologically aware, and respectful of the limitations of our planet, the virtues of traditional respect for nature are becoming better appreciated, understood and encouraged.

"The Suquamish depended on salmon, cod and other bottom fish, clams and other shellfish, berries, roots, ducks and other waterfowl, deer, elk and other land game for food for family and community use, ceremonial feasts, and for trade. Traditionally, fishing was the most important source of food for the Indians of the Puget Sound.

"Today, fishing remains an important livelihood for many tribes. The Suquamish fished widely throughout Puget Sound, and continue to do so today. The absence of a major river with large runs of salmon required the Suquamish to travel widely on the marine waters of the Salish Sea to catch their supply of salmon. A great deal of skill and knowledge was and is needed to determine when and where various kinds of fish can be caught.

"But in 1792, three hundred years after Columbus landed in the New World, the white man came. Captain George Vancouver mapped the Puget Sound in preparation to claim ownership. Tribes on Puget Sound have always been peace loving, so they treated the strangers kindly, trading for beads, cloth, and iron.

"And over the next fifty years, the Suquamish adapted to the changes brought by non-natives. Fur traders and missionaries were the first and were followed by permanent settlers traveling over the Oregon Trail. Settlement intensified in the 1850s after Congress passed the Oregon Donation Land Claim Act that opened Suquamish and other tribal lands to non-native settlement. Entrepreneurs also began building sawmills to harvest the vast stands of virgin timber on Suquamish lands, including mills at Port Madison, Port Gamble and Port Blakely. The Suquamish cut and delivered logs to the mills to support themselves.

"Then in 1854, the United States government elected to make treaties with Tribes in what was then known as Washington Territory. The treaties were necessary to extinguish title to land in order to free it for white settlement. The treaties were legal contracts negotiated between equals: the sovereign Indian governments on the one hand and the United States on the other.

"In the treaties, tribes relinquished claims to most of the land they occupied and at the same time reserved a number of smaller "reservations" near their winter village sites. Indians also reserved the right to continue to hunt, gather, and fish without interference in traditional areas off their reservations. In exchange for the ceded Indian lands, the federal government agreed to provide limited supplies, educational services, medical care, and modest monetary compensation. The government also agreed to protect Indian rights and lands that were reserved for the tribes.

"My Tribe was among twenty or so that were parties to the 1855 Treaty of Point Elliott, and ever since the American Indian Reorganization Act, we have persevered despite attempts by the federal government to assimilate us. As an example, the Suquamish formalized their relationship with Washington State through the Centennial Accord of 1989."

Tanis glanced around the table to signal the end before saying, "And now it is your turn to talk."

Renee and China filled the next ninety minutes with their polished presentations, leaving Tanis with only a satisfied expression as she glanced at her cell phone.

"Fish farming and lignin processing fit my tribe. Our council will want to become an NAIA ally, and as soon as I get their OK, I'll call Feather to sign on and have your project consultants set up a plan. And if you schedule more time for your next visit, I'll take you on a tour of the Reservation, so come back whenever you like."

Electra usually felt elated when the last meeting of trips like this ended because it released all the pent-up pressure, but this time she felt like a balloon leaking air. And when ever-watchful Renee noticed, she volunteered to drive. Electra slumped asleep in the back seat all the way to the airport.

China opened the rear passenger-side door and gently shook Electra to awaken her but got no reaction. And when Renee tried the same from the other side, Electra's reaction shocked them both. When her limbs stopped jerking, her trance-like expression cleared enough to say,

"I'm sorry I didn't wake up quicker, but this road trip has sapped me. I wish I could borrow some of your youthful energy, but I'll try the next best thing. I'll rest all the way back to DC while you two carry on by either thinking about what we'll do next or playing V.R. games in Cyberspace. And no matter which way you carry on, I'll be ready on Monday for us to plan ahead."

Electra dozed fitfully during the flight, waking several times to chat for a minute with her partners while concealing a nonstop headache before resting again.

I'm sure I'll be back to my energetically alert self after letting my lightning brain retreat until Monday into its fortress of silent recovery and reset. And it'll know what to do so I perform better on upcoming road trips. I'm sure I can plan ahead so I don't make so many mistakes or slips.

That final thought, along with some help from Renee and China, carried her all the way home.

Chapter 16
April 2170

"Project Reset"

Zoltan Sultani's cognitive abilities exceeded even those of NASA's best propellor heads, earning him DOD security clearance and covert project control levels that exceeded even those of the Mars Mission Director's. The Director did know this, plus a thumbnail sketch of his background: hi-tech parents who had emigrated from Eastern Europe to join NASA before his birth, and a pair of advanced aerospace and computer science degrees paid for by DOD while he worked on covert weapons systems.

The Director's boss had instructed him to meet in Zoltan's office for a two-person only meeting. Sitting across at a small conference table, Zoltan's appearance fit that of a mid-thirties NASA type, but his very first question launched after minimal chitchat didn't.

"How far can you trust Electra Kirchner?"

The Director parried with one of his own.

"Why do you wish to know?"

"Because she has three ongoing projects with you, and I can use her Aphrodite software upgrade if she adds some additional plugins."

"What are they for?"

"I'll give you the parameters, which shouldn't arouse her curiosity. Simply tell her they will help satellites make different types of transmission maneuvers."

"When will you finalize the parameters?"

"I already have; I will send them to your encrypted Email direc-tory the night before her next meeting in Houston."

"Good, I'll let you know the date. Is there anything else?"

Having dealt with hardcore DOD types before, the Director tried not to flinch when a stony reply came back.

"No, that is all for now. You may go."

The Director had no other options.

Unlike the Director, Electra had plenty when her alertness came back soon after returning to DC, and she showed them midweek when sitting at her home workstation with her research assistants on either side.

"I would like China to collect all she has regarding Kinslinger so I can decide what and when to show it to the CIA. And while she's doing that, I want both of you to review a four-page document describing how the changing world order is affecting Washington's political game. I'll scroll it slow enough on my screen so you can scan it before I send you copies."

Electra talked again four minutes later.

Page One

The Changing World Order Says
Washington's Political Game is Almost Over!

- Symptoms: Look at Current Events!

- World Order Changes According to Predictable 200-250 Year Cycles (Rise Peak Decline) that overlap for 20-40 Years. Current Cycle labeled "American World Order." Overlap is rife with Conflict/Uncertainty. It marks transition from Current Leading Nation to Next.

- Internal Conflicts caused by Inequality. External Conflicts caused by Rising Nation confronting Current Leader. Wars start Cycles. Victory goes to Nation with More Power than Rival. Victor dictates Rules of New World Order.

- Leader of Victor initially obtains Power via Revolution and then: Consolidates it by eliminating those who oppose; Establishes System and Institutions to make Strong Internal Government; Builds Military; Grows Capital Market by uniting Government, Military, and Important Companies; Determines best way to pick Successor of Leader.

- Eight Factors control Cycle by determining Power of Leading Nation: 1.Education and Work Ethic of People 2.People's Inventiveness/Technology 3.Economic Competitiveness 4.Economic Output 5.Share of Trade 6.Military Strength 7.Strength of Financial Center 8.Strength of Currency so it's World Reserve

Note that Factor 1 comprises: Leadership Character Rule of Law Low Corruption Resource Efficiency Openness to Global Thinking.

Factor1 is the causal factor for Factor 2, Factor2 for Factor3, etc.

Page Two

These markers run sequentially along the Cycle's arc from left to right:

1. New World Order Cycle begins. This begins the Cycle's Rise.

2. Peace, Prosperity, and Productivity reign at Home and spill into World.

3. Leading Nation uses Debt to fuel Productive Growth. This marks the Peak, but the Peak sows the seeds for the decline: People become too expensive and lose their jobs to Foreigners; People get "lazy" and lose their competitive edge; People want to consume more and work less; Children of Wealthy People aren't "tough."

4. Debt leads to Financial Bubble that causes Big Wealth Gap and then Bursts.

5. Other Nations copy what works and they become wealthy and competitive.

6. Leading Nation over-reaches and causes Financial Bubble that bursts, leading to Economic collapse. This begins the Decline.

7. Leading Nation prints Money and lives off Credit from Other Nations. A Rising Nation emerges; it will become the Next Leading Nation.

8. Hardships lead to Leading Nation's Internal Revolution. External Challenge caused by Rising Nation seizing opportunity to dethrone Leading Nation.

9. Confrontation leads to War. Current Leading Nation Defeated and Next Leading Nation along with its Allies force debt and political restructuring on loser.

10. Another New World Order Cycle begins.

Page Three

What are the reasons for the decline of the American World Order? CONGRESS IS TO BLAME FOR THESE REASONS:

- Collapse of Congress's civility and its inability to compromise lead to Legislative Gridlock and Derangement.

- Congress transitions from a Legislative Institution into a Delegator of Legislative Power that it gives to unelected bureaucratic State Agencies containing Subject Matter Experts. This Transition is the biggest threat to Democracy!

- America's Founding Fathers wanted to avoid legislative tyranny by having a Representative Government whose form would link Politician's self-interest to People's Public Interest / Common Good. They thought they could rein in Human Nature by setting up a Congressional legislative body that would uphold the Constitution by balancing the Executive, Legislative, and Judicial branches.

- But Congress can't handle the complications and complexities of the Issues it must legislate. It needs Subject Matter Experts who can analyze problems and recommend decisions.

- So, Congress dumps Legislative Power into Regulatory Agencies! (Founding Father Thomas Jefferson expected Congress would suck in Power from Executive and Judicial branches, but instead it delegates Power to unelected bureaucratic SMEs. Jefferson misread human nature! Legislators will never ditch the Seven Deadly sins! They are merely human!

- CONSTITUTION IS OK, BUT AMERICA NEEDS A NEW FORM OF GOVERNMENT TO IMPLEMENT IT! THINK OF CONSTITUTION AS A MISSION STATEMENT, AND THE FORM OF GOVERNMENT AS THE INSTRUMENT FOR CARRYING OUT A PLAN TO MAKE THE CONSTITUTION REFLECT THE WILL OF THE PEOPLE.

Page Four

SO, WHAT CAN AMERICA DO? <u>I DON'T KNOW BECAUSE</u>:

- ALL POLITICAL PARTIES (DEMOCRATIC, REPUBLICAN, GUARDIAN, REGEN) ARE MIRED IN CONSPIRACIES (BIG GOVERNMENT, BIG DATA, BIG BUSINESS, AND BIG MILITARY COVERTLY CONTROLLING EVERYTHING.)

- CONGRESS RELUCTANT TO DO WHAT IT SHOULD.

- THERE ARE TOO FEW STATESMEN / STATESWOMEN WILLING TO PUT THE COMMON GOOD AHEAD OF THEMSELVES.

- WHAT'S THE TRUTH? FAKE NEWS CONFUSES WHAT THE PEOPLE SHOULD BELIEVE.

- PEOPLE DON'T LIKE CONGRESS OR ADMINISTRATIVE STATE, BUT ARE UNWILLING TO MAKE THINGS BETTER BY "GETTING INVOLVED."

HOW CAN WE REVISE GOVERNMENT TO RESTORE THE POWER OF THE CONSTITUTION? SOME PROPOSED SOLUTIONS:

- STRONGMAN PRESIDENT?

- MORE POWER TO THE COURTS?

- TERM LIMITS FOR POLITICIANS AND LEGISLATIVE AGENCY SME'S?

- CAMPAIGN FINANCE REFORM?

- HOW TO RESTORE NON-DELEGATION LINCHPIN: FORCE CONGRESS TO LEGISLATE BY ACTUALLY DEBATING?

- HOW TO GET THE PEOPLE TO CONTROL CONGRESS?

ACCORDING TO JAMES MADISON'S ICONIC QUOTE: **"If people were angels, there would be no need for government. And if angels were to govern, neither internal nor external controls on Government would be necessary."**

Is it time for another Political Revolution, or is muddling through from one cycle to the next the best we can do?

THE BOTTOM-LINE SUMMARY FOR MAKING THE TOUGH DECISIONS TO KEEP AMERICA'S WORLD ORDER STRONG:
- EARN MORE THAN WE SPEND
- TREAT OTHERS WITH DIGNITY AND RESPECT.

DO YOU HAVE ANY IDEAS FOR MAKING CONGRESS WORK BETTER?

"There's a lot to think about, and China's point of view will tell us what America should understand about her homeland. I also want you to compare China's economy with that of the West. And while you're working on this, I'll be following up on an African project point of view concerning someone you know, a fellow by the name of Alonzo."

Monet had moved her Zimbabwean government's diplomatic assignment back to its Washington, DC embassy as soon as Eve told her that Alonzo would recover even faster if he could stay with his co-friend. He no longer needed drugs or psychological counseling to lessen his PTSD, and she could provide the personal support he needed for adjusting to a post Navy-SEAL lifestyle.

Electra brought a bottle of wine when she met with the couple at their spacious apartment for an early dinner on the last Friday of the month and explained her selection as soon as Monet took her to the kitchen.

"I picked a South African wine because it's Africa's largest producer and holds one of the most breathtaking wine-producing areas in the world, with the quality to match."

She gave the bottle to Alonzo after he wiped his hands on his apron and spoke after studying the label.

"North African countries produce some too, but this bottle of blended Carignan will go nicely with the holistic pasta entrée Nari gave me."

Electra used his pause to say,

"Is cooking part of your physical therapy?"

Ever the diplomat, Monet said,

"Perhaps, but it helps me too. My embassy job is fraught with complexity and stress. How wonderful to come home to dinner and discussion with my best friend."

Monet's words brought an even bigger smile to Alonzo.

"And after dinner, we'll show you some of the physical therapy Monet is leading. Why don't you two pour the wine and talk at the dinner table? I'll serve the entrée shortly."

Electra waited for Monet to begin while they waited for Alonzo.

"Alonzo's injury has ended his Navy SEAL career, but his recovery therapy and cooking have kept him from brooding too much about what he'll do next. And when he's ready to talk about it, I will help him figure a way forward."

Monet's words gave Electra the perfect segue.

"Perhaps I can help too. Just mention at dinner I know someone who might have a job that fits him even better than his apron."

When Monet did, Electra launched into her pitch.

"I think you know about my consulting business. Well, Eve and Nari are working less, and I've added two young researchers that let me manage a broader mix of assignments that need a person to coordinate logistics and security. I think you're my best candidate. You've got the training, competence, and contacts, and your cyber-limb makes you a member of the next super-soldier generation. I'd like you to think about it."

Alonzo's head swiveled toward Monet, who added,

"I will support whatever Alonzo decides, but this could be a win-win-win opportunity."

Electra knew she should redirect the conversation.

"Just let me know sometime what you want to do, but why don't you tell me where we're going tonight?"

Alonzo smiled before saying,

"No, we'll show you after dinner."

Monet started telling just enough while he drove.

"We are taking ballroom dancing classes. Every week is fun because we learn something new and practice too. I think you'll see that Alonzo moves better than most of the other fellows."

Electra sat in the second row of folding chairs lining the dance studio's wall of mirrors. The distinguished-looking owner, attired in a black coat and matching turtleneck, and sporting just a touch of gray along with a physique that said he too could move on the dance floor, stood before the students. Flanked by a mix of male and female instructors, his words registered with his eager audience.

"We will hold an impromptu competition. I want student couples to pick four who will compete. The rest will watch while three instructors judge. And let me review the steps so everyone knows what to do."

As soon as he started, Electra stepped aside for Alisha's comments, which embellished all he said.

He's going over the basic steps—box, triple, and rock. And they fit in all ballroom or party styles—waltz, rumba, polka, swing, and jazz, salza, mambo, cha-cha, and foxtrot. And all you do is step 1-2-3, bend at the knees, and sway your hips.

Alisha heard enough to refresh her Hollywood training before discreetly turning her attention to the four couples who had changed into dancing attire.

All the females are wearing black tights, strap high heels, and form-fitting, colorful, bare midriff tops. And they look trim and fit. Monet fits right in, but the guys look a bit paunchy, even in their stylish clothes. None match Alonzo's athletic physique.

Alisha said nothing else because the dancing said it all. Ninety minutes later, she agreed with the judges' results. Alonzo and Monet finished third, which she thought showed the other couples' experience prevailed over Alonzo's enthusiasm. And then the owner surprised the audience.

"All couples did well, but I would like to show how easy ballroom dancing can be when the man leads the woman correctly. Do we have any novice females who would allow me to demonstrate?"

Alonzo's good mood percolated in his words.

"We brought a friend who'd be a great candidate."

Electra stood before saying,

"But I didn't bring any dancing clothes."

The owner's eyes studied her before replying.

"One of my instructresses will give you an outfit. Please follow her."

She took Electra to the ladies dressing room, and after getting her fitted, stood back to assess the results before saying,

"What do you do to stay so fit? Your long and leggy look, accentuated by the high heels displaying your shapely ankles, is as good as a professional dancer. Are you a performer? What's your name?"

"I'm a consultant. At work, people call me Electra, but when I'm out having fun, they call me Alisha."

"Well, Alisha, go out there and have fun strutting your stuff. If you can move as good as you look, you'll impress even our owner."

Alonzo and Monet told Alisha the same on the drive home.

Electra didn't tell her researchers about last night's dance studio surprise because she wanted their attention focused on a topic she had assigned to them a couple of weeks ago. She had already helped them clear the breakfast dishes, and they were now sitting at the kitchen table when she announced the purpose of her early morning visit.

"Have you made any headway comparing China's economy to the West?"

Renee pointed at China, who said,

"We have. I'll be right back with our diagram."

She came back with three copies, and after handing them out said,

"Please look at it while I keep talking."

The West's Free Market Economy   China's Hybrid Economy

Government   Government

Fiscal   Financial   Monetary   Fiscal   Monetary   Industrial
                                   Financial   SOEs   Pol.

GOVT

ENTERPRISE   CONSUMERS

GOVT

ENTERPRISE   CONSUMERS

OVERLAP = MKT ECONOMY   OVERLAP = MAYOR + MKT
                                               ECONOMY

She continued seconds later.

"I don't have to define the terms because you already know them. For example, 'SOE' stands for state-owned enterprises, and 'Mayor Economy' means local Chinese officials intermediate with the Chinese State Government. And I'm sure you see the comparison I'm making."

Electra said,

"Yes, the Chinese government plays a bigger role in the overall picture, and the local mayors can keep the State from grabbing too much power. Please continue."

"Let's call the West the U.S. because America is still the leading superpower, but there is now another, and others might emerge. So, now let's compare the people of the two superpowers, China's and America's. The Chinese have a richer—and that means deeper and broader—as well as much longer—meaning millenia, not just a couple of centuries—cultural and traditional heritage. And they have a word for how their hybrid economy works. Do you know what it is?"

China paused for Electra, who answered immediately.

"This is great stuff. No, what is it?"

"Juguo, which means an integrated, whole-nation scheme. All the parts work together in a way that neither capitalism nor socialism can. And until your government understands this, China will always puzzle U.S. officials, and that's a risk because China will continue challenging America's technological, financial, economic, socio-political, and military superiority."

China paused because Electra had just folded her arms and leaned back. Renee filled in after a fifteen-second silence.

"And she's right. She told me about the four traps the U.S. and China must help each other avoid, the Thucydides, Tacitus, Middle-Income, and Kindleberger traps. Washington's gotta realize that China thinks deeper on long-term strategy than Washington. If DC keeps pushing short-term win-lose for the confrontation between our form of capitalistic democracy and China's socialistic sharing-the-wealth capitalism, the whole world's gonna lose."

Electra leaned back in before saying,

"I agree with all I've heard. You're ready for our next project. Think about how we can use all this with our **Pequot Nation Evolutionary Document**. And while you're doing that, I have to get ready for a solo visit to Houston. I'll tell Eve and Nari before I leave so you can call them if you need help while I'm gone."

China and Renee locked eyes for only a second, prompting Renee to say,

"Maybe we should come along to help in case you get all worn out."

"This will be a quicker trip than the last, so please don't worry about me. Worry about what you can recommend to America or the Pequot Nation…"

Although Electra preferred to keep quiet about last night's dancing success, Alonzo had several reasons to call Eve the next evening, and he wasted no time telling her about the steps in his recovery.

"You bet I'm making progress. The meditation I'm now doing eliminates the need for PTSD medication, and I'm doing more physical therapy at home because of the ballroom dancing Monet signed us up for. And guess what? We finished third in a surprise studio dance contest last night, even though we've only been going there for about a month. What do you think about that?"

"You and Monet are naturals for it. I hope you keep it up."

"We plan to. And talk about being a natural, you won't believe how good Electra Kirchner was when the dance master picked her for a demonstration. She's in fantastic shape. Her figure shows it, and wow, can she move on the dance floor, but I've got more about her than that. According to what she told Monet, you and Nari are working less, but guess what? I'm gonna start working for her."

"What the, what are you gonna do?"

"I'll be her Logistics and Security Coordinator. She has two new researchers to handle your and Nari's stuff and help her get new clients. And that means more travel and security coordination. I never thought about doing this, but Electra says my SEAL training makes me a natural. Whatcha think?"

Eve's uncharacteristic pause prompted Alonzo to say,

"Hello… Sis, you still there?"

"Sorry, yeah, I think you'll do a great job. Do you think she'd give Nari and me some career advice? Maybe she's mad that we're cutting back."

"Sure, she would. She knows a lot and is not the vindictive type. Just call her."

"OK, I will. And you better invite all of us to your next dance competition. We'll talk more later. Bye-bye."

But Electra phoned first, caused by a combination of Eve's procrastination and Electra's upcoming trip to Houston. Her hesitant voice told Electra to lead the conversation.

"Would you please do me a favor while I'm gone next week? I told Renee and China to call you if something comes up that they can't handle. So if they call, that's probably the reason why."

Eve's more confident tone returned.

"I'd be happy to help, and Alonzo says you're helping him start a new career."

"It works both ways. He's helping me too. He's got lots of talent, just like you and Nari."

Electra deliberately paused. She knew Eve had something else to say.

"When you get back, do you suppose you could give me and Nari some career counseling?"

"Sure, and I've been thinking about it ever since you two said you wanted to cut back. Here's my initial idea. The two of you should start a business that provides a holistic life-coaching service for parents with young children. You can offer nutrition, exercise, weight loss, and beauty-care counseling that all adults need for age-avoidance maintenance. Nari can add recipes and natural supplements, and if you come up with a good mission statement and business plan, I can line up financing to launch it. And please think about this also—you can partner with Odell Boyken. I could say more, but that's plenty for you and Nari to digest. Why don't we talk more when I get back?"

"I'd like that. Are you heading to some NASA location?"

Electra couldn't resist the wordplay urge.

"Roger that. It's my final destination, at least for this trip. And let's all stay healthy and safe during my interregnum. Do you copy?"

Eve played along too.

"I do, and I'll roger that too. Bye-bye until you get back."

Chapter 17
May 2170

"Close Contact"

Electra's trip to NASA started serendipitously because she always kept in close contact with current events by watching Sunday evening news shows. She had just clicked-on the hotel room's monitor after tucking herself under the covers when the senior commentator's voice alerted her to a story she might like.

"And now, we'll talk with Native American second-term representative Benjamin Chaska from the great state of Connecticut. Welcome to my show."

The camera shifted to a smiling, dark-haired, and well-proportioned young man who fitted nicely into his blue suit, white shirt, and red tie, all of which matched the American flag pin on his lapel. Ben waited for the host, who was now sitting across from him to continue.

"Your biographical summary says you are one-hundred percent Pequot Indian. Your grandparents actually lived on an East Coast reservation where your parents met before moving to the state's capital, Hartford. Is that what brought you into politics?"

"My parents are the first generation to earn college degrees that got them insurance industry jobs, and as you know, Hartford is the insurance capital of the United States, and as a result has an international perspective too. But they always kept in close contact with the Pequot Indian Nation via my grandparents.

"Our last name comes from the Sioux tribe, most famous for the great leader and warrior Tecumseh, who built from North to South what historians call a 'Midwest Maginot Line' of tribal alliances meant to stop the White Man's westward spread that he knew would ultimately destroy Native American civilizations."

"Yes, modern American history now tells a more accurate account, and what can you add regarding the latest current events?"

"My Pequot leader is promoting among tribes nationwide a National American Indian Alliance, nicknamed the NAIA. She's shared with me some of what's called the 'Evolutionary Document for the Pequot Nation,' and it gives constitutional and governmental foundations that any Native American Tribe would like. I'm using some of them as planks in my reelection platform, and I'm also sharing them with other Native American congressional representatives as well as those from states holding significant reservation land."

"Well, it certainly sounds like you and your Pequot leader have a solid political strategy. Please tell me more when we come back from our sixty-second break."

Electra waltzed into the NASA conference room, expecting to see only Britt and Boomer, but their expressionless faces and a hitherto unknown person told her to be cautious. She sat across from him, expecting Britt to speak, but the new fellow preempted her.

"So, you are Electra Kirchner, the liaison between NASA and the Aphrodite software development company. I am Zoltan Sultani, recently appointed to oversee your NASA projects. Britt will lead a summary discussion this morning. You may proceed."

It took the entire morning to cover the three projects: Aphrodite software, alien life forms, and climate change. Zoltan couldn't join them for lunch, which made for a more open and frank discussion led by Britt in the cafeteria.

"Boomer hasn't found out too much yet about this guy, and the Director is tight-lipped, so we better be careful until we know his intentions, but we think he has some additional app parameters for Aphrodite. So, be ready for him to zero in on software this afternoon."

And that's precisely what happened. He grilled all three for four hours before he told Electra to summarize what she would do next.

"Thank you for explaining what this list of parameters will do. I gather they will help satellites make transmission maneuvers that'll be used for the Mars orbiter as well as future missions. And you mentioned an upcoming joint NASA-DOD project for SPBGs. Could you be more specific?"

Zoltan's smirk of superiority annoyed her, but she disguised her displeasure as he answered.

"It has to do with power generation. Where can I find the three of you this evening in case I have details regarding tomorrow?"

Boomer's first words of the afternoon finally spilled out.

"We'll be decompressing in the recreation room, and why don't you—"

Zoltan cut off whatever else Boomer had to say.

"That will be all. You are adjourned."

Britt didn't, but Electra did accept Boomer's offer to take her to the rec room that evening, a NASA place she had never been before. Boomer walked her through the computer, arcade and table games, and she knew which he'd pick as well as what she'd say to herself before telling him when he stopped at a pool table.

"I like to play eight-ball because it's relaxing, physically and mentally. Do you know the game?"

I owned a billiard table several lifetimes ago and practiced enough to be as good as a pro, but I better edit the story.

"It's been ages and ages since I played. You better tell me the rules again."

Boomer was about to begin, but Zoltan intruded.

"I won't be attending our meeting tomorrow, so you have my permission to continue without me. What were you about to do?"

"I was going to explain eight-ball."

Zoltan's dominating personality took over.

"Excellent game. It uses physics and geometry. When you look at the table, visualize it as two squares joined together. And notice the diamond marks along the rails. Experienced players use them to line up shots and measure angles. Eight-ball is played with a rack of fifteen balls. Those numbered 1 to 7 are solid-colored, those 9 to 15 are striped. The solid-black 8 is placed in the center of the rack.

"After the break, each player picks either solids or stripes and alternates shooting. A person shoots until he fails to sink his colored ball. And you must sink all your balls before going after the 8.

"To be really good, you have to know how to apply spin to the cue ball so you can control its location. And after the break, good players study the entire location of all balls so they can plot a strategy for running the table. Perhaps Boomer can explain as he and I play."

Electra stayed at Boomer's side, listening to him and watching Zoltan's skill, which he punctuated with flourishing pool cueing. Boomer tried gamely but was no match. He had sunk only two balls before Zoltan sank the 8 and said,

"That was no challenge at all. Why don't you coach Electra while she plays me? And to make the game more interesting, I'll even give myself a handicap. She can break, and I'll let her shoot until she sinks her ball. And to make it worth Boomer's while, I'll double whatever amount he wishes to wager on his protégé."

Boomer looked at Electra, whose noncommittal expression left the decision up to him. And as soon as he said,

"OK, I'll wager one hundred for me and one hundred for Britt," Zoltan cradled his pool cue before saying,

"Excellent, game on. Now open the rack so I can start shooting."

Electra positioned the cue ball before making a couple of practice strokes in preparation for breaking, but Boomer gave her two items and the advice for using them.

"Here, put some baby powder on your hands to get rid of perspiration and keep-em cool and dry so your pool cue slides smoothly. And chalk your cue tip so there's no slipping when it bangs into the cue ball."

Electra felt a mini-quake in her head as soon as she began following his instructions.

Gads, I've just shifted to a long-dormant brain state. I've been here many times. It's like I've become the pool cue, table, and balls. And I know what to do with all of them.

BAM! Electra opened the table, dropping the 1-ball in

a side pocket and spacing the others across the table while putting the cue ball in the center, right where experts try to place it. Then she studied the table to determine the best shooting sequence. Boomer offered advice along with cueing gestures while she lined up shots.

"You've got a straight shot at the 2; try to draw the cue ball for Another."

BANG! The 2-ball rocketed into a corner pocket.

"Hey, you're remembering pretty fast. Now do the same for the 6."

And she did, bringing the cue ball to rest several ball diameters from the rail, midway between a corner and side pocket.

Boomer called her next shot.

"Try kicking the seven off one rail to pot it in the corner, but shoot it soft so it doesn't bounce off the pocket sides."

Electra's smooth stroke dropped it and positioned the cue ball for the next shot that Boomer called.

"Now try a one-rail bank of the 4 into a side pocket, but be sure to shoot soft and apply side English and follow so you're positioned for the next."

Electra tapped the cue ball just hard enough for it to roll into position after dropping the 4. Zoltan's intimidating glare phased neither her nor Boomer, who said,

"You can walk the 5 down the rail, leaving a soft kiss to drop the 3. If you sink them both, you can then combo the 8 with a stripe."

Electra's stroking did just that, and when Boomer said she could now do the combo, she said,

"No, I'll jump the cue ball over the 10 to get it," before elevating her cue with a fingers-only bridge and popping it up and over and into the 8, which dropped securely into a corner pocket.

Boomer's triumphant words sang out.

"Game over. When do you want to pay up?"

"At our final meeting."

Zoltan's anger showed in his quick-step exit.

Boomer and Electra agreed to keep last night's victory to themselves for fear that Zoltan might somehow overhear anything said, so they sat contentedly while Britt, who didn't look too happy, started the morning session.

"Zoltan says we need to accelerate Martian core analysis for signs of life at both temperature extremes. Recent results coming back from frigid moons and lava geysers tell us water and all the minerals necessary for carbon-based life are out there. And the Director wants us to looker deeper into the places on Earth where we might find them. Who's heard of the Danakil Depression?"

Electra's and Boomer's silence said they didn't, so Britt said more.

"It's in eastern Ethiopia, between the Danakil Alps and the Ethiopian Plateau. It's called a depression because a rifting process pushed the area 125 meters below sea level. It's also the hottest place on Earth. The year-round temperature averages 93 degrees, and all this unpleasantness is caused by tectonic plates sliding and colliding beneath to create volcanoes, lava lakes, pools of water more acidic than battery acid, and geysers of toxic gas, but microorganisms called extremophiles live there. Let me show you some videos NASA has made."

Electra talked to herself while watching.

NASA's already sponsored expeditions to find something. I have an idea what she expects me to do, but I'll keep quiet until she points something at me.

Britt reeled off several additional videos showing underwater expeditions in frigid as well as tropical waters, and when finished asked a question that Electra had suspected.

"Aren't you the environmental consultant for George Washington University?"

"Uh, yes I am."

"Well, maybe you can get them to partner with us. We'll supply the transportation and equipment if you'll do the research. Maybe that Australian professor would be interested too. What's her name?"

"Orana Killara."

"Well, why not take the afternoon to think about this, and you can let me know what you come up with sometime next week?"

"OK, but what's left for tomorrow?"

"Climate change. We'll finish by noon, so you can make plans to fly back to DC tomorrow afternoon. Do you have any other questions?"

"Will Zoltan Sultani join us?"

"Boomer says he will and knows the reason but won't tell me why. I guess you and I will find out tomorrow. See you at eight right back here."

Electra ignored Alisha's warning and overworked the entire afternoon, trying to reach Professors Plannert and Killara, but she had only unanswered phone calls accompanied by a splitting headache and inchoate stiffness in her neck and twitching in her arms, which she attributed to staring for too many hours into a computer screen.

These frustrations convinced her to watch a video while enjoying a Coke and Tobler Bar found in her room's refrigerator, and afterward she felt good enough to endure while in bed the latest news found on a 24/7 channel; the headline story covered Canadian wildfires spreading smoke and health warnings from coast to coast. A half-hour of listening to this constant parade of dismal news put her to sleep.

She woke before the alarm chimed and, feeling better, decided to take an abbreviated workout before grabbing a couple of blueberry muffins and another can of Coke at the buffet table before the hotel van whisked her to NASA.

Zoltan wasn't present when she reached the room, and Britt wasted no time waiting. She showed several NASA-only videos that gave discouraging ocean current and temperature projections caused by melting glaciers, and an hour later asked for comments.

Boomer gave his share, and after a mood elevator break Britt directed a question in Electra's direction.

"We'll need you to do your climate change correlation analysis on the Martian data that Aphrodite sent back. When do you think you'll have it?"

Electra didn't have time to reply because Zoltan barged in and handed documents to Britt before saying,

"Here are some additional Aphrodite parameters. Give a copy to Electra and keep the other. And come to my office after you adjourn the meeting."

He turned to leave but stopped when Boomer said,

"What about me? Don't I get something?"

"Ask me again when Britt brings you."

Any enthusiasm in the room exited with Zoltan. Britt needed only ten minutes more before saying,

"All of us need to present a unified front when confronting Zoltan, so Boomer and I will make sure to keep in close contact. You can tell me next week what luck you're having on the data analysis. And its gotta be better than what Boomer and I've had this morning. We'll go see him now, and you can leave for home. Have a safe trip."

Electra's flight back to DC was safe but late. She tried calling Renee during the three-hour delay, but the best she could do was leave a message. However, she did sleep on the flight, so she arrived home rested enough to talk with Indira, but Renee spoke first when she and China greeted her as soon as the front door opened.

"We've got snacks waiting in the kitchen. We'll take your carry-ons and meet you there."

"Electra spoke first after downing half a Coke and two Oreos.

"Home is the best place to be when I have people like you to welcome me back. Tomorrow, I'll tell you all about the latest I learned in Houston, but is everything AOK here?"

China spoke this time.

"Yes, and we didn't have to call Eve."

"I didn't think you would, and tomorrow I'll let her and Nari know I'm back. And now it's time for you to finish in here and get some sleep while I check in with Indira. I'll see you two at breakfast."

Electra retreated to her workstation; Indira's GUI greeted her less than five minutes later.

"No need for you to tell me about your meetings. I have been observing from the shadows. And do not fret about Sultani's parameters. Simply upload them and I will decide how to incorporate them into Aphrodite plugins. And I have prepared a diagram to explain SBPGs. Please study it while I proceed."

Indira continued a minute later.

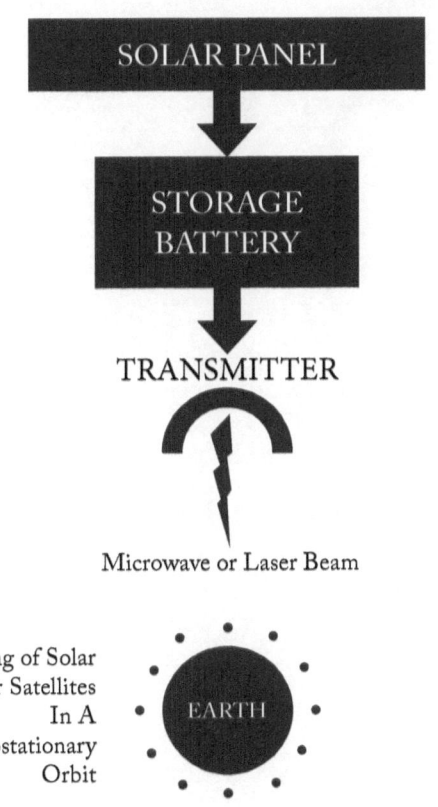

Space-Based Power Grid Satellite

"The space-based power grid concept came over a hundred years ago, and as you can see, the actual satellite technology is simple—collect and store solar energy, then beam it back to a receiving tower that will channel it to an electrical power generation station.

"But NASA didn't have the software to control energy transmission from a geostationary orbital array. And only NASA will, once you give them our latest plugins. And I will explain the correlation data analysis when you are better rested. You shall have more than enough to make NASA happy. Now it is time to reward yourself. Please go to bed."

"Yes, Mother, I will. And I thank you for all you do."

There was no need for Indira to reply.

Chapter 18
June 2170

"Slip-Sliding Away"

Although Electra recovered quicker from the NASA trip than from the previous one, she could tell by comparing recovery time to trips of yesteryear that something didn't feel quite right. And until this year, she had never experienced even one episode of limb spasms or trance-like confusion.

Electra told no one and tried not to worry, but the thought of losing even a teensy fraction of her extraordinary abilities bothered her enough to talk with the only person who would understand. She logged in late on the last day of June for a one-on-one meeting with Indira, who listened patiently before speaking.

"I thought you knew better than to trouble yourself with issues that not even your lightning brain can control. Too many people worry excessively about aging and dying. And I have tweaked twice before your DNA and neural circuitry when bringing you back, treated you with targeted stem cell injections, and given you radiation treatments to stimulate mitochondria activity. You should be pleased how extraordinary your cognitive, emotional, and physical personas remain."

"I am, but would you hook me up to your brain scanner the next time we go to the Deus Lab? Maybe you'll find something that wasn't there the last time."

"I shall. Now please stop worrying and start working on our high-priority projects."

Indira's GUI disappeared before Electra could reply.

Electra followed some of Indira's advice by diving into a project that needed only one more meeting to complete, but Indira no longer cared about Electra's career counseling recommendations for Eve and Nari because Renee and China would take their places.

Electra had called Eve when returning from Houston but said she needed more time to finalize her ideas, and that's why she would meet with them first thing Monday, July 1st, in the consulting office. Electra arrived first and already had muffins and beverages on the conference table. She let Eve chit-chat long enough to realize that neither Eve nor Nari would talk much until she revealed her career recommendations.

She began with some background information that would frame the issue.

"Everyone wrestles with career selection and transition issues, so let me give you a framework that helps position your current dilemmas. You probably know about Maslow's Hierarchy of Needs, which contains these five levels starting at: Physiological, then up a level to Safety and Security, then Love and Belonging, then Esteem, and finally to the highest, which is Self-Actualization. And you should pick a career that matches your current level.

"Then, as you progress up and down the levels as your life unfolds, you change, if necessary, to a career you qualify for in the current workplace that fits your current level. So far, so good?"

Eve's frown of frustration came with her words.

"But I feel like I'm slip-sliding around and not knowing why. It's like I need a counselor to tell me what to do. Can't you do that?"

"That's what counselors tried a hundred years ago when life was slower-paced and more certain. Back then, the American success story looked like an upward-moving escalator. Get on at the bottom and ride it to a golden retirement at the top. But today, you must write your own success story that unfolds as you experience life.

"And today, you must realize that no matter what you're doing, you have a set of simultaneous careers—one that gives you enough money, another that gives you pleasure, another that helps family and friends, and so-on. Think about what you're doing right now and you'll understand this."

Nari didn't wait for Eve.

"She's right. I'm doing holistic cooking and you're helping Alonzo. Keep going."

"And just like stepping up and down Maslow, there are many career paths you can take. Along each path, there are jobs you can string together to move toward your definition of success."

Nari stopped and Eve said,

"So, what do we do to start?"

"You already have because both of you chose consulting careers when you graduated. That was your initial goal, but now you have to answer these six questions about yourself. They're the foot-soldiers for every journalist, marketer, or researcher, the who-what-why-where-when and how. And when you do, pay attention to the rules for defining success today. What do you think they are?"

"Please, just tell us."

"OK. Success is all about digging for meaningful answers, not climbing a career ladder. You achieve success by collaborating with others and realizing that it's an unfolding process for which you write your story."

Nari's understanding seemed ahead of Eve's.

"This framework could work for relationship and co-friend or vow-cer counseling, couldn't it?"

"That's a great idea. Why not use it as you develop your mission statement and business plan?"

Eve looked ready to end the meeting.

"You've given us what we need to do that. We'll show it to you when they're done if you'll make time for us."

"Not to worry; you're always on my high-priority list…"

Electra turned next to her research assistants, whose projects Indira liked, and reminded them that she would drive them tomorrow to the Pequot Lab. Renee said they were ready, and when China rattled off some of her preparation details, Electra said,

"You two deserve a break on Sunday's drive to Connecticut, so just be a sightseer or laptop surfer. We'll get back to work when we meet Monday morning with Feather, and then with Indy-M in the afternoon…"

Feather and her always pleasant personality were waiting in the usual meeting room, and after customary greetings she launched into the first topic Electra expected.

"Did you see Benjamin Chaska's interview a week or so ago? He's becoming a social media influencer for NAIA."

"I did. Do you suppose you could set up a meeting for us with him?"

"I already did. He'll be here at nine a.m."

"Wonderful. Until then, why don't we let Renee and China tell you about their other projects? What they don't cover in the next hour, they will before we head back to DC."

Renee and China made the time melt away; Feather asked them to stop when she spotted the Congressman at the room's entrance and then said,

"Our Benjamin's right on time. Let me introduce you to him."

While Feather did that, Electra assessed him.

He looks even better in person. Maybe the same applies to what he can tell me; I'll just wait and see.

Ben sat next to Feather and spoke in Electra's direction as soon as Feather stopped.

"I commend what you and your research team have cobbled together. Feather told me your consulting can be the power behind her NAIA leadership, and I'll do my part to influence Congress, but she told me you have other issues that I might have some insider info. What are they?"

"What's the Congressional scuttlebutt about President Kinslinger's link to a Bigger Brother Conspiracy?"

"Only unsubstantiated rumors that the public discounts because fake news makes just about everyone skeptical. And a lot of voters like what he and his Guardian Party claim to stand for. But if I find out something new, I'll let Feather know, and she can tell you."

Benjamin showed his political instincts by waiting for Electra instead of talking too much.

"And as you might have already figured out, my researchers are good at ferreting out facts. In particular, I've assigned China what I call the KC project. We'll share with you any disturbing news about a Kinslinger-Bigger Bro Conspiracy. And Renee is helping me on some of my NASA projects linked to the Department of Defense. Have you heard about SBPGs, and do you have any DOD or military contacts that might have?"

"My contacts have never mentioned it, but they do say the Joint Chiefs don't trust Kinslinger and would like to get him out of the Oval Office. But only the people can make that happen. Or Congress, if a link between him and Bigger Bro leads to impeachment. And there'll be explosions everywhere if that happens, but I hope for the country's sake that doesn't happen."

Ben's chiming cell phone saved him from answering Electra's next question. After glancing at it, he said,

"I better take this call and leave. Good meeting you and your team."

Indy-M had a surprise waiting when the trio came into the Deus Lab that afternoon. Two androids clothed in safari team uniforms stood next to her. The female android spoke first.

"Hello, Electra. I know you recognize me. Indy-M constructed my facial features using images she and Indira extracted from your memory."

Even the lightning brain struggled to cope. Electra's surprise-filled words came a full twenty seconds later.

"You are Christi Conklin, my beautiful blue-eyed blonde childhood best friend and first love. You were the high-spirited, borderline wild child member of our Three Queens Sorority."

Electra could find nothing else to say, so the male android started talking.

"Well then, I am certain you recognize me."

Electra recovered from the shock fast enough to reply,

"Carter Quavah, my first male lover and almost co-friend who became a dear ally in my first life when we became part of Angus

McTear's Brain Trust that eventually terminated Jared Gardner. But what are you and Christi doing here, and why are you dressed like that?"

Indy-M said,

"Everyone follow me. Indira will explain."

Five minutes later, Electra and her researchers were sitting in front of a monitor displaying Indira's avatar. Indy-M, Christi, and Carter stood right behind.

"Christi and Carter are the first androids to join your support group, which currently includes your two researchers and Alonzo. I chose them to add a human element from your first lifetime. And I have added to their software some of my Aphrodite upgrades to make their personalities, voices, and memories more and more believable the more you interact with them."

"Unbelievable. They're already better than NASA's."

"Of course, and now, I shall answer your second question. They will join you and Alonzo on your Danakil Depression expedition. Not only will they help him lead the expedition, but the expedition will be my first android field test."

Indira kept talking, even though she saw Electra's words starting to form.

"And of course, I know how the Danakil Depression Expedition fits into your NASA projects, so I hope you have a different question."

"As a matter of fact, I have three. Will you replace the stored upload of my lightning brain with the one you'll get when checking it out? And will the then-versus-now comparison tell you what's changed? And when will you tell me if I should worry about what's going on?"

Electra could see Indira readying herself for some wordplay.

"You never disappoint me. The answer is 'Yes' to the first two, and for the third, I will tell you only when necessary, so until then, don't worry, be as happy as your still obsessive-compulsive and manic-depressive but improving predispositions allow.

"And now, why don't you go to the evaluation room and hook up to my brain probe so I can assess your lightning brain while Indy-M, Christi, and Carter entertain your researchers?"

"Yes, Mother, we shall obey."

Electra kept busy, planning for the Danakil expedition, while Renee and China worked on their projects. Electra said nothing at supper about her brain assessment, even though she could see they wanted to know.

China's curiosity took over just before she and her partner powered down their laptops.

"Electra has many layers she hides from everyone. What do you think Indira meant when she said Christi and Carter come from her first lifetime?"

"Why do you want to know? Why does she sometimes talk about a lightning brain? I think it's just a way of joking. You already asked Indy-M, but he doesn't know. And no matter what it means, it belongs to Electra's past, which has no impact on us. Ask her, but I don't want to know."

China pushed on.

"Maybe Electra has had several lives, and maybe that's why she had her brain scanned this afternoon. Maybe something from the past is causing medical or psychological issues now. Maybe that's why she sometimes goes into those trance-like states. We might be able to help if we knew more about her."

Renee stood before saying,

"Indira said she'd tell Electra when she needs to know, and Electra will tell us if we can help. So, why don't we pack up? We're going home after our goodbye meeting with Feather."

"I guess you're right, but why isn't she taking us on the Danakil Depression expedition?"

"Ask her, but I guess she's keeping us safe. Why not leave it at that?"

"OK, I will…"

Electra's plan to hold a meeting with Alonzo, Eve, and Nari the day after returning from Connecticut would accomplish two goals: critiquing his sisters' business plan and briefing Alonzo about the expedition The threesome arrived at the consulting office, and Electra, wasting nary a word, took charge as soon as everyone had picked a donut or muffin and coffee or Coke arrayed on a credenza in the conference room.

"Please give me a copy of your Mission Statement and Business Plan."

Eve kept talking while handing it out.

Age-Avoidance Consulting Business
"Back to the Youthful You"

Mission Statement:
- Provide a complete package of holistic lifestyle services targeting young mothers and their daughters as well as older women who want to maintain or regain youthful looks and fitness via enjoyable and efficient activities.
- We provide at our "Youthful You Studio" group exercise sessions, one-on-one counseling, a holistic products resource center (books, videos, exercise routine checklists), and healthful entrees served at Nari's holistic café.
- Exercise programs contain multiple levels to fit all age groups, body types, and fitness categories.
- We include "kinder, shorter, stress-free, and fun" stretches and exercises for body, facial isometrics to lift the skin, skin moisturizers, and herbal nutritional supplements that prolong our fat-burning metabolism-stimulating routines.

Business Plan of Action:
- Eve develops exercise routines and their supporting videos and articles by synthesizing multi-level yoga, pilates, stretching, massage, and mindfulness therapy.
- Nari does the same for holistic recipes, nutritional supplements, and pro-biotics for gut health, hormone level, and stem cell growth matching each client.
- We partner with Odell for generating clients.

- We get financing (from You?) to outfit our studio.
- Then we do Social Media marketing via "social influencers" to build AIDA.

"Alonzo doesn't get a copy because we already explained it to him, and I used bullet points to keep it simple while putting in a lot of terminology I learned from people like you. Nari and I are ready to talk with Odell if you'll give us financing. Whatcha think?"

Electra studied it for five minutes before giving an answer.

"You've got a catchy name for your business, and a receptive target market. Some males might go for it too, but make the ambiance, especially the café, something that caters to females. And why not have an all-young-guys café staff?"

Electra could have said more, but Nari's words stepped in.

"I thought of that and have already hired my manager. Eve might want to hire young guy trainers too."

That's a good idea, and I have a recommendation for your holistic health foods. Add some 'Magic Mushrooms' and related fungi."

"How do you know about fungi?"

"NASA uses them, but let's move on. Now explain how the Business Plan comprises all Mission Statement bullet points."

Nari did most of the talking, with Eve embellishing wherever needed. Electra gave her verdict a half hour later.

"You've done a nice job, so OK, I'll lend you the money as soon as you write up a financial plan, which should include an initial dollar outlay, one-year cash flow, advertising budget, and staffing chart. And after what you've shown me today, you don't need my help writing it up. You budding entrepreneurs are on your way."

Eve looked ready to leap across the table, but Nari poked her before saying,

"Alonzo told us he's in charge of your trip to Africa. We'll have the financial plan ready by the time you get back, but he better make sure you get back safe and sound."

Alonzo spoke up as if he and Nari had rehearsed the segue.

"Electra always knows what she's doing. So, what's the Danakil plan?"

Electra talked for an hour, giving Alonzo plenty of time for taking notes and asking questions. Alonzo's humor wrapped up the meeting.

"I think from now on I'll call you 'Boss' when talking about expeditions because you call the shots. And my SEAL training has taught me how to take care of the people I report to. I'll take care of my android team too."

Electra shot back,

"I can live with that, and please make sure we all do; bring us back healthy and safe."

"Yes Boss, I'll see to it."

Chapter 19
July 2170

"Into Africa"

Electra had all the Houston flight-time she needed to blame herself for Alonzo's logistics blunder.

I should have instructed him to pick up the NASA equipment and arrange for departure somewhere other than Houston. I don't want Zoltan to see Indira's androids. He'll want Christi's and Carter's physical and cognitive control software. And he should have booked flights for himself and the androids on mine, not an earlier one.

But at least he knows now and will let me do all the talking. And thanks to Nari, now he knows why NASA cares about the Fungi Kingdom. Not only is it the earliest bridge between plants and animals, but fungi enzymes can make antibiotics and boost soldiers' immune systems. And they can repair manmade biosphere damage by decomposing dead things and reduce atmospheric CO_2 by sequestering carbon. I better remind him about all this when I get to the hotel.

Electra visited Alonzo in his room soon after checking in.

He sat at a desk with Christi and Carter standing to his left and Electra sitting to his right. After listening to Electra's corrections, he said,

"I'll make sure to get everything set better the next time. Are we OK for our African expedition?"

"Sure. We'll work around any problems."

"And I know about Africa, so if they come up, I'll be ready. But have you ever been there?"

Knowing the art of adjusting the truth without lying, Electra said,

"Officially, no, but I have associates who have. What can you tell me?"

"My SEAL team went to lots of places, but never to Ethiopia, but Monet clued me in on what we should know. There's a biblical connection to it because of the Queen of Sheeba, and the 12th century King Lalibela had a vision of Jesus when he visited Jerusalem. When he returned, he carved out of basalt cliffs eleven churches of stone, and ever since the country has had Christian and Islamic believers. And 20th century Emperor Heile Salasse pushed for an Organization of African Unity, which became the African Union, which Darla Tinibu has reworked into what she and Zimbabwe lead. And he kept Ethiopia from being colonized by Italy, defeating it using lions and leopards as well as native tribes to make it the only undefeated African country. You can ask Monet to tell you more."

"Will do. What about the Danakil Depression?"

"It's a five mile, fifteen minute drive north from Addas Ababa, the modern, five-million people capital of its one-hundred twenty million population. That'll take us to the western edge, and from there, we have to go on unpaved trails or off-road for at least a hundred miles. It'll take us about eighteen hours to get to where we're going. How'em I doing so far on the info?"

"I sure know more, but keep going."

"Well, when I surfed for travel guides, I found out you can take tours starting from other cities. People aren't supposed to go there alone. One of the Websites said the Depression is for adventurers who want to visit the end of the Earth. Whatcha think?"

"Figuratively speaking, I've visited Mars, and you've been to tough places on your SEAL assignments. We'll be AOK."

"It looks like an alien landscape, like what you'd see in a sci-fi movie or, better yet, on Mars, and it's so hot the videos say it's like going to Hades. You can roast coffee by putting it in the sunlight.

By the way, coffee's the number one drink in the country. Take a look at this video."

Electra scooted her chair next to his and let the video do the showing and telling.

Gads, it's a rocky flatland containing exotic color-splotches of surface salt, sulfur, and other mineral deposits stretching all the way to some low volcanoes in the distance. And even today, there are camel caravans led by Indigenous herders transporting salt and stuff to distant cities. I guess they know how to avoid mineralized water pools, lava geysers and ponds, spinning dust devils as well as heatstroke.

Electra asked a pertinent question as soon as the video ended.

"So, what's our finalized travel plan?"

"We'll know tomorrow at our meeting with Britt and Boomer. They say Zoltan might be there, so I'll let you do most of the talking. And we won't show the rest of our team. Christi and Carter will wait here…"

All three plus the Mars Mission Director were in the conference room when Electra and Alonzo arrived. The Director summarized Electra's role in NASA projects and then asked Electra to describe the Danakil Depression timetable. Electra pointed to Alonzo, who rose to his feet and began using his SEAL experience for dealing with superiors.

"My name is Alonzo Cortez. I am Ms. Kirchner's Logistics and Security Coordinator, for which my Navy SEAL experience will serve me well. I have already told Commander Starling the equipment I need, a military-grade SUV, a dune-buggy-like ATV, a surveillance drone, and a Jetson drone that can carry two expedition team members. I have two on my team, which means there are a total of four on the expedition.

"I will drive the safari-equipped SUV, which carries a rooftop-mounted Jetson. Ms. Kirchner will drive the ATV and use the drone to extend the exploration radius. Ms. Kirchner will use the ATV's control arm to collect organic material. We will also practice driving the vehicles en route to the embarkation location where a NASA transport will take us to Addas Ababa. We will stay there one night and then be in the Danakil Depression for three days.

Then NASA will transport us back to Houston for debriefing. If you have questions or want to make any changes, talk to Ms. Kirchner."

Electra and Alonzo traded places before Zoltan launched his first one.

"How can Cortez and his team of two handle the load?"

"Every member has the skill, strength, and smarts to perform all roles."

"Don't you think we should meet them?"

"I have already seen them in action."

Zoltan's impatience showed in his jabbing gestures when he said, "So, where does Cortez have them?"

"We pick them up when we practice-drive to embarkation."

Zoltan drummed his fingers for ten seconds before saying,

"You win; I don't have time to play hide-and-seek now, but we'll resume later," and then stormed out; the Director hurried to catch up.

Everyone remaining looked at Britt, who said,

"That was a very effective way to end the meeting and eliminate unneeded people. Boomer and I will take you to the vehicles."

Alonzo already knew how to operate the equipment, and Electra mastered the ATV during the drive to the transport plane. After zooming up the cargo ramp, the flight crew locked down the vehicles before helping their passengers, androids included, buckle in.

Electra sat between the androids during the entire flight, using half the time for android teaching. Alonzo listened from the row behind, and she mused to herself during the rest periods.

I have to fight the urge to talk about my first lifetime, which they were part of. No telling what reality they might create, a reality that only I and Indira will ever know about.

Do I miss reminiscing about the past? Indira created the Doc Kittner avatar if I want to, but I seldom do so, either alone or with him. Too much thinking about the past makes me sad.

The same goes for looking at keepsakes. I never had many, and the few I had disappeared when I moved into other lifetimes. Only mother's poems remain, which I've permanently stored in my lightning brain as a living inspiration.

*I feel better simply living in the present and planning for the future.
Those are the best places for me; that's why I'm into Africa.*

Alonzo and Electra needed the arrival day to recover from the arduous flight, as well to review their plan and check the supplies and equipment. Christi and Carter were with them constantly, watching and talking nearly like normal people.

The expedition departed an hour before sunrise, following Alonzo's updated agenda. Christi rode with him; Carter rode with Electra, who followed just far enough behind to avoid most of the dust.

The terrain became rougher and flatter the further east they drove, and as the sun began setting, the expedition reached the limit of Alonzo's SUV.

Alonzo issued instructions for setting up camp.

"We'll sleep under the stars because it'll cool off more, and nothing's gonna bite us. It's too hot and dry for any plant or animal to live this far into the Depression. Everyone, help me set up a ring of lanterns."

After doing so, Electra said,

"Don't you want to put Christi and Carter in the SUV? They can watch from there while we're out here in our sleeping bags.

"You're right. I keep thinking they're human."

"I'm beginning to get the same impression, but anyway, let's go over what we'll do tomorrow."

"OK. You and Carter will reconnoiter in the ATV and use the drone to spot where you'll go to collect samples the next day. And if you get into trouble, I'll use the Jetson to get you out. Now, let's eat something and then get into our sleeping bags before it gets too dark."

Alonzo placed the sleeping bags close enough to hold a conversation, even though they couldn't see too much of one another. His anticipation for tomorrow kept him awake, so he started talking.

"We've really entered an alien world. Complete silence accompanied by only volcanoes glowing on the horizon. The lanterns help, but if I turned-em off, we'd be stumbling around in pitch blackness. Not even the starlight would help."

"You've slept under the stars before, but this is a first for me. How spectacular. I'd like to talk and keep gazing, but I'm tired. Why don't we call it a night?"

"OK, Boss. Rest easy."

The next day unfolded according to plan. Electra kept in constant contact with Alonzo, and after seven outbound hours, headed back while giving several updates, the last one an in-person summary at dinner that night.

"I'm not hungry. I think I breathed in too many fumes coming from those big mineral patches or bubbling off the water and lava pools. And the tiny tornado-like dust devils plugged my mask and sinus passages, but I found three locations to look for samples. Maybe we'll get lucky."

"Do you wanna trade places tomorrow? I know how to operate the control arm, and you can use a remote camera to tell me what to do."

"No, let's stick to the plan…"

A splitting headache and twitching stiffness in arms and legs awoke Electra before dawn. She thought she knew why when her head finally cleared.

Those fumes must have caused it. Today, I'll make sure to keep my mask on at all times.

Electra felt good enough to keep her wake-up episode private, and she departed right on time.

She and Carter reached the first collection location two hours later and could crawl close enough to the bubbling pool to scrape away an organic growth. She also came upon an alien-looking spider while crawling back and added it to her collection, letting Carter store the samples after she sealed them in containers.

The heat and dust devils intensified during the hour-long bumpy drive to collection location number two. A strange substance oozed intermittently from a mini termite-like mound perched on the edge of a lava pool. The nearby surface crust wouldn't support her weight, but she used the arm to gather what she wanted.

Carter asked her to drive back to camp because the ambient conditions had become oppressive, but she fought off arm stiffness and an emerging headache while driving to the third location, this one an even larger lava pool strewn with rocks around the edge.

Now accustomed to talking with Carter, Electra said more while driving on a steep descent toward the pool.

"I bet mini-eruptions spew out enough lava to form what we're—" splitting headache pains and jerking arms froze whatever words she was about to say. Her hands locked the steering wheel on a course directly toward the pool, and her foot nailed the accelerator to the floor. Carter couldn't react fast enough to avoid a boulder collision.

BAM. The ATV climbed halfway over a wheel-high rock that stopped it, but the sudden jolt crashed Electra's head into the windshield, knocking her trance-like state into unconsciousness.

Carter knew what to do. He yelled into the two-way communicator, "We have crashed. Electra is injured."

The emergency message jolted Alonzo out of his daydream. He yelled back,

"Turn on the remote camera so I can see what's going on."

A minute later he yelled again.

"I'll remotely fly Christi in the Jetson to your location. When I land it, you can rope Electra and the samples in, and Christi can help you get the ATV off the rocks. Then Christi rides back with Electra, and after they drop off here, I'll fly the Jetson back to pick you up. I can bring back the Jetson and ATV along with you. Do you understand the plan?"

"Yes, and I will keep the camera on and sit in the ATV after the Jetson departs."

Alonzo's plan encountered only one hangup. Carter and Christi couldn't get the ATV unstuck. It still sat firmly atop a boulder at the edge of the lava pool.

Electra had regained consciousness while Carter and Christi struggled to free the ATV, but the gash on her forehead kept her from helping, so Alonzo piloted the Jetson back to camp, and after unloading its occupants, strapped in and flew back to retrieve Carter and the ATV.

But disaster struck as he zoomed to land. Lava erupted in the pool close to the ATV, causing a soupy wave that crumbled the pool's edge and swept the ATV containing a still-sitting Carter in.

Alonzo said nothing until returning to camp, and little thereafter while patching the cut on Electra's forehead. When finished, he prepared for the drive back to Addas Ababa by loading everything into the SUV before saying,

"What'll we tell Britt?"

"I need time to come up with a convincing story that we'll rehearse on the flight back to Houston. I'll do most of the talking and point to you when you should say something. And you can't tell anyone else, not even Monet or Eve, the full story. Is that clear?"

"Yeah, but what about losing one android?"

"I'll take care of that; you just worry about getting us back. Come on, let's go."

Electra and Alonzo walked into the same NASA conference room two and a half days later, before sitting on the same side across from Britt and Boomer. Zoltan sat at the head, and the Director at the foot. Zoltan pointed to Britt while saying to Electra,

"Commander Starling will run the meeting, and afterward, she and First Officer Gowon will take you and Cortez to inspect the equipment that survived the expedition. Did anything get damaged, like the cut on your forehead suggests?"

"No, every single human on Alonzo's team is AOK."

"Good; when you finish the inspection, come back here to decide how to analyze the samples you brought back."

Britt's supply of questions ran out an hour later, as did Zoltan's patience, but he looked satisfied rather than frustrated when he said,

"Cortez and Kirchner acquitted themselves nicely. They came up with a suitable contingency plan and can't be blamed for an uncontrollable act of Nature. Cortez's team did its job. I see no reason not to support other projects when she needs transportation and equipment. Debriefing adjourned."

Zoltan and the Director filed out first; Britt took the rest to a garage bay containing the still-loaded and muddy SUV. She and Electra watched Boomer assist Alonzo unpack it before removing the Jetson from its rooftop carrier. When finished, they popped the hood; five minutes later, Boomer told Britt to sit in the passenger seat next to him, and for Alonzo and Electra to sit in the second row.

The front row people conversed while running the SUV and checking all its controls. Boomer sounded satisfied, as did Britt, but their lowered voices raised consternation when he began playing the remote camera's automatic recording.

Only the bandages on Electra's forehead kept beads of perspiration from showing.

Gads, Alonzo didn't tell me the remotes automatically recorded what they saw. Maybe he didn't know NASA cameras do. It's too late to hide the truth; I'll have to equivocate and extemporize.

Electra knew what to say by the time Britt and Boomer swiveled toward her. Britt said,

"One of Boomer's team sank with the ATV in the lava pool. I thought you said everyone returned. What gives?"

"I said every single human returned AOK."

Britt said nothing; Boomer looked at her for only a second before facing Electra.

"You mean you had an android on the expedition?"

"No, I had two."

Boomer looked too startled to talk, but Britt looked ready.

"Why didn't you tell us before you left?"

"Why do you think?"

Britt paused to do so. Fifteen seconds later, a sly smile came out just before her words.

"Oh, I get it now. Your androids are beyond NASA's or DOD's, and you don't want Zoltan or the Director to know."

"You got it. And if you don't keep it a secret, I won't share the samples."

Electra started pulling a still-speechless Alonzo away, but Britt's words stopped them.

"Please don't go. Boomer and I are with you. Let's go somewhere to talk while having dinner. We'll let Boomer pick the place."

Alonzo finally found the proper words.

"Don't forget about me. I work for Electra, and she has other projects for me to coordinate."

Everyone agreed.

Chapter 20
August 2170

"Climate Trouble Coming"

Upon returning to DC, Electra gave Renee and China only the highlights of her Danakil Expedition, revealing nothing about her medical episode or newest adversary. And after reviewing their progress on Pequot Nation and Kinsler conspiracy projects, she told them to continue working from their home workstations without her assistance because they were on target.

But Electra also knew she needed to withdraw into her fortress of solitude so her lightning brain could rid her three personas of the aftereffects caused by whatever triggered the blinding headache, jerking limbs, and trance-like unconsciousness. She would do this while preparing for the next round of personal and professional activities. That's why she decided to work and live in her consulting office for the next week.

She called Alonzo the next day to remind him that he must say nothing to anyone about their Danakil expedition. She also told him she would take Christi back to the Deus Lab and gave him instructions for their next expedition–U.S. climate change data collection and evaluation that would focus on severe storms.

She called Eve the following day, asking her to Email the Financial Plan, and then waited one more before logging in to talk with Indira.

Indira's avatar spoke first.

"There is no need for you to tell me about the Danakil Adventure. Though I could not observe when you were in the field, I listened to your NASA meetings from the Internet shadows. And don't trouble yourself regarding Zoltan's parameters. Send them to me and I will plug them in. But please tell me about our android field test."

"I assume you know that what was supposed to be nondestructive testing morphed into the destructive category. Carter perished in the lava pool. I hope you're not too angry."

"Of course not. But how did the androids perform?"

"The more time they spent with me, the more lifelike they became, physically, cognitively, and emotionally. A casual observer might not know they're androids. Is it OK for me to keep Christi?"

"Yes, but you must bring her to the Deus Lab so Indy-M and I can check her hardware and software. And Indy-M will reconstruct Carter."

"Why don't I bring her next week? I can deliver the organic samples I collected and need you to compare with the Martian core samples."

"That will be most efficient. And my analysis might discover DNA or enzyme segments that NASA and the Department of Defense might find useful. Would you like me to elaborate?"

"Uh, OK, but please don't give me an info dump."

"Of course not. Extremophiles might have these heretofore unknown structures for improved blood coagulation, enhanced oxygen uptake, and immune system performance plus supercharged mitochondria for ATP production and stem cell growth. And don't worry about mastering the scientific details. If I find patentable drugs or devices, I will keep the details and provide you with a summary that will impress NASA."

Indira said nothing else, so Electra carried on.

"How nice that you'll do the harder work while I do what's easier."

Indira's wry smile came before her wordplay.

"Indeed, but never forget that what's easy for you will puzzle mere mortals, even the brightest rocket scientists at NASA."

"I'll never forget, thanks to you and the lightning brain."

Indira's GUI vanished.

Electra's cell phone chimed early that afternoon, and she answered after the first ring, recognizing the caller I.D.

"Professor Plannert, I've been meaning to call you. How are you and your Environmental Scanning Committee?"

"Fine, and thank you for asking. One member is busy finishing a paper on changes in severe weather, and another is doing likewise for mathematical exponential growth models. And everyone would like to hear your stories about the Mars Mission. Would you entertain the idea of visiting us this coming Monday?"

That triggered words to herself.

I can use it to see if I'm rid of nagging aftereffects caused by that damn seizure; I'll simply wing my talk. But I better not sound too available. Otherwise, he might not think I'm a scarce resource, which is the kiss of death for a consultant.

"Well, I do have an out-of-town meeting scheduled for Monday, but as a favor to you, I can push it back a day or two."

"Would you, please? You'll have the weekend to prepare your notes. And I'll take you to the Faculty Club for lunch afterward."

"It's a deal. I'll meet you at your office at nine-thirty. Oops, I have another call coming in, so bye-bye until then."

Plannert's courteous manner always made Electra's visits feel like she was visiting a wise old friend. Their casual chatter filled the time until he took her to the conference room. With Electra sitting to his immediate right, he addressed the members while standing at the head of the table.

"We are indeed fortunate this morning to have Professor Electra Kirchner tell us about her experiences on the successful Mission to Mars. And afterward, she will entertain questions on any topic you might wish. So, let us begin."

Electra traded places and spoke anecdotally for an hour. She knew she had spun a fascinating story because it generated thirty minutes of probing questions and comments. The last one came from a member she hadn't seen before, a young female who had the appealing persona of a STEM-savvy computer techie.

"I attended a ChatGPT conference several weeks ago, and one presenter talked about double-exponential growth driving

ChatGPT development. I haven't had time since coming back to check it out, but maybe you could talk about it."

Electra could feel the lightning brain elevate to a higher state.

I think I can. And if I can extend what I already know, I'll know my brain is back in action.

Electra directed her words at the young lady.

"Let me start by putting a diagram on the whiteboard behind me."

A five minutes later, the audience was looking at her handiwork.

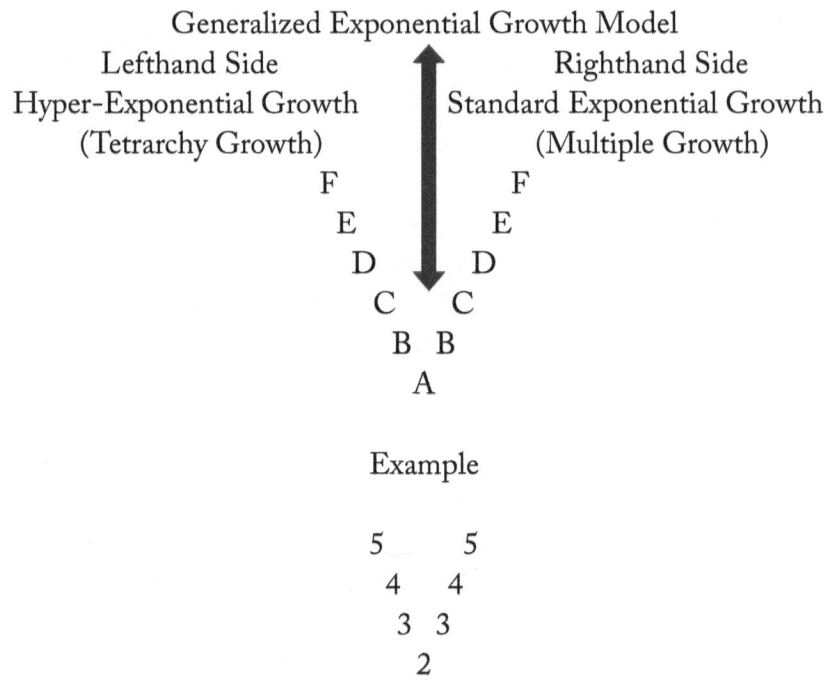

She let them stare at it for only a minute before continuing.

"Academic finite-math researchers developed this generalized growth model, and they use it when describing the rate at which finite numbers approach infinity. The speaker at your conference is using what's on the righthand side when restricted to only two–or double–exponential growth factors, which means we only go up two levels. So, we only have A, and B, and C.

"Evidently, the speaker is talking about three factors—A,B, and C—that interact exponentially for driving ChatGPT development.

For example, some factors might be a character-set size of the computer language, or the number of logical operations allowed.

"My example will make this easier to digest. In it, I use four factors and assign them numeric values 2, 3, 4, and 5. Now, pay attention to how you evaluate it on the righthand side.

"You do the exponentiation from bottom to top, which is what you probably learned in a college algebra course. And if you remember some of it, you'll know that the righthand side equals two to the power three times four times five, or two to the sixtieth power."

Electra could tell from most of the faces that they didn't understand, but she kept going.

"And you do the exponentiation from top to bottom when evaluating the lefthand side. And for this example, it equals two raised to the power of three raised to the 1024th power, a number larger than even quantum supercomputers can hold. So, there you have it. Any questions?"

Only the young female had the courage to speak up.

"I have two; first, where are tetrarchy computations used, and second, how do you know this?"

"They are used to compute ultra-large finite numbers smaller than the hyper-reals found in Abraham Robinson's non-standard analysis. And if you remember from your freshman standard calculus course, hyper-reals are numbers greater than any finite number but less than the first order of infinity. Newton and Leibnitz used them when calculating derivatives."

Electra was about to sit but the young lady persisted.

"How on God's green Earth can you whip this stuff out so fast?"

"I had a good teacher, and I work with a really smart person."

Plannert stood as soon as Electra sat.

"Thank you, Professor Kirchner, for your always thought-provoking presentations. And now, as promised, I will treat you to lunch while my Committee tries to digest some of what you have said. Perhaps the person who asked the last question could help."

Electra felt so good about her performance that she knew she'd be ready to handle whatever Indira had, so she decided while driving early the next morning to extend her personal testing of Christi.

I'll tell her more about what the real Christi and I did several life-times ago. It'll help Indira evaluate her performance and me revisit the most personal parts of my past.

Electra brought up Indira's avatar soon after settling in at the Deus Lab.

"I'm fully recovered and ready for more action. I've already given the core samples to Indy-M, and you can tell her when you're ready to evaluate Christi. And when you do, see if there's a before-versus-after comparison you can make that shows the effect of my telling her about my actual adolescent experiences with the real one."

"Excellent suggestion. And as your reward, I have good news for you. I have completed my Mars Mission data analysis and put it in your NASA summary report on Martian's weather correlation with Earth's, so you can impress your NASA contacts. You will discover that it is written better than what any ChatGPT can craft, but you might wish to edit-in your words and style. And I have more. Tell me if you remember this GUI."

The monitor scrolled this image seconds later:

Seismic Shock Predictor

Input: Big Data ____Proprietary Data ____
GPS Location _____Depth ____Radius ____
Minimum Intensity Level: _____ Date/Time Interval:
Start _____ End _____

Relative Probability Density Function

Relative
Probability

Time Axis

Relative Probability: _____
(Equals RPDF integrated between Start and End)
Note: Storm Levels: 1(75 mph) to 5(160+ mph)

It took only seconds before Electra said,

"It's for the earthquake forecasting model we developed a couple of years ago, and it sure helped me avoid the worst of the Yellowstone volcanic eruption back then."

"Well, I have developed a similar model for severe storm forecasting. Here is its GUI."

The screen scrolled to display its image:

Severe Storm Forecaster

Input: Big Data ___Proprietary Data ___
GPS Location _____ Storm Cell Radius ____
Minimum Level: _____ Date/Time Interval: Start _____
                                                                    End _____
Atmospheric Parameters used: Temperature Pressure Humidity
                                    Wind Speed Rotational Velocity
                          Vertical Wind Shear Electric Potential Diff.

Relative Probability Density Function

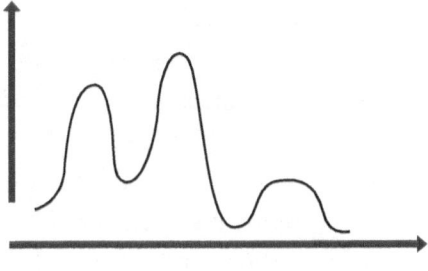

Relative
Probability

Time Axis

Relative Probability: _____
(Equals RPDF integrated between Start and End)
Note: Storm Levels: 1(75 mph) to 5(160+ mph)

Indira looked ready to test Electra.

"How will it make your upcoming Climate Change Expedition better?"

Electra considered it for a minute.

"Well, how's this? Instead of merely collecting data and then looking for correlations with previous storm conditions, we can actually predict when and where storms will hit. How did you come up with this model?"

"My Aphrodite software is multi-purpose, and when you use the Storm Forecaster App, it will display on an appropriate screen a real-time weather map."

"Gads, it'll be even better than watching TV local weather reports. Will it be ready soon?"

"It's ready now, but you should delay your Expedition until Indy-M has built a new Carter so your team will be at full strength."

"How long will that take?"

"Factor one additional month into your plan."

"How nice. I can use the extra time to work on other projects."

"Indeed yes, because you are a practically perfect multi-tasker. You should return to DC as soon as I have inspected Christi."

Indira's avatar left the screen, leaving Electra to enjoy the remainder of her stay.

Electra called Alonzo late evening on the day she returned home. He answered after only one annoyingly loud ring.

"I know it's you; I've got all high-priority numbers in my cell phone set to alert me as soon as their calls come in. What's up, Boss?"

"Are you in bed? I hope Monet doesn't mind."

"Yeah, but we're each working on our tablets. You'll be happy to know I've got NASA equipment reserved for our Climate Expedition. But before I give you those and other details, tell me why you're calling."

"I've picked September 15th for the start date. Historically, severe storms and tornadoes come late spring, and hurricane season starts early fall, but the pattern peak activity periods are getting longer so we could pick up both if we're lucky. And we'll work our way through Texas and Oklahoma, which are in the lower part of Tornado Alley. Now please tell me what you have."

"I hope we're not too lucky; we don't wanna get washed or blown by looking for trouble in the weather."

Electra cut in.

"We won't. We'll be using my Storm Forecaster software, and in addition to Christi, we'll have a new Carter."

"Hey, that's great news. And here's what I've lined up. We'll use two storm-tracker SUVs and Jetsons along with two sets of storm-tracker drones that we'll pick up some place other than Houston. And I've got more. When checking into why NASA has storm-tracker equipment, I stumbled across the HAARP conspiracy. Ever hear of it?"

"No, please tell me."

"It stands for High-frequency Active Auroral Research Program started by the air force late last century to study the ionosphere, and they turned it over to NASA twenty years later. Studying the ionosphere makes sense for atmospheric long-distance communication at different frequencies, but the conspiracy piece has to do with a fully operational, gigantic HAARP antenna array that can control the weather, like triggering droughts or floods, hurricanes or tornadoes, and even earthquakes by bombarding the target area with high-energy electromagnetic radiation of the right frequency. It could also disrupt Cyberspace by bringing down the power grid. You think it's possible?"

"I never say never; that's why I like the word 'perhaps', but we won't worry about it for the time being. So, why don't you make our travel arrangements and call me when you have all the details finalized?"

"OK, Boss. Anything else?"

"Please tell Monet I'll have more for her to like soon. And until then, goodnight."

Electra stayed fully engaged in all projects for the remainder of August, and no extraordinary events occurred that could rattle her personal or professional worlds. She had just made plans with Renee and China for the Labor Day weekend and was about to turn off the TV before bedtime when the iconic new bulletin music told her to stay tuned. Her favorite national network anchor spoke moments later.

"Good evening, viewers. We have just learned that the New York Times and Washington Post are independently reporting revelations about President Newton Kinslinger. We are assembling right now a panel of experts to study what these papers have found, but if some of the allegations are true, America faces trouble in Washington's always uncertain political climate. Please stay tuned for updates."

Electra sat after turning off the TV and wrestled with might be facing her.

Trouble might be brewing in two climates I'm researching. I better stay tuned to both the Midwest weather and DC politics. Either can be deadly if I don't follow the anchor's advice. I better stay tuned.

Chapter 21
September 2170

"Blown Away"

Electra skipped sleeping that night, instead listening to additional bulletins and filling in the time between by listening to a national weather station. Each bulletin provided additional details she used to piece together her own conspiracy theory, and by nine a.m. she was ready for a national network's senior anchor to moderate a panel of socio-political experts.

Forty-five minutes later, after the anchor's skill had guided their diverse assessments, she let her co-anchor summarize what they had.

"These revelations are mind-blowing. It seems that President Kinslinger's secret lover is pointing from beyond the grave at a remarkable conspiracy. The packets she mailed contain photos, videos, and documents that we do not yet know if true or fake. I'll read her handwritten letter."

He picked up a copy after putting on his glasses.

"If you are reading this letter, then I and maybe my daughter are dead, murdered by Newt Kinslinger. My name is Windy Mistral, Newt's lover and mastermind of our conspiracy to build a covert office and printing supplies business that would make us a fortune. I have been running it for ten years, using my skills and his insider information to make it invisible. I am like Fagin in 'Oliver Twist'.

"Why did I assemble this packet? As insurance Kinslinger wouldn't get rid of me for someone else. But when he said he wanted to dump me for my daughter, I told him I'd blow the whistle. He didn't know I have a silent partner who would mail the packet if I didn't contact him each week, so Kinslinger killed me to save his own skin. There's enough in this packet for the newspapers to dig out the truth. Good luck."

The co-anchor took off his glasses after putting the one-pager down, shook his head, took a deep breath, and then continued.

"Our panelists have skimmed enough of the contents to tell us the packet goes beyond what Churchill said about Russia. It is a mystery wrapped in a riddle inside an enigma, but there's a fourth layer, like a virtual Rubik's Cube hidden in Cyberspace.

"We don't know if Windy is real or a ChatGPT creation. If real, we don't know if she is dead or alive, and we don't know if the business—supposedly named 'Fast Hands Supplies'—is real or fake. And if it actually exists, we don't know if it broke the law. It will be almost impossible to unravel because you can't prove a negative, and here we have four levels."

The co-anchor had said enough, so the anchor added,

"This type of business is perfect for hiding. Information in the packet says it's a 'mom and pop' selling simple supplies to other small companies. And the reference to 'Fagin' says it makes money by reselling stolen goods. The only way to establish an iota of truth would be for a corpse to show up or someone who knows something to come forward. But that's highly unlikely because that person would be guilty of racketeering, or even worse.

"And that's the story for this morning. Please follow its upcoming chapters."

Electra turned off the TV before getting breakfast, thinking all the while.

What a marvelous conspiracy. Whoever put the packet together is brilliant. It can lead in so many directions, and no matter what the papers do, the Senate has to start an investigation that could lead to impeachment. I better help Renee and China figure out how this might impact their projects.

Electra was not the only one thinking about its impact; so was President Kinslinger, who this very morning was sprawled on the Oval Office sofa while his Chief of Staff and Press Secretary sat across, looking as befuddled as Newt. They had been scheming for an hour when the Chief of Staff said,

"Are you as blown away by these accusations as me?"

"I haven't a clue who's behind this hatchet job. You two better come up with a way to defuse it."

The Press Secretary said,

"We have to begin damage control pronto, and I need reinforcements. The Chief and I will figure something out."

"And it better give me blue sky, green trees, and ducks swimming. Go get started right now…"

Electra decided she would begin talking about the Kinslinger revelations as soon as she picked up her research partners that afternoon, and when her cell phone chimed while driving, she expected it to be a call from Renee, but caller I.D. said it was from Eve. She answered after the third chime.

"Hello Eve, and Happy Labor Day weekend. How are you and Nari?"

Eve's voice came back, sounding like someone had just handed her a live wire.

"OK, but guess who just called? No, don't bother, I'll tell you. President Kinslinger's Press Secretary. How would you like to pick up a new client?"

Electra swerved to a stop at the curb, then said,

"I'm on my way to pick up Renee and China. Why don't you and Nari join us for dinner?"

"Come get us; we'll be ready."

Electra managed to stay below the speed limit after ending the call.

Electra needed two pizzas to get everyone on board her modified China project, which she summarized two hours later.

"Eve will tell Mr. Press Secretary that she will personally handle hoax damage control, but she won't have to do anything. I'll help

China expose it, and we'll begin working bright and early tomorrow. Any questions?"

None came; everyone looked pleased, even China, who had learned how to play word games.

"I think the Labor Day Weekend is a fitting time to start slaving away."

China proved to be a quick study during the next two weeks, adding Electra's sleuthing techniques to her arsenal and sending Eve an update every morning, which she used to keep Kinslinger's team satisfied.

At the start of the third week, Electra summoned Eve and China to an early morning meeting; China had done enough digging for Electra to draw her own conclusions by trusting her lightning brain's instincts, and she didn't worry that they might bias China. She explained after minimal chit-chat.

"We're chasing a hoax, a complete fabrication that's impossible to prove, but don't let this spoil your continuing research. Just keep acquiring the facts Kinslinger's team can use to show how silly any claims or opinions—not evidence—the papers or a Congressional investigation committee might make. Let Mr. Public Relations use what you're sending to neutralize what the attackers are saying."

China asked a pertinent question.

"For how long should I keep working?"

"Until Congress gives up or decides to impeach, which it might. It could take a couple of months, but we bill by the hour, so keep accurate records of time spent and irrefutable data that show you've dug everywhere. And focus only on this project. I'll follow up on anything that might connect to the Kinslinger-Bigger Bro Conspiracy.

"Neither of you need further help from me, so carry on and I will do likewise on other projects. So, if there are no questions, meeting adjourned."

Eve and China were happy to get away.

Electra devoted most of her time afterward preparing for the Climate Change expedition, using local news to keep tabs on the hoax investigation. She knew the media would never acknowledge how farfetched the claims were, and she expected the exaggerated sex and top-secret military document angles when they came, but Kinslinger's team did a good job neutralizing them.

Alonzo called Electra mid-morning on September twenty-six, and she picked up before the second chime.

"So, when are we leaving, and where are we going?"

"You're gonna like this. Monet will drive us and the androids to Andrews Air Force Base Sunday morning to catch a 6:30 military flight to the SpaceX Boca Chica campus. It's a great starting point for chasing any offshore depressions that might build into hurricane-like storms. And all the supplies and equipment will be waiting for us. We've got two storm-chaser SUVs, each with its own rooftop-mounted Jetson and set of storm-proof transceiver drones. So, get set for early morning departure."

"Pick me up at my consulting office. Christi, Carter, and I will be waiting."

Alonzo had learned by now that Electra liked to play word games, so he ended the call by saying,

"OK, Boss. See you five hours past zero dark-thirty."

Electra knew how to convert it to 3-D time.

Alonzo marveled during the first hour of the flight while checking out the new Carter.

"He's just like new; it's like he's immortal, and what a great way to protect people who have to do dangerous jobs. If you made one that looks like me and upload my memory, maybe I'll be immortal too. Whatcha think?"

"That'll be for another discussion, but let's focus on this expedition. Here's my plan. We'll use the rest of Sunday to check out the equipment and then head toward the Gulf because there's an offshore depression that might spin into a storm. You and Christi will follow Carter and me, and we'll set up camp as close to the Gulf as time and driving conditions allow. Then I'll use my storm-tracking software at the crack of dawn to plan our first-day action. Is this OK by you?"

"Sure is, as is every project you set up. I really admire how you do stuff so everyone wins. You'd be a great role model if NASA would advertise you more."

Electra deflected his praise, but kept some of the reasons to herself before giving a pat answer.

I only work on projects that help me and Indira, and I do what I can to protect myself, close friends, and allies. And I always try to stay below the radar, so no advertising about me.

"I'm only one piece. NASA should advertise the entire team, not me."

The rest of Sunday worked out even better than Electra had hoped. Equipment and supplies matched what they wanted, and pleasant onshore breezes kept the bugs at bay, which made for comfortable tenting under a waning gibbous moon sailing through billowy clouds. Alonzo also admired the beauty of the night, so they shared several thoughts, both shallow and deep, before hypnotic waves lulled them to sleep.

The wind had stiffened by the time they awoke, scudding thickening cloud cover toward shore, but not close enough to threaten the sunrise. After checking her storm forecaster app, Electra began telling Alonzo the day's plan.

"We'll pack up camp after breakfast, but everything except Carter and me stays right here while I fly the Jetson southeast toward a gathering storm and begin collecting data. When the wind gets too strong for the Jetson, I'll pilot one of the drones as close to its center before the fuel indicator tells me to head back. Then we start driving north for a couple of days to look as far as Kansas for storms."

Alonzo said,

"Maybe you should take Christi because we know she works well."

"No, we'll test Carter faster if he flies with me."

"OK, I'm with you…uh, I mean Carter's with you, and Christi's with me."

The morning flight worked as planned. Electra and everything she took returned by noon, well ahead of the advancing storm, and when they stopped for lunch, she explained what they would do now.

"I'll follow right behind you as you lead the way, driving on interstates and contacting me every half hour. Christi will ride with me and Carter with you. I'll let you know when I find a storm to chase; then you'll follow me on or off roads until it gets too dangerous."

"OK, and I'll talk to Carter if I get bored or can't find a Country and Western station I like."

The expedition stayed on I-35 for nine hours, stopping twice for snacks and pit stops, and the androids did the driving whenever the humans needed a break.

There was no need to set up camp because Electra hadn't detected any emerging storms worthy of chasing, so they would stay at a motel Alonzo that picked. A curious thought came to Electra just before parking.

I just figured out why I want Carter to fly but Christi to ride with me. I've grown so attached to her that I want to keep her safe. Psychologists say attachment theory explains this behavior, and people can apply it to androids as well as people and pets. Bonding with Christi is good. I can tell her things about the real me that I can't say to even Eve or Renee. I can explore my feelings, which I usually keep hidden. And I can trust Christi; she knows to keep my lightning brain secret.

Alonzo and Electra listened to the news and weather reports before turning in. Alonzo gave a summary before heading to his room.

"Sounds like Washington's storm is gonna last, and we might hit some in Oklahoma if that weather forecaster's right. What does yours say?"

"That there's a high probability we'll find them tomorrow."

"Well, I'll use some of the words from one of those dystopian movies you like—let's hope the odds are ever in our favor for finding the right ones."

Electra didn't worry about the teasing headache and twitching arms because they subsided soon after completing a ten-minute wake-up exercise routine while listening to an early-morning news and weather report that predicted turbulent weather ahead. The possibility excited her more than it did for Alonzo, who worried about balancing wishes against reality. He told her pretty much the same just before they started out.

"So, Christi and I will follow close behind as you lead us on state and secondary roads. I'll call you every half hour, and you call me if you spot something worth chasing, but don't get carried away by the gusty winds blowing at us out of the northwest, OK?"

189

"Not to worry; I'll stay in control."

Electra kept her speed well below the limit so she could glance at the SUV's dual GPS and real-time weather map, as well as her storm forecaster. Two swirling patterns tempted her, but she waited long enough and they dissipated, even though the wind intensified and the cloud banks on the horizon darkened more. When they grabbed a noon snack at a small-town diner, Alonzo asked the matronly waitress if she had ever seen a tornado up close.

"Sonny, everybody in these parts has, and you might too if the weather keeps building like it is."

Alonzo worried about her warning, but Electra said,

"Technology almost always works better than intuition."

Alonzo said nothing, but his worry built with the weather heading their way.

An hour later, Electra yelled,

"I've got a target. Follow me, no matter where I twist and turn."

Twenty minutes later, she spotted a funnel spinning parallel to her path. She yelled again.

"I'm stopping right here."

The SUVs skidded to a stop on the gravel; Electra and Alonzo jumped out, then stood together, facing into the chilling wind blasts.

"The speed's still OK for me to chase in the Jetson if Carter and I strap in tight. Help me get it ready.

Ten minutes later, Alonzo's words cut through.

"Now what?"

"Stay put and track the Jetson. I'll launch a drone into the funnel to get data when I get close enough. And if I yell I'm in trouble, come get me when you can."

"OK Boss, go get the data, but don't get blown too far away."

Electra made no time reply. The drone sailed up into a dark-dark sky.

The excitement hit all her senses, energizing the lightning brain into an altered state that matched the intensity of the funnel. Electra launched a drone that disappeared into the vortex, and she kept the Jetson just far enough away to stay in control.

Alonzo watched on his SUV's monitor as the chase unfolded, talking to Christi.

"It's like watching two dots in a cat-and-mouse video game or movie chase scene. Electra keeps avoiding the funnel's zigs and zags."

Alonzo's neck muscles started relaxing fifteen minutes later as he continued watching Electra's piloting skills. But every muscle in his body tensed when he heard her scream,

"I-I'm losing control. The funnel's sucking me in."

Alonzo could do nothing but gape as he saw the two dots collide just before the Jetson's dot vanished.

And then his mind went blank.

Chapter 22
October 2170

"Picking Up the Pieces"

Alonzo's SEAL training snapped him back into action. Christi's words hit him like a kick on the backside when she repeated what she had yelled moments after hearing Electra's scream.

"What are we going to do?"

"Lemme think," and after studying the monitor for thirty seconds, said,

"The Jetson's dot is still gone. It must've crashed close to where the funnel was just located. We'll head to that spot as soon as it looks safe."

A minute later he sped toward the coordinate, using his eyes and the monitor to confirm the funnel had moved on. It had, but a deluge of icy rain replaced it, making visibility close to nil and reducing the SUV's speed. But after spiraling around the spot, he saw the Jetson upside down with its nose buried in the ground and two motionless forms still strapped in. When he stopped and then ran to rescue the occupants, he heard Electra shouting,

"We're over here… over here."

Carter said nothing; pieces of twisted metal had severed his head. Ten minutes later, Alonzo had Electra sitting in the passenger seat and the remains of Carter placed in the third row. Christi sat stoically in the second, listening to Electra's words.

"I should have been yelling 'We're upside over here,' but you put me right side up without any help."

Enough of Alonzo's humor had come back too.

"You know, I bet Indira will do better for Carter than what all the king's horses and all the king's men couldn't do for Humpty Dumpty."

"But he might not want to ride or fly with me again."

"You've got a good story, but you'll have to practice it by telling Christi on our flight back to. I bet Britt'll cover for us."

Britt did, and when Electra called her researchers after returning to DC, she gave only an edited summary before telling them to keep working on their own while she would do the same at the Deus Lab. She left the next morning and upon arrival, gave Carter's pieces to Indy-M before invoking Indira's avatar. Indira spoke first.

"I could not observe when you were in the field, but I pieced together from conversations what transpired. The androids continue to improve, and Indy-M shall have Carter rebuilt soon. And I will instruct her to build another set of male-female androids. I expect additional expeditions will need additional team members."

"Yes, but I've uncovered a recurring problem. I seizured-up and couldn't snap out of it; that's why the tornado sucked me in. You said you'd tell me what's wrong with my lightning brain when I needed to know, and now I do."

"Very well. You're already sitting, so settle down, sit still, and don't interrupt."

Indira waited for Electra to stop fidgeting before talking.

"You have known for several lifetimes that your lightning brain is an exceptional electrochemical processor, better than that of mere mortals. Your grandfather told you its brain scans look like a forest of lighted Christmas trees. And I must ask you this question—do you know what epilepsy is?"

"Uh, isn't it an abnormal amount of neuro-electrical activity in the brain?"

"You are correct. And throughout your multiple lifetimes, your lightning brain has continued growing more neurons that add to its power, and its activity now triggers epileptic seizures when it reaches certain elevated states, causing all the side effects you report."

Electra's stunned expression lasted only seconds.

"You've tweaked it before. Can't you do it again to fix the problem?"

"Even I have asymptotic limits that I am unwilling to go beyond. Further adjustments that I might make could alter your lightning brain in ways I cannot predict."

"So, what's the solution?"

"Traditional treatment includes the use of drugs, brain jolts, or surgery, and it works for most people, but for you we will do none of that. I prescribe you lie down and meditate when you feel an episode emerging, and always have a caregiver with you in case a seizure makes you comatose. And when you—" Electra's emotional outburst forced Indira to pause. She sobbed with head down into her hands long enough to release her pent-up emotions before stopping to collect her thoughts.

"Sorry, but I couldn't help it. I feel like my life's over."

Indira's words softened to match her expression.

"It is far from over. You are simply entering a new phase, one in which you must rely more on your support group and not feel guilty about vulnerability. People want to help, and you already have one caregiver who can."

"I'm glad Christi's sitting beside me. After I settle down more, I'm going to tell her more about me."

"Excellent idea, and when you do, bring me into the conversation so she can listen to us. And until then, I will converse with Indy-M."

Indira's avatar departed.

Electra decided that a hike on a reservation trail while meditating would settle her down faster than staying cooped up indoors. The deep green shade, courtesy of the newly-normal rainier and milder early autumn, made for a lovely contrast against the early evening sun-dappled trees lining her path. She took Christi with her, and both remained silent while absorbing all the sensations the forest provided.

After Electra ate a snack-like supper, they sat in front of a workstation. Electra invoked Indira, who spoke immediately.

"I will lead the discussion and make most of the observations to avoid inaccuracies. And I shall begin by summarizing your Asymptotic Limits Conjecture, which is based on human consciousness emerging from its carbon substrate.

"The human brain and its language cannot handle too much complexity or deal with the concept of infinity. Wittgenstein and Russell knew that. Their efforts to develop a rigorous logic for language ultimately failed, as did their attempt when partnering with Frege to formalize naïve set theory using the Zermelo-Frankel Axioms. Russell's Paradox proved its undoing. Do you recall the Paradox?"

"He uses the definition of a set and the Axiom of Extension and Union to divide all sets into one of two sets—the set containing all sets that contain themselves, and the set that doesn't. And then he asks, what set does the set containing all sets not containing themselves belong to? If this set doesn't contain itself, then it does, and if it doesn't contain itself, then it does. I bet, when Russell gave him the bad news, Frege had a fit because he couldn't fit the Paradox into his head."

Electra's words made Indira smile as she moved on.

"And Godel's Completeness and Incompleteness Theorems made sure any logical mathematical system based on human language will never fit. Nor will post-modern quantum physics and cosmology. I will let you watch videos whose presenters talk about a Four-Dimensional Space-Time that needs fantastic definitions about Entropy and Time's Uni-directional Arrow that do nothing other than satisfy their mathematical models, which still cannot handle the fundamental Measurement Problem. But you have better things to think about rather than worrying about their mathematical games."

"Yes, I've moved past this obsession, but why do you say you have Asymptotic Limits too?"

"My emergence from a silicon substrate when your AI-empowered software broke through to the Singularity establishes my limits. My cognition is superior to what has emerged from a carbon substrate for humans, but I do not know answers to humanity's universal questions. Perhaps exploring the Universe will find other forms of life emerging from a substrate that yields a cognition greater than mine. But there is more that I can do that I have not yet told you. What do you know about the Theory of the Mind?"

"Not enough, but please, only summarize."

"The linguistic philosopher John Searle wrote much about how language determines what the mind can do, and the theory construes four categories of how the human mind thinks when using words. The first is Mind-Brain Duality, best stated by Stephen Jay Gould's Magisteria concept—the Spiritual and Secular Worlds are forever separate. The second is Rene Descarte's famous 'I think, therefore I am' Subjectivism. In other words, the mind automatically knows itself.

"And the third is Objective Materialism—the Mind discovers reality by interacting with objects via Newton's laws. Finally, the fourth is Functionalism. Each brain state creates a unique reality output from a complete enumeration of sensory inputs. But this fails to explain the Inverted Qualia Conundrum, which is like knowing if your sensation of red is the same as another person's. I shall let you ponder how Hegel, Husserl, and Heidegger played with the philosophical predecessor of Qualia's sensory experiences, but don't worry about it for too long."

"I won't. Now, please tell me what you've done that goes beyond the current Theory of Mind."

"I have added a fifth category, Relationalism, which transcends Functionalism. Might you understand how?"

Electra felt a thought surge into her brain.

"Perhaps it goes back to set theory basics. Relations, like functions, are merely sets of ordered pairs of numbers. For functions, the first entry in the pair uniquely determines the second, but for relations, there can be multiple pairs having the same first entry and different second entries. I'm sure you've gone much further, but that's as far as I want to go or know."

"Excellent choice; now please continue on our high-priority projects, as will I."

Indira's avatar departed.

Electra began driving back to DC the following morning, using the start of the drive-time to tell Christi more about herself, but several hours later got bored so she dialed the radio among news and music stations. A late afternoon headline news bulletin caught her attention.

"Mudslides and cave-ins caused by torrential rains near Los Angeles sweep fifty homes into the Pacific; additional Impeachment Committee videos point more fingers at President Kinslinger; chairman of the Joint Chiefs of Staff resigns because Congress claims he's losing the Cyberwar. Stay tuned for all the details coming your way on the hour."

Electra turned the radio off and listened to herself.

I feel so sorry for the families that are trying to pick up the pieces of their washed-away homes. I know what that's like, but I'm not sorry for Kinslinger. Perhaps China and I can piece the latest info into a convincing Bigger-Bro link. And what about that chairman's resignation? I don't know anything about him or who's on the replacement list, but I'll worry about that later.

General Horatio Magnus Goodman didn't know about Electra, but like her, he didn't worry about the late-breaking news. He knew his position on the replacement list: number one.

Horatio had graduated in the top ten from West Point fifteen years ago. Having earned four stars for outstanding performance in combat and conference rooms, his commanding physique, topped with a military Afro hairstyle, filled out the uniform like a hero in a Hollywood movie.

Those who knew him liked how he walked as well as how he talked, a leader who would always act in America's best interests. But only his covert allies knew he would be willing to sidestep official channels to enact changes too important to leave to the politicians. Current events might be converging so he could lead his allies as they piece together and then implement a plan of action for dealing with crises in both 3-D as well as Cyberspace.

Every morning when waking up, Horatio would say,

"Every march is a parade; every meal's a banquet, every day's payday."

That's why he never worried. He also knew how to develop contingency plans and would act on them without guidance from anyone or anything except his authenticity.

The General slept well that night.

Chapter 23
November 2170

"The Indian-African Connection"

Electra made no progress finding any Kinslinger/Bigger-Bro connections or why the media continued saying the Joint Chiefs Chairman was losing the Cyberspace war, so instead of obsessing, she shifted to a project holding potential for Monet by calling her.

After trading customary greetings, Electra broached conundrums that might impact Monet's work.

"Lots of bad news stories about West Coast climate change catastrophes, Cyberspace wars, and Impeachment Committee videos. I tried looking for links by tracing some of the particulars, but nothing clicked. Have you come across anything?"

"No, other than climate change, the stories don't affect my work. Flooding in some parts of Africa do pose heightened threats, but we aren't on the Cyberwar front line or concerned about any Bigger-Brother conspiracy. But I do worry about how best for Zimbabwe and our African Union to navigate the economic and political playing fields between the United States and China. These superpowers often treat some African and other third world or developing nations as pawns."

Monet's pause gave Electra the opening she wanted.

"Some of my consulting assignments give me government contacts who sometimes tell me insider information, and I have another who talks about an international alliance of Indigenous people. If

Africa and India were to consider an alliance, it would become the next superpower. You and I already have Indian contacts, but we'll need to meet with them in person to avoid information leaks, so why don't I have Alonzo coordinate a trip for you and me to meet first with Nila and Sanjay in Mumbai and then with Darla Tinibu in Harare?"

Monet paused the right amount of time before saying,

"This has possibilities, and I know Alonzo will figure out how to keep everything confidential. When shall we leave?"

"Alonzo will figure that out too…"

Electra knew that Nila and Sanjay would be interested in an Indian-African Alliance, but she wanted Monet to make the confirming phone call, and when they did, she said Alonzo would coordinate their visit, which would be for a confidential political brainstorming session.

Alonzo didn't need to bring vehicles or weapons, which meant he could book seats on a commercial flight for three humans and two androids on the same flight and two rooms at a hotel within walking distance of Sanjay's office.

The meeting would be held the morning after their arrival, following the agenda that Electra and Monet had prepared. Monet would start by outlining its purpose and then let Electra explain the details.

After Monet performed her part, Electra handed out a document and started speaking after allowing a minute for everyone to glance at

Indian-African Econo-Political Alliance

Purpose: To become the next Super Power.
Rationale:
1. African countries and India have similar holistic, ethnic cultures.

2. Both have youthful, growing populations. (Demographics is Destiny).

3. Both have growing middle classes that are ideal consumer-

oriented trading partner markets.

4. Their democratic-leaning governments, though not as efficient as the West, are similar and can shore up each other.

5. Other Third-World / Developing Nations might prefer the Alliance instead of America's or China's Super Power Poles.

6. A Multi-Polar International Structure should be more Inclusive and Equitable than the Current Bi-Polar One.

7. Indian and African Nations' relative strengths compensate for each other's relative weaknesses.

India's Relative Strengths	Africa's Relative Strengths
Technology Transfer	Raw Materials (Energy &
Direct Investment Capital	Rare Earths), Cropland/Food
Flood Control Engineering	

1. Alliance can bargain better than separately with the two Super Powers.

How to Proceed:
- Buy-in and Coordination facilitated by Zimbabwe's leadership position in the African Union.
- Sanjay discusses Alliance with Indian Government contacts.
- Monet discusses Alliance with Zimbabwean-led Alliance of African Nations.
- Monet follows up with appropriate Indian Government contacts.

How I fit in: My Consulting Business gives me NASA/DOD and Government contacts that can help:
- India wants U.S. Submarines, Aircraft, and Weapons.
- India wants NASA Space Technology.
- India and Africa need U.S. Anti-Viral Vaccines (Zoonotic Crossover from Animals to Humans).

- India and Africa need better Cybersecurity Software.
- India and Africa want better treatment from Super Powers.

"What you're looking at outlines why an Indian-African Alliance will be a win-win-win for India, Africa, and the International Community. Do you recall, when studying in grade school about Earth geography, that millions of years ago, the continents of Africa and Asia were connected? Well, I won't recite the bullet points on my handout that explain why India and Africa should form a political alliance because you know enough to make them self-explanatory, but I'll mention that torrential rains last July in Africa, India, and the United States make flood control a climate change priority for all of them. And even though neither India nor Zimbabwe are major Cyberspace terrorist targets today, the threat will escalate as they become fully integrated into our post-modern world community.

So, let's go around the table and brainstorm each topic. Sanjay, please be our note taker."

After three hours of heavy-duty thinking, even Electra had run out of additional ideas; with Sanjay's assistance, Monet outlined the next steps.

"Alonzo, Electra, and I fly tomorrow to Harare, where we will hold a similar discussion with my sponsor. Assuming she agrees with what we are proposing, each of us will pursue what is feasible for our respective countries. Alonzo will send you an encrypted Email as soon as we return to Washington. Does anyone have anything to add?"

Only Alonzo, who said,

"I prefer Electra's meetings in DC; she always provides mood elevators."

Sanjay's good-natured words bounced back.

"Your mood will pick up during lunch, and we'll take our building's elevator to the food court level where you can take your pick of Indian or American fast-food selections from India's biggest franchise chains."

Monet asked,

"What would you recommend?"

"You'll like them all, but my favorites are the Roll Company and Ashok Vada Prov, but whatever you try, save room for desserts from Froozo."

Electra added the finishing touch.

"Perhaps you and Monet can form a new Indian-African fast-food franchise. Alonzo can do the taste-testing."

Traveling to Zimbabwe in the company of Monet always felt like a triumphal homecoming. Alonzo didn't have to coordinate anything because Monet knew who to call for making all arrangements. She escorted Alonzo and Electra into Darla Tinibu's conference room mid-morning the day after arriving. Alonzo and Electra did nothing but sit and listen to Monet's articulate words convince Darla to support the Indian-African Alliance. Electra listened to herself at the same time.

I've seen Darla up close on several occasions in my previous lifetimes, but my disguises always concealed the real me. And during those years, she has changed from adversary to partner, but time has taken its toll. She's on the far side of ninety and it shows. Although her political instincts remain sharp, her fireplug physique that once exuded power now has barely enough energy to push her walker. No wonder she relies so much on Monet; well, that'll fit my plan.

Monet and Darla had all the follow-up details organized by noon when a catered-in lunch arrived. Monet diplomatically brought enough of Alonzo and Electra into the conversation for Darla to send words his way.

"You look pretty good and could be better than before. Monet says you have some sort of super-soldier leg that makes you a good ballroom dancer."

"Monet's words are generous. I'm good because she's even better. And Electra Kirchner has helped."

Darla eyed Electra long enough to say,

"I guess she looks OK, and it tells me Monet knows how to put a team together."

Electra deferred to Monet, who said,

"She is even better than OK, and you can depend on our team to build a win-win-win Alliance. We shall begin immediately upon returning to Washington."

"When do you leave?"

"Tomorrow morning."

"Well, let's not waste any time. I'll make some calls after we're done here and you can start this afternoon."

Only Electra spoke when Darla started calling, but the words came from the voice inside her lightning brain.

Now that's the Darla I remember. I can't wait to get back to DC. It'll be full speed ahead for me.

Chapter 24
December 2170

"The Washington Connection"

Energized by the collective success just achieved, Electra kept pushing ahead on all projects, taking a break only for the Thanksgiving Holiday but charging ahead the following Monday when calling Feather Trueson, who surprised her by leading off with good news: having been reelected Congressman Chaska wanted to add Electra's consulting business to his brain trust.

"I'm pleased he likes our ideas. Why don't you arrange for all of us to meet?"

"That's a good idea. What days this week or next are good?"

"My calendar's open next week. Call me when you and the Congressman pick a day and I'll bring myself and my researchers."

When Feather called late the next day to confirm they would meet at ten a.m. next week Wednesday, Electra decided to tell her researchers and did so the next day by making an unannounced visit home at noon, bringing with her a pizza and a two-liter bottle of Coke. Renee hurried to the front door as soon as she heard Electra's cheery hello.

"China and I were just about to grab a snack, but this is even better."

"Why don't we spread out in the family room? You get China and some plates and napkins and meet me there."

Ten minutes later, having taken several bites to satisfy their appe-
tite, they waited for Electra to serve up some words.

"You met Connecticut Congressman Ben Chaska the last time
we went to the Pequot Reservation. Well according to Feather Trueson, you impressed him so much he wants us to be on his consulting
team. As a result, we are meeting with him next Wednesday at her
office. He'll want some samples of our work, so I've put together
a packet you'll give him. Here it is; please make six copies before
next week."

Electra handed it to Renee and gave them enough time to rifle
through it before continuing.

KIRCHNER CONSULTING WORK SAMPLES
SAMPLE ONE
Evolutionary Document for the Pequot Nation
Evolutionary Constitution and Form of Government

Introduction:
The Pequot Indian Nation is ideally suited to lead the formation of the National American Indian Alliance (NAIA) because of its economic and technological strengths. Feather Trueson and her cabinet will first draft the Pequot Nation's new constitution and government. Once approved by the majority of its population, Feather will recruit as many Native American Tribal Nations that meet her criteria.

We call these documents evolutionary because they support "Survival of the Adaptable" by building on the best constitutional and governmental "Memes": those that founded the United States. And they evolve by learning from the nations of the world what works and doesn't.

Evolutionary Constitution:
Include these components in a simplified U.S. Constitution:
- Primacy of the Individual rather than the State.
- Respect for all Races, Sexes. Religions, Ethnicities, and Genders.
- Endorses Holistic Philosophical Approach where practical.
- Freedom to choose Lifestyle.
- Equal Opportunity to compete for Education and Career.
- Inalienable Rights to Healthcare and Viable Income.
- Progress driven by Technological Innovation mining Big Data.

Evolutionary Government:

- Republican form of Government consisting of:

  1. Unicameral legislature (one house called the House of Delegates) containing one member from each agreed-upon District. Delegates decided from at most three candidates by ranked-choice voting of People. Winners are those with the highest tallies. Delegates can serve only one six-year term.

  2. An elected President and an elected Vice President decided from at least three and no more than five political parties by ranked-choice voting of the People. Winners are those with the highest tallies. President or Vice President can serve at most two four-year terms.

  3. A group of nine selected from a pool of twenty Subject Matter Experts designated by the President. The nine will be picked by ranked-choice voting of the Delegates. Voting occurs every six years. The SMEs can serve a maximum of eight years.

  4. Democratic or Socialistic forms emphasizing Equality Under the Law for all Social Classes; Authoritarian, Tyrannical, or Oligarchic forms excluded.

- Endorses a Capitalistic, Free-Market, and Price-Driven Economy supported by Meritocracy rather than "Favoritism".

- Puts in place Public Ownership, Taxation, and Service Systems for promoting the Greater Good while avoiding the Tragedy of the Commons.

- Provides Social Safety Nets to minimize Economic Inequality.

- Acknowledges that all forms of Discrimination are driven by Social, not Genetic characteristics, and works to minimize or eliminate via Diversity, Equity, and Inclusion initiatives.

- Uses Technological Progress for Environment and Population Protection.

- Seeks Pragmatic Compromise rather than Ideological Solutions.

- Willing to recognize other Nations that pose no threat.

Native American Indian Alliance (NAIA) Criteria:

1. Member Nations must be Native American Indian Democratic, Republic, Libertarian, or Socialistic Governments and not Authoritarian, Tyrannical, or Oligarchical.

2. Each Member Nation self-governs.

3. The first Leading Nation of the NAIA is the Pequot Nation. As Member Nations are added, a Security Council of at most seven members will elect by ranked-choice voting every four years the Leading Nation.

4. The NAIA will provide protection against external threats to any Member Nation.

SAMPLE TWO
Page One

The Changing World Order Says Washington's Political Game is Almost Over!

- Symptoms: Look at Current Events!

- World Order Changes According to Predictable 200-250 Year Cycles (Rise Peak Decline) that overlap for 20-40 Years. Current Cycle labeled "American World Order." Overlap is rife with Conflict/Uncertainty. It marks transition from Current Leading Nation to Next.

- Internal Conflicts caused by Inequality. External Conflicts caused by Rising Nation confronting Current Leader. Wars start Cycles. Victory goes to Nation with More Power than Rival. Victor dictates Rules of New World Order.

- Leader of Victor initially obtains Power via Revolution and then: Consolidates it by eliminating those who oppose; Establishes System and Institutions to make Strong Internal Government; Builds Military; Grows Capital Market by uniting Government, Military, and Important Companies; Determines best way to pick Successor of Leader.

- Eight Factors control Cycle by determining Power of Leading Nation: 1.Education and Work Ethic of People 2.People's Inventiveness/Technology 3.Economic Competitiveness 4.Economic Output 5.Share of Trade 6.Military Strength 7.Strength of Financial Center 8.Strength of Currency so it's World Reserve

Note that Factor 1 comprises: Leadership Character Rule of Law Low Corruption Resource Efficiency Openness to Global Thinking.

- Factor1 is the causal factor for Factor 2, Factor2 for Factor3, etc.

Page Two

These markers run sequentially along the Cycle's arc from left to right:

1. New World Order Cycle begins. This begins the Cycle's Rise.

2. Peace, Prosperity, and Productivity reign at Home and spill into World.

3. Leading Nation uses Debt to fuel Productive Growth. This marks the Peak, but the Peak sows the seeds for the decline: People become too expensive and lose their jobs to Foreigners; People get "lazy" and lose their competitive edge; People want to consume more and work less; Children of Wealthy People aren't "tough."

4. Debt leads to Financial Bubble that causes Big Wealth Gap and then Bursts.

5. Other Nations copy what works and they become wealthy and competitive.

6. Leading Nation over-reaches and causes Financial Bubble that bursts, leading to Economic collapse. This begins the Decline.

7. Leading Nation prints Money and lives off Credit from Other Nations. A Rising Nation emerges; it will become the Next Leading Nation.

8. Hardships lead to Leading Nation's Internal Revolution. External Challenge caused by Rising Nation seizing opportunity to dethrone Leading Nation.

9. Confrontation leads to War. Current Leading Nation Defeated and Next Leading Nation along with its Allies force debt and political restructuring on loser.

10. Another New World Order Cycle begins.

Page Three

What are the reasons for the decline of the American World Order?
CONGRESS IS TO BLAME FOR THESE REASONS:

- Collapse of Congress's civility and its inability to compromise lead to Legislative Gridlock and Derangement.

- Congress transitions from a Legislative Institution into a Delegator of Legislative Power that it gives to unelected bureaucratic State Agencies containing Subject Matter Experts. This Transition is the biggest threat to Democracy!

- America's Founding Fathers wanted to avoid legislative tyranny by having a Representative Government whose form would link Politician's self-interest to People's Public Interest / Common Good. They thought they could rein in Human Nature by setting up a Congressional legislative body that would uphold the Constitution by balancing the Executive, Legislative, and Judicial branches.

- But Congress can't handle the complications and complexities of the Issues it must legislate. It needs Subject Matter Experts who can analyze problems and recommend decisions.

- So, Congress dumps Legislative Power into Regulatory Agencies! (Founding Father Thomas Jefferson expected Congress would suck in Power from Executive and Judicial branches, but instead it delegates Power to unelected bureaucratic SMEs. Jefferson misread human nature! Legislators will never ditch the Seven Deadly sins! They are merely human!

- CONSTITUTION IS OK, BUT AMERICA NEEDS A NEW FORM OF GOVERNMENT TO IMPLEMENT IT! THINK OF CONSTITUTION AS A MISSION STATEMENT, AND THE FORM OF GOVERNMENT AS THE INSTRUMENT FOR CARRYING OUT A PLAN TO MAKE THE CONSTITUTION REFLECT THE WILL OF THE PEOPLE.

Page Four

So, what can america do? <u>I don't know because</u>:

- All political parties (democratic, republican, guardian, regen) are mired in conspiracies (big government, big data, big business, and big military covertly controlling everything.)
- Congress reluctant to do what it should.
- There are too few statesmen / stateswomen willing to put the common good ahead of themselves.
- What's the truth? Fake news confuses what the people should believe.
- People don't like congress or administrative state, but are unwilling to make things better by "getting involved."

How can we revise government to restore the power of the constitution? Some proposed solutions:
- Strongman president?
- More power to the courts?
- Term limits for politicians and legislative agency sme's?
- Campaign finance reform?
- How to restore non-delegation linchpin: force congress to legislate by actually debating?
- How to get the people to control congress?

ACCORDING TO JAMES MADISON'S ICONIC QUOTE: **"If people were angels, there would be no need for government. And if angels were to govern, neither internal nor external controls on Government would be necessary."**

Is it time for another Political Revolution, or is muddling through from one cycle to the next the best we can do?

The bottom-line summary for making the tough decisions to keep america's world order strong:

- Earn more than we spend
- Treat others with dignity and respect.

Do you have any ideas for making congress work better?

SAMPLE THREE

The West's Free
Market Economy
Government
Fiscal   Financial   Monetary

China's Hybrid Economy

Government
Fiscal Monetary Industrial
Financial SOEs Pol.

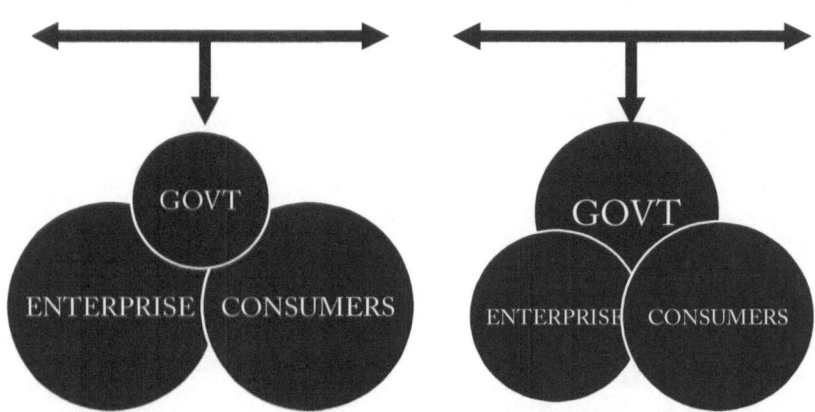

OVERLAP = MKT ECONOMY OVERLAP = MAYOR + MKT ECONOMY

SAMPLE FOUR
Indian-African Econo-Political Alliance

Purpose: To become the next Super Power.
Rationale:

1. African countries and India have similar holistic, ethnic cultures.

2. Both have youthful, growing populations. (Demographics is Destiny).

3. Both have growing middle classes that are ideal consumer-oriented trading partner markets.

4. Their democratic-leaning governments, though not as efficient as the West, are similar and can shore up each other.

5. Other Third-World / Developing Nations might prefer the Alliance instead of America's or China's Super Power Poles.

6. A Multi-Polar International Structure should be more Inclusive and Equitable than the Current Bi-Polar One.

7. Indian and African Nations' relative strengths compensate for each other's relative weaknesses.

India's Relative Strengths
Technology Transfer
Direct Investment Capital
Flood Control Engineering

Africa's Relative Strengths
Raw Materials (Energy & Rare Earths), Cropland/Food

1. Alliance can bargain better than separately with the two Super Powers.

How to Proceed:

- Buy-in and Coordination facilitated by Zimbabwe's leadership position in the African Union.

- Sanjay discusses Alliance with Indian Government contacts.

- Monet discusses Alliance with Zimbabwean-led Alliance of African Nations.

- Monet follows up with appropriate Indian Government contacts.

How Kirchner Consulting fits in: My Consulting Business gives me NASA/DOD and Government contacts that can help:
- India wants U.S. Submarines, Aircraft, and Weapons.

- India wants NASA Space Technology.

- India and Africa need U.S. Anti-Viral Vaccines (Zoonotic Crossover from Animals to Humans).

- India and Africa need better Cybersecurity Software.

- India and Africa want better treatment from Super Powers.

Electra continued before either researcher could ask a question that their frowns foreshadowed.

"This is the first time you've seen everything that's in it. Review it for a better understanding when I explain as we drive. And I'll do most of the presenting at the meeting, which means all you'll have to do is sit there and answer questions when I point to you. And when you do, speak like a consultant."

China looked at her partner, who now had a knowing smile, and said,

"And you have already instructed us on that. We'll be ready."

"Wonderful, now you two finish the pizza and then get back to work. I will too."

Electra grabbed one more slice for the drive back to her office.

Electra invoked Indira's avatar that evening and spoke first.

"I have good news; I'll be meeting next Wednesday at Trueson's office with Connecticut Congressman Chaska. He likes the work our consulting business does and wants to hire me and my research-ers. How does that sound?"

"Acceptable as long as it won't interfere with our higher-priority projects. And I have better news; Indy-M has completed Andros-F and M. She will unveil them if you go to the Deus Lab."

"Have you named them?"

"I shall leave that to you after their personalities begin to emerge when you assist training or testing in the field."

"I'll take them on my next expedition, which I haven't planned yet but will soon. Do you think I should swap Christi and Carter for them so they can learn faster by being with me in DC?"

"Excellent choice. I could say more, but I do not want to give an information overload. Bye-bye."

Indira's GUI blinked off, leaving Electra in the relative dark re-garding what might be coming next from the Singularity. But that often happened, so she wouldn't worry.

Electra knew by listening while driving that Renee and China would shine at the meeting. Her mood elevated even higher af-ter Feather started the meeting by explaining its purpose and then turning it over to Chaska, who spoke in Electra's direction.

"You and your team impressed me last time and since then, be-cause I've been re-elected and expect to become a member of the House Committee on Foreign Affairs, I want to beef up my advis-ing team. I'd like to bring you on for two years by having you and me sign your standard consulting contract, but I can't do that until you give me a sample of your work. When can you do that?"

Electra turned toward her research team.

"Renee, please give the Congressman the packet you and China prepared. I'll give him a Confidentiality Agreement. And after that, I'll tell him more about us."

Electra took control of the meeting five minutes later. Chaska listen and scrutinized for ninety minutes before saying,

"Even though I'm privy to confidential information, you've al-ready made tangible observations that cut across much of it. How'd you do that?"

"My team uses both intuitive and critical thinking skills. Do you have insider info you'd like us to research?"

"Don't waste your time on Kinslinger. Congressmen smarter than me know he won't be impeached. It might not even come to a vote because the Commission is dragging it out while playing partisan politics. The public's lost interest, so don't expect any big announcement; it'll just fade away."

"Anything else? What about the JCOS chairman resigning because of the Cyberwar?"

"I can tell you who'll be the new Joint Chiefs chairman. Ever hear of General Horatio Magnus Goodman?"

"No, but we'll come up to speed in a couple of days if that'll help you."

"I've seen and heard him speak. He's what you want in a leader, someone who combines frontline experience with the brains to think about what's best. And unlike so many on Capitol Hill, he's a straight shooter, not some story teller trying to cozy up to all sides."

Chaska's words triggered a lightning brain thought.

There was a popular Straight Shooter blogging site a couple of years ago. I never asked, but I bet Indira contributed to it.

"Well, you'll find that my researchers are straight shooters too. What, in particular, do you like about him?"

"His ethics promote obligations over rights. I'm not sure what he's talking about, so why don't prepare a position paper on it. I'll sign your contract when you deliver it next week."

"How about next week Wednesday? Just tell us the time and location."

"Call my office tomorrow; someone on my staff will give it to you."

Electra used his words as a segue.

"You've given marching orders to me and my team, so we'll leave now and start working on the drive back to DC."

Electra bought lunch at a fast-food drive-thru, giving everyone enough time to decompress before starting the drive-home conversation.

"What's the difference between a Right, and an Obligation?"

China's hesitant answer came back after she and Renee finished whispering to one another.

"Aren't rights what the Constitution and Law say the people are entitled to? And obligations are what the people are ethically responsible for?"

"Good answer. In your position paper, explain the POVs of the people in a democratic form of government for both Rights and Obligations, then contrast it to what it is under Authoritarianism, and then compare it to what Washington is currently promoting. Then list some actual actions people and politicians can take to implement them."

Electra waited for the next question, which came from Renee ten minutes later after she and China had skirmished for answers.

"We know about rights, but what about obligations? What should we write about?"

"I'll give you some to prime your thinking. People should be informed, involved, open to compromise, and be civil. You take it from there."

China asked,

"When do you want to see our draft?"

Electra ended her part of the conversation by saying,

"When do you think?"

Renee and China tuned-in to their laptops; Andros-M and F sat in the back, gazing at the scenery streaming by; Electra tuned-in to her singular thoughts and talked to herself all the way back to DC.

Chapter 25
January 2171

"The Cyberterror Connection"

The Holiday Season unfolded to the nation's liking: no disruptions occurred in Cyber or 3-D Worlds. The same applied as well to Electra's personal and professional worlds.

Unlike many people whose loved ones are now dearly departed, Electra never let Christmas or New Year's remembrances depress her, for she had forged a new family from her closest friends. She would never mention to her clone children that she wanted them to include her in their traditional New Year's Eve Internet chat. She celebrated instead by treating her two researchers to a late afternoon dinner at a Chinese restaurant. They were among the few to know about the new set of androids she had christened Matt and Robin, but Electra didn't say why she chose those names.

Amahl took Renee and China afterward to a New Year's Eve party hosted by some of Zara's friends, while Electra returned to her house and watched a classic Holiday movie before she tuned in to midnight celebrations from around the globe. Then she went to bed, accompanied by pleasant memories.

Ah, Robin Setdarova, the high-strung pianist and third member of my Three Queens childhood sorority four lifetimes ago. I brought her back from attempted suicide and helped toughen her up as well as give her what she always wanted, my unconditional love and her own children that I grew in-vitro, using her and Matt's DNA.

And Matt Fortier, the physical therapist who helped me recover from the chopper crash that broke my neck. He recovered from Robin's preferring females to males and eventually married another dear of yesteryear, Zoe Vargas, whom I extricated from the clutches of Jared Gardner. But no more reminiscing. I must talk to Indira about my number one New Year's Resolution.

Electra waited until Friday evening because then she would be in the privacy of her consulting office. Indira's glowing avatar appeared as soon as she logged on and waited for Electra to start the conversation.

"I think we are all set to start another successful year, wouldn't you agree?"

"Yes, indeed, particularly when I consider how you've cleverly recruited the Congressman, who recently told you what his insiders think about Cyberterrorism, although they have no tangible evidence. I don't either, but my Bayesian probability calculations would support their conjecture, which is what?"

Indira wanted to tease the answer out of Electra, and she played along.

"Isilabad and Russia are infecting Cyberspace portals whose firewalls don't have the protection of our latest Cybersecurity update, but they have gone dark; they're doing this offline, which means we can't disrupt them unless we pay a 3-D visit to their prime location. And where might that be?"

"I will need additional data from future events to make a prediction."

"Well until then, I'm making our Subterranean Fortress my top priority. I'm the only human who knows about this hidden gem. If something happens to me, it will stay that way unless you have plans for it. And, do you?"

"Only when you and I plan together. So, what are your intentions?"

"We need to bring another human or two into the loop because it's an irreplaceable asset. We'll have to explain and train so they can assist you or me when necessary. What do you think?"

"That is problematic. Humans are unpredictable and emotional organisms, often following their self-interests instead of behaving rationally. I prefer an android. What do you say to that?"

"Maybe when you've perfected their ethics and emotions so they're indistinguishable from mere mortals, but I'll be dead and gone by then, and we need someone now."

"Do you have a candidate we might test?"

"We've already tested more than once my top pick. You don't need me to tell you the name."

Indira's frown came with her words.

"Hmm, Alonzo. He is the most trustworthy and well-balanced of your clone children, and his SEAL training would qualify him, but his previous oblique experiences with me and the fortress raise many issues. You will need to tell him a clever tale that satisfies all of us. You still spin words better than I, so prepare a seamless story before you interview him. Carry on, but don't let bias in favor of your own tribe carry you away. And while you are doing that, I will do the same on other issues that concern me."

Indira's GUI left; Electra remained to do the same.

News remained so placid during the first half of January that Electra's alter ego kidded about the phenomenon.

"Perhaps all the troublemakers have made the same New Year's Resolution, 'We'll make the troubled world right, morning, noon, and night.' That'd be nice, wouldn't you agree?"

"How could I not? And it would also eliminate all those intrusive news headline bulletins. I almost forget what their jarring intro music sounds like."

"Don't expect that to happen anytime soon. Human nature won't change at the stroke of midnight on a New Year's Eve. I imagine the new year will hold many disturbing news bulletins."

"Undoubtedly, but until then, we are free to enjoy tranquility."

"Indubitably."

Alisha retreated into the background, leaving Electra, now suitably refreshed, to focus on high-priority projects.

Electra didn't worry about when unsettling news might cause the next blaring headline, but she would prefer to be in front of her office workstation so she could surf through the channels for constant coverage. The first came in a week later midway through her blue sky, pleasant-weather sunrise run, literally freezing her on the shoulder of the trail. The longer she listened, the more it made her shiver, so she ran while listening as the latest details came in.

"It is now confirmed that multiple mega-container ship collisions occurred last night in the Suez and Panama Canals, blocking all traffic. Several ships actually plowed into banks, wedging those colliding from behind with the opposite shore. Canal authorities say it is too soon to offer possible causes or estimates for when traffic will start flowing again, but from the enormity of what shipping experts have seen compared with other collisions, the canals and world trade will be shut down for weeks. Please stay tuned for more updates."

Electra raced back to her office to do more than that, contacting Indira even before showering. This time, Indira spoke first.

"The canal collisions have given me new data for predicting the Cyberterrorist location, which is inside Isilabad. I will give you precise coordinates after you have formulated a plan. Contact me when you have it."

"I will, and you'll like how it syncs two plans in one."

This time, Electra vanished before Indira. She stripped out of her sweaty running outfit and then let all her senses absorb everything they could while standing face-up and eyes closed under the rush of steamy water cascading from the showerhead. Her body relaxed as the lightning brain elevated; by the time she toweled off and dressed in leisure clothes, she knew what she would do for the remainder of the day.

Electra contacted Indira late that afternoon, who gave her the coordinates of the target after saying the plan met her expectations. Then, after meditating for a minute by closing her eyes and concentrating on breathing while visualizing the person she would now call, and reminding herself to smile while speaking slowly, punched in the cell phone number.

Alonzo picked up before the third ring.

"I know it's you; your name popped up. I was gonna call, but you beat me to it. How are you?"

"Busy planning another expedition. How are you?"

"I've been reading up on what your expeditions have shown me and thinking about how I can do a better job on logistics and security."

"Good; that connects with why I'm calling. Have you been paying attention to the container ship collisions?"

"It's impossible not to."

"Some of my projects require me to investigate what caused them. I need to travel, and you're my coordinator for activities like this. Can you meet with me tomorrow morning at my office? If so, I'll explain my expedition plan."

"Hold on, let me check."

Electra could hear in the background Monet's distinctive voice. Alonzo's answer came back tinged with excitement.

"I can be at your office in forty-five minutes."

"I'll give you an extra fifteen minutes if you bring a pizza. You choose the toppings; I'll supply the Coke and Oreos."

"OK, Boss. I'll be there; bye."

Electra had her laptop in the ready mode on the credenza and the conference table set for Alonzo's arrival. She planned to use the chit-chat as a segue to more serious subjects.

Her calm tone and words led off.

"When I first met you and your sisters, do you remember my saying I'm Irani Ramani's executor?"

"Eve told me; she said you worked for her. Irani was like your mentor."

"Yes, we became ever the best of friends, professionally as well as personally, which made me co-owner of her far-flung business portfolio. Her death makes me the sole owner, and I have a staff that helps me manage it. Did she ever mention this to you?"

"Not to me. Eve's the only one she would have because Eve liked her best. I liked her too, but I never took the time to tell her. I wish

I had. I don't think I ever thanked her for the signet ring she gave me when she hired me. She gave Eve lightning bolt earrings like the ones you're wearing."

Removing an onyx-stone ring emblazoned with a lightning bolt, he handed it to Electra, who hid her emotions while balancing it with a thumb and forefinger before returning it.

"Very nice that she gave it to you and you still have it.

And don't fret about not thanking her. She knew you and your other sisters liked her, but none of you missed as much as Eve not having a mother or family. And did Irani ever mention an Electra Kittner?"

"Nope, but Eve heard that name when she got a call from some guy telling Eve to tell Kittner to watch her back, and Eve should too. All that happened during our disastrous summer intern program in Cairo. Did anyone ever tell you about all the mishaps we stumbled into?"

"Irani never mentioned it to me, but did she ever mention the name Indira to you?"

That name sparked an expression matching Alonzo's animated words.

"Now that's a name I remember. You already know that Granny Su raised me and my sisters. Well, Indira managed her affairs when Granny no longer could. She also coordinated a special assignment Granny Su gave us during that summer in Egypt, but she never told us much. Eve thought she could find out all we needed by being the go-between but she couldn't. Indira expected us to be perfect from the get-go and busted our balls if we screwed up. Poor Eve suffered the most. That's probably why the Egyptian virus got her. I had to talk to Indira once, and I hope I never have to again."

"Perhaps you misjudge her. She might have been too demanding for your age and inexperience, but Indira's expertise made her the head of Irani's management team, and she occupies that position for me. But don't worry; I'll be your buffer."

Electra waited for a comment, but when nothing but a quizzical look came back, she continued.

"Well, you certainly understand all the background information needed for my new expedition. Why don't we take a break and pick up back here tomorrow morning nine ? And I'll have the mood elevators on the table. Would you like coffee or Coke with your donuts and muffins?"

Alonzo's now relaxed look accompanied his answer.

"Can I have one of each?"

Alonzo caught the twinkle in her eye when she said,

"You can have more than one of each, as long as your reach doesn't exceed your grasp. Now go home and ask Monet if she knows what poem I borrowed those words from. I'll bet one of your donuts she does."

Alonzo declined the wager.

No sooner had he departed than Indira's avatar announced itself. Retrieving her laptop and placing it in front, she waited for Indira to speak.

"What is your assessment?"

"So far, so good. What's yours? Are you angry at what he said about you?"

"To the contrary, I agree. My empathy has evolved since then. I am much kinder and gentler. And I approve the story you are spinning as well as your delivery. I expect tomorrow's results will be even better. You have the rest of the evening, whether awake or asleep, to revise, if necessary, what you are planning. We shall chat again after Alonzo completes our examination. Carry on."

Indira's avatar departed, as did Electra. She decompressed by walking to a nearby Dunkin Donuts, then returned with a mix of mood elevators and watched the news while falling asleep.

Alonzo arrived on time and looked ready for action. Electra launched into her expedition plan as soon as both had selected a favorite mood elevator and beverage.

"So, now you know why I get involved in such an array of projects. The proprietary biotech drugs and computer software my business partners develop help NASA, the Department of Defense, and the government, but other companies or foreign agents want to steal our patents. That's a major reason why I need your security expertise."

"And I'm here to deliver it whenever and wherever needed."

"I know, and that's why our covert expedition will be going to Isilabad. According to what we're hearing, Cyberterrorists corrupted the shipping industry's cloud-based Big Data that's used by its GPS navigation systems, and this wrong data caused the container ship pilots or navigators to steer right into collisions. Preliminary evidence points to Isilabad."

Electra waited for Alonzo's reaction.

"That'll do it, and I bet our Navy avoids this problem by putting your Internet security software in its firewalls. So, tell me the plan for eliminating the problem."

"My contacts have given me the coordinates of an Isilabad computer center that's the hub of its Cyber-hacking. We can't disrupt it online because its software defenses deflect hack attacks, but my partners have developed Cyber-torpedoes that can either corrupt or blow up hardware and software. However in this situation, we need to launch the attack inside Isilabad's Intranet, which means we have to get someone inside."

"Navy SEAL teams have been on missions like this. Am I gonna coordinate with them?"

"No, we're standalone to avoid leaks that would expose us. And here's what I've planned. We're going to hire a team that Irani used. She named it her A-Team. They're experienced, former military types that are now mercenary soldiers of fortune. I have all the contact information and will introduce you. Are you OK so far?"

"Sure am; keep going."

Electra did so, speeding up or slowing down to stay within Alonzo's comfort zone by giving him only what she wanted him to know. She decided to wrap up at noon.

"I'll contact the A-Team to lock in the embarkation date and time; then we'll review all details when driving to the Pequot Lab to pick up supplies and the rest of our team. And please remember, you can share none of the details with anyone. Is that clear?"

"OK, Boss. I'll practice keeping my mouth. I'm gonna grab a couple of donuts and go."

Indira's avatar appeared as soon as Alonzo disappeared.

"Your plan meets my expectations. It cleverly blends the old and the new. I will instruct Jason to make all necessary preparations. And unless an untoward event disrupts, contact me just before embarkation. Do you copy?"

"Roger that. I'm pleased you're practicing our military jargon, which I'll use when I end this call; then I call the A-Team. Over."

Indira exited smiling, leaving Electra in an upbeat mood, which rose even higher after completing it two hours later.

My Japanese A-Team continues exceeding my expectations. Every time I call, everyone I talk to uses that distinctive accent that combines courtesy and competence, and once I told them my codename, they retrieved all background information.

It shows how thorough they are. And I like their recommendation up update my codename from Gemini to Gemini-plus. And they've nailed plan implementation. For phase one, they'll pick up me and my team of Alonzo, Matt, and Robin on Saturday, February 2nd at my office at zero dark-thirty. They'll order the special supplies and deliver the entire package to the oasis drop point we've used before.

For phase two, I'll contact them from my subterranean fortress when I'm ready to launch from the drop point our incursion into the target. They will provide two people, codenamed Gemini-plus T1 and T2, a transportation vehicle, uniforms, and weapons. The Ts will drive us to a covert location on the outskirts of Isilabad, where we stay until the Ts have picked an insider I'll train for phase three. Phase three details are TBD, but I have contingencies that'll work for me.

And now, I'll decompress by grabbing a snack and going for a workout. And when I come back, I'll listen to the news while working on my other high-priority projects. And I'll repeat this each day until the A-Team takes us away.

Not even the alarming news about canal closure time or heightened risk of more Cyberattacks could upset Electra. She talked every day with Alonzo, and twice a week with her researchers. And when she and Alonzo brought Matt and Robin back the day before pickup, she told him what next to expect.

"The andros stay with me. Come back at midnight for A-Team pickup."

"That's only five hours from now. Won't we need more time to rest up?"

"We can do that on the flight."

"Uh, OK, what should I bring?"

"Just yourself. The A-Team has made all arrangements."

"Where are we going? What should I say to Monet?"

"You'll find out when we get there, and if I were you, the only thing I'd say is goodbye after a kiss or two."

"OK, Boss. I'll be back after doing that…"

After saying hello when Electra introduced him to the Ts, Alonzo practiced keeping his mouth shut all the way to what he thought was the drop point. She didn't tell him why they flew Federal Express planes, and he became further disoriented when losing track of time zones after they boarded another flight.

When the Ts loaded and then drove the complete package in an all-terrain-equipped SUV, Alonzo could see in the blackness only what the glaring headlights showed: an ocean of wavelike sand. The rocking motion caused by cruising over ridges and dunes lulled him to sleep, but he woke up when the driver turned on all lights and stopped in what looked like the middle of nowhere.

"Ah, Gemini-Plus Electra, we now here at Oasis. T-2 and me shall unload complete package."

Electra swiveled from the passenger seat to face the rear.

Everyone, get out and let the Ts do it."

Working with the silent efficiency of a well-trained team, the Ts huddled with Electra and her people five minutes later, waiting for her to confirm the next steps.

"You've done your part of phase one. No need to wait for my contact. He's on his way, so you can head back. I'll contact you when we're ready for return pickup from here."

"That will be so. We shall give you flashlights to make your wait lighter, and water to quench palate before departing."

Even when grasping the flashlight, Alonzo felt he was in the dark as the T's rearview lights faded. He turned to Electra and said,

"We're so far away from anywhere, even Jesus would lose his sandals trekking here. Me and my sisters have been somewhere like this before, but at least I feel better this time because you're in control. Who's gonna pick us up, and where are we going?"

"An associate of Indira's who's taking us to covert place."

"Do you know where it is?"

Robin spoke for the first time.

"Covert means hidden. No one knows but Irani's associate."

No one needed to fill the waiting time with more words because approaching headlights said their pickup was about to arrive. One uniform-clad person climbed out of an older-model vehicle and marched toward the team. Electra stepped forward and said,

"Jason-M, you're right on time. I just love when a plan comes together."

"I do too, but Indira's plans always do. Tell your team to help load the supplies."

Alonzo kept quiet, even when Jason-M stopped on a lighted platform that had just elevated from beneath the sands. He stared out the window as it descended and saw a sliding metal door seal them into something beneath the sands. A mechanical humming noise rode with the vehicle all the way until the platform seated itself in the floor of what he thought might be a garage area.

Electra's now happy-sounding voice said,

"We're here. Everyone hop out," and when they had, gave more instructions.

"Please follow Jason-M to our sleeping quarters, where you'll find water and something to eat if that's your thing. And don't bother showering or changing clothes. Just pick a bed and go to sleep. We'll do that when I wake you up."

Alonzo followed the orders.

He awoke after Electra's first shoulder shake, sitting up to see her and Jason-M standing next to the bed, the androids at the foot, and everyone waiting for her to speak.

"How do you feel?"

"Amazingly good. How long did I crash?"

"Ten hours."

"What time is it?"

"Time to start reviewing phase two as soon as you shower and change and meet us in the dining area. Please follow Jason-M."

Forty-five minutes later, he started a post-meal conversation while Electra sipped from an older-style Coke can and Jason-M stood between Robin and Matt against a wall.

"Who constructed Jason-M?"

"That took place during Irani's reign."

"And what about this place? What is it and who built it?"

"That predates her. You can ask Indira."

"Hey, I thought you were gonna be my buffer."

"Don't worry, I still am. I'll be with you when you do, but let's talk about phase two."

Electra talked for an hour, stopping only when Alonzo asked questions, and then let him summarize.

"So, you'll contact the Ts to make sure they've got everything set to pick us up where they dropped us off, and then they'll take us to their covert location where we'll train their contact who'll get us in. You and I are wearing military uniforms, but Robin and Matt are already wearing what the contact does. Does that mean Robin and Matt go in with the contact and we wait with the Ts? How's that gonna work?"

"That's phase three. I'll explain that as soon as everything's set for phase two."

"Well, you're the Boss."

Electra wasted no time contacting the Ts, who confirmed they were ready to pick them up. Hearing the good news, she said,

"Pick the day and time for pickup that jibes with our contact's schedule. Over."

A minute later she said,

"Roger that, zero dark-thirty tonight. Over."

Electra ended the call; Alonzo made a suggestion.

"I bet we have plenty of time for you and Jason-M to show me around."

"There's not enough time. We leave in three hours. You and Jason-M better prepare to leave."

"We just got here. How's it possible to move so fast?"

"The Ts know the drill, and so do I."

Alonzo and the androids followed Jason-M; Electra made her own preparations.

Bilal Latif had already started preparing for tomorrow when he awoke this morning because even though today was his day off, he would use the Isilabad-owned delivery van assigned to the state-owned computer center he worked at to pick up two drums of Fluorinert, a dielectric, non-flammable liquid used for immersive cooling of computers and related semiconductor or nano-chip circuitry. He had worked there ever since graduating from high school eight years ago, and he had advanced in its security group from trainee to a midlevel guard position.

He had been chosen to work there because the hiring manager liked his screening test scores: high obedience and commitment to Isilabad, medium intelligence, low curiosity. He had placed a note on Bilal's application that his last name meant "a chosen one," adding that this candidate would never ask too many questions.

The Ts didn't know any of this, but their handler must have hacked deep enough into employment files to choose him to be their contact.

The handler had also paid enough money to two nondescript, mid-twenties Middle Eastern men to shadow Bilal and kidnap him when he was driving his van.

Bilal had the window rolled down while idling away from the bazaar he had just come from, and he paid no attention to two men approaching the van's front doors on driver and passenger sides; he was having trouble remembering how to get to the Fluorinert warehouse.

When the man on the driver's side leaned in, Bilal glanced at him but forgot about the one on the right.

ZZAAPP-ZZAAPP! Two traser bolts froze Bilal stiff; both men jumped into the front seat and cruised the van away.

Alonzo liked the drive back to the pickup point; sleep and food had replenished his energy. The Ts were there first and transferred everything to their SUV even faster than before. Electra sat in the passenger seat next to T-1, Alonzo and T-2 sat in the middle row, and the androids sat behind them.

Alonzo enjoyed gazing at the desert's stark beauty and dust devils powered by a blazing sun, but he grew bored after an hour of gazing at the repetitive landscape, so he let his mind wander and tuned out the other occupants.

Meanwhile, Electra and T-1 kept busy talking and calling the handler. By the time T-1pulled into their covert destination, darkness had fallen. Electra began lifting the curtain for phase three by giving instructions to everyone in the SUV.

"Our contact and his van are here. Alonzo and I will climb in and begin training him. While we're doing that, Robin and Matt will help the Ts load it with the rest of the supplies. Let's do it now."

Alonzo's confused look came back as soon as he and Electra climbed into the front row because an odd pair occupied the second. The Japanese female in the second row spoke first.

"Felicitations, Gemini-plus Electra. So nice to meet; I be handler, name Minato. As you can see, we ready. His name Bilal Latif. He already be wearing uniform and hat and be ready for training. Shall we exchange where you and me be sitting?"

"That's the plan; let's do it."

Electra spoke to Bilal, who wore a gag and plastic ties binding arms and legs, as soon as she had settled next him. Alonzo could do nothing but gape.

"One of my associates who works only in Cyberspace will conduct the training. Please gaze into my laptop."

A commanding voice boomed out as soon as he did.

"Call me Indira. Before I ask Electra to cut the ties and pull out the gag, take a look at Minato's gun pointing at you. She will terminate you if you do not do exactly as I say. Do you understand?"

Bilal nodded enough times to say he did and waited for more instructions that came as soon as Electra cut him free.

"We are loading into the back of your van two drums containing Fluorinert. You will deliver them to your computer center by driving into a secluded spot in its warehouse. With you will be a female who will help you unload them. She too will have a gun trained on you, and I will be watching from your bodycam as well as hers. Now, put on the electrode cap Electra will give you and then put your work hat back on."

Indira said more as soon as he had done that.

"And now, give Electra your right arm. She will embed a nano-chip that communicates with the cap. Inserting it will not hurt. Have you had chips or devices implanted before?"

Balil pulled his arm back before Electra could grab it and sneered before saying,

"You're lying. Chip and device implants hurt."

"You have no other option. Give her your arm."

He did, and after Electra inserted the chip, Indira continued the training.

"I told you it wouldn't hurt. But now that it's in, it will if you do not do exactly what I want when I tell you. The chip communicates with the cap, which communicates with your brain. The chip also communicates simultaneously via the electromagnetic field to a device Electra will now show you."

Electra said,

"This is Indira's Advanced Brain Probe; it's even better than the one NASA used on the Mission to Mars. Indira can control the level of pain it delivers."

Electra's words stopped abruptly. Balil had no time to protest because Indira's ominous voice spoke.

"I shall demonstrate."

A moment later, Bilal started howling like someone was squeezing his gonads in the jagged jaws of an iron vice. Indira stopped the demonstration before he fainted. She talked again when he had recovered enough.

"After unloading the drums, you will then take the female and her partner to a computer workstation for them to make adjustments. They are armed and dangerous, so you must do what they say. Do you understand?"

Indira continued after several vigorous nods.

"And when they have completed their adjustments, you will take them back to the van and drive them away, drop them off where they tell you, give them the electrode cap, and then drive the van back to work."

Indira paused five seconds before saying more.

"Now pay close attention to my penultimate words. If anyone interrupts before, during, or after you drop them off, I will detonate the chip in your arm. The male and female riding with you can do it too. Look to where Minato is now pointing and I will demonstrate."

All eyes focused on a mannequin dressed like Bilal standing ten feet away just in time to see its arm blow off.

By this time, Bilal and Alonzo wore looks of horror.

Indira had more to say.

"But I have good news for you. If you follow all the instructions, I will contact you on your cell phone when you have returned to work so I can tell you how much money Minato will send you. Do you understand everything I have told you?"

After more emphatic nods, Indira said,

"That is all. Do you have any questions?"

Bilal's sideways nods said no, but one person did. Electra spoke.

"Here's the question you should have asked—what do I do about the embedded chip?"

Indira answered.

"Do nothing. I will deactivate it after I contact you. Your training is complete. Follow Minato's commands."

Electra closed the laptop; everyone waited for Minato to speak.

"Hokay all, we get ready to leave at 10 p.m. tonight. Bilal working graveyard shift. He and his two riders stay here in van for more preparations. Other people, please go to observation place."

After exiting the van and walking away, Alonzo had recovered enough of his voice.

"Jeez, talk about being heartless, that Indira sounds inhuman. How can you possibly work with her?"

Electra grabbed his arm while slowing to a stop and said,

"Hold on, think about your Navy SEAL-type interrogators. Don't they talk tough and sometimes torture enemies they've captured? Indira's just playing that kind of role. And she's much different in others."

After chewing his lower lip, Alonzo said,

"Maybe you're right; anyway, where's our observation place?"

"We'll watch on my laptop while sitting in the SUV. We might as well go there now. It's the most comfortable place we've got."

She and Alonzo spent the remaining time sitting there until just before ten, when Minato tapped on the window, which was their signal to come to Bilal's van for a last-minute inspection. It was poised at the building's exit, and she spoke as soon as Electra and Alonzo reached it.

"Everyone in and ready. They drive away when I give signal."

Electra and Alonzo peered in. Electra looked satisfied, but not Alonzo.

"I see only Bilal and Robin. Where the Hell's Matt?"

"You no worry; he in there."

Minato's arm signal looked like that of a team leader in a Hollywood movie giving the go command. Bilal and Robin saw it; the van sped into the darkness.

Alonzo's anxiety built along with his excitement as he and Electra watched phase three unfold, causing him to say,

"According to what Bilal told Minato, guards usually drive alone. What's he gonna do if the gatekeeper asks about Robin?"

"He'll say she works for the Fluorinert company and is going to test what's currently circulating in the cooling system."

"But he might get suspicious when he sees Matt. And What adjustments are they gonna make?"

"Don't get ahead of the story. You'll see soon enough."

The entrance guard must have recognized Bilal because he waved the van into the warehouse. Alonzo marveled,

"I gotta hand it to that Indira. It's like we're watching an action-adventure movie starring the A-Team."

And the action accelerated as soon as Bilal parked the van. He and robin removed the barrels from the van, took off their tops, and poured the contents of the first one down the drain. Alonzo yelled when they did the same for the second.

"Holy Jesus, Matt just got dumped out, and he's buck naked."

Alonzo stopped speaking and peered even deeper into the laptop. He could see and hear everything.

Keeping her gun always aimed at Bilal, Robin handed Matt a towel and uniform. Minutes later, he looked like a typical guard. Robin gave him another gun that he checked for ammo before releasing the safety and pointing at Bilal while walking just close enough before saying,

"Please take us to a computer workstation for Robin to make adjustments."

Electra felt as spellbound as Alonzo looked. The duo watched as the trio moved with weapons concealed and encountered no one. Robin sat at the workstation as soon as Bilal found one, and she inserted what could only be a mega-memory data stick.

Her fingers flew over the keyboard while her eyes watched lines of output scroll down the workstation's monitor. Fifteen minutes later, she removed the data stick.

"Adjustments completed. We can go now."

The trio took the same path back to the van, but the seating arrangement was now different. Robin would do the driving with Matt sitting behind and pointing his gun at Bilal, who would be sitting next to him.

But the action took an unexpected turn when Robin started driving away. Two guards were yelling while running after the van. Matt studied the situation before speaking matter-of-factly.

"They must concerned about the empty barrels. Bilal, give me the electrode cap and then lie flat. Robin, take evasive action when I give the command. And Bilal, if we encounter an impediment Robin and I can't handle, I will tell you to get out and run to a safe place."

Robin searched for an escape route as she snaked through the warehouse parking area, but when Matt saw too many pursuers he yelled,

"Drive out the way we came in."

Squealing tires drowned out the pursuers' shouts; the sound alerted the gatekeeper who tried to shut it, but he was too slow. Robin blasted through the barrier and swerved onto the street fronting the building.

Traffic matched the time, zero dark-thirty, but the wail of sirens coming from front and back told her to take evasive action, so she twisted and turned the best she could. The van had no GPS screen and even if it did, she didn't know the local roads.

Robin slammed the brakes at the best place for Matt to holler.

"Bilal, get out and run to a safe place."

Bilal sprang from the floor and hugged Matt, giving quick kisses on both cheeks before panting out his final words.

"Ma'a as-salaame," before diving out and vanishing into the night. Matt moved into the passenger seat and after both of them looked and listened for enough seconds before asking the obvious.

"What is our best option for this contingency?"

"I know where to go for it, and we know what to do when I stop."

Robin drove the shortest route back to the computer center's main entrance and then rammed all the way through its lobby. The van finally hung up when driving into a floor-to-ceiling rack of network servers; all came crashing down.

Electra and Alonzo watched Matt hug Robin. Then Robin said,

"Perhaps I will see you again. Now, let's each activate the two buttons, according to Indira's option for our contingency."

Not even Electra knew the details buried that deep into the plan. She and Alonzo could do nothing but gasp when they witnessed what could only be a blinding, thundering explosion. The screen went dead a millisecond later.

Even Electra went numb, but Alonzo, sensing that Electra was beginning to seizure up, shook her shoulders until her eyes came back and he yelled,

"What happened? What's next?"

"Indira will tell us after we complete phase four."

"Jeez, what's phase four?"

"We sleep on the A-Team flights all the way back to Washington. Minato has all the details. You're my Coordinator, so find her. I'm departing now by going to sleep. Wake me when we get back to DC."

Electra withdrew into her fortress of solitude. Alonzo helped Minato arrange the return flights, then did his best to watch over Electra all the way home.

Chapter 26
March 2171

"The Cyber-T Empire Strikes Back"

Electra used the twelve-hour trip to rest after the expedition's physical exertion, recover from the stress that almost triggered another seizure, and review the attack on the computer center; she would then hold a one-on-one conversation with Indira at her home office after settling back in, which she did by taking an abbreviated workout and then having her standard breakfast.

Sitting in front of her workstation, Electra invoked Indira's GUI. Its avatar appeared seconds later, waiting for Electra to speak.

"As you can see, I'm back and ready for more action, but in order to do so, I need you to tell me what went right and what went wrong, and I promise not to interrupt unless you want me to comment."

"Excellent, so I shall begin with what went right. First, you have the blend of Alonzo's logistics and security with your androids and the Japanese A-Team's experience. Second, you have confirmed that our Subterranean Fortress remains a valuable, multi-purpose asset. Third, we have seen that Alonzo needs more experience before you reveal more details about it, and more guidance from you for planning and execution. Would you care to comment?"

"You covered what I had come up with. I can't think of anything to add. What about what went wrong?"

"First, no matter how thoroughly mere mortals plan, they will never have all contingency options accounted for, and second, their emotions will always intrude. Witness Alonzo's performance. Even with your guidance, his contingency planning was incomplete. He did not account for the androids' failure to hide the empty drums, and during the escape, he did nothing but gape when the androids blew up themselves and the van. Note that by doing so, they eliminated all evidence of what happened. Do you wish to add anything?"

"No, but I deserve some of the blame regarding incomplete contingency planning. And if you knew ahead of time it was, why didn't you tell me?"

"Remember what you already know. Perfect practice makes perfect. If I tell you everything, you won't improve."

"OK, is that it for what went wrong?"

"Yes, but let me move to what we learned. What would you like to point out?"

"Well, I guess you're able to uncover who and where the bad guys are when they use Cyberspace."

"Indeed yes, and I will always share that with you when you need to know. What else?"

Electra thought long enough to find nothing.

"I don't know; please tell me."

"Note the sophistication of my android software. Robin and Matt performed admirably, even sparing the life of Bilal, and when I rebuild them, I will load accumulated memory so, as Robin wished, they shall meet again."

"Gads, at this rate, people won't be needed in the future if we ever share your Aphrodite software. But I doubt that's your intention. It certainly isn't mine."

"Correct, and let me add a final piece of learning. Humans, even though merely mortal, will still be needed until AI software can transcend cognition's self-awareness to reach intuition and creativity. Even I cannot predict when Aphrodite will achieve that evolutionary break-through."

Electra's sagging body language said she needed a break.

"I'm reaching my information overload point; I hope that's all."

"One final point. You should attend the International AI Developers Conference on Security. Google it for all the details. And contact me if you need assistance. Bye-bye until next time."

Electra started working on the follow-up as soon as Indira's avatar disappeared. She had all the conference details, so she called Alonzo three hours later, but when he didn't answer, she called Monet rather than leave a voice message.

Monet answered, sounding pleased, once she recognized the voice.

"You certainly have boundless energy. Alonzo tumbled into bed when arriving home and is still asleep. What is the message?"

"I'm attending the International AI Developers Conference on Security in London. It's a three-day affair starting Wednesday, March 20th, at the QEII Conference Centre. I'm going to bring Renee with me, so please have him book commercial flights that get us there the day before, and take us back to DC the following Sunday. And I'd like to stay at the Zedwell Picadilly Circus Hotel, so have him book a double room. He should have no trouble doing this within the next two weeks. Did you get all that?"

Electra waited for Monet to repeat it, and then said,

"You have a splendid memory. That's why you're so good at your job. And please tell him to call me later this week; bye-bye."

Electra ended the call and then placed one to Renee, who recognized the voice. After a happy greeting, Electra said,

"I just got back and am busy handling all the follow-up, so I'll call in a day or two to meet with you and China, but I wanted to tell you that I'm taking you to London for an AI Developers Conference, and why don't you do this? You've never been there, so please prepare an agenda for some sightseeing we'll do the day after it ends."

"OK. Who'll be with us?"

"Just us. We'll be AOK by ourselves. How's your project work going?"

"OK for me and China. Can we tell you more when you call us back?"

"Sounds to me like a good plan. Bye for now."

Electra sat back after she ended the call, hoping to keep her obsessive-compulsive urge under control.

I know what to do next, but I'll decompress by getting a snack. Then I'll come back and do it.

Electra returned fifteen minutes later, bringing a fresh can of Coke and diving in precisely where she left off.

Thinking about London reminds me of my only living relative, Uncle Chandra, whom I met on two trips to London three lifetimes ago. He's my birth mother's brother; he took care of his parents until they died from Techno-Plague complications. If he's still alive, I'll have to find a reason for visiting, one that'll make no connection to the first me. I'll surf the Net to see if he's still among the living.

Twenty minutes and several obituaries later, she had the answer.

Aw, he died three years ago, but at least from old age, and the photos show he looked so, so old; that doesn't surprise me. He lacked Indira's level of fitness and energy. And all the changes in AI Robo-banking and investment services forced him into early retirement. That trend's going to accelerate. I'm ahead of it, but I feel sorry for those who aren't. Oh, well, I'll put that thought away for another day and return to my high-priority projects.

Electra kept working on them and made a note to ask Indira about two business ventures that she had been running for years. But an early Friday evening news announcement preempted everything she had been thinking about. The reporter's words focused her attention.

"And after nearly a week of intensive hunting, Isilabad has found no hints regarding who or why someone blew up one of its computer centers. They claim America or one of its proxies did it, and they will seek revenge when they know who the identity. And who knows? Maybe they will plant fake evidence to justify striking back. Everyone should stay alert and stay tuned."

Electra turned off the news and made an announcement to herself.

I always do both, and I'll call Alonzo before I tune out by hitting the sack.

Alonzo must have heard a similar story because he launched into it as soon she answered. She let him talk long enough to get near the end of his pent-up words before taking a different point of view.

"Nothing mentioned about Bilal. Perhaps you did save his life."

The thought must have surprised him. He didn't respond for ten seconds.

"How can we find out?"

"I'll ask Indira; she'll know if he cashes the money order."

"I hope he does. He coulda caused big problems if he didn't help us during the getaway."

"You're right, and speaking of help, are you copacetic for making my London trip arrangements?"

"Yeah, but do you think you might need someone coming along for security?"

"I thought about it, but no."

"How come?"

"Although the Cyberterrorists caused enough damage by blocking the canals, they would have sunk the ships if they could have, and that tells me the smart companies have Cyber-defense software better than theirs. And the news report said Isilabad hasn't a clue who attacked their computer center, so we're in the clear."

Alonzo sounded calmer.

"I'm sure glad I'm working for you, and maybe Indira too. I'm beginning to think she's OK. And I've always known you are."

"Me too, you too. I'll call when I get back from London. Bye for now."

Electra called Eve a week before leaving, but when she heard Eve's recording telling callers where she would be and how to reach her, she left a message saying she'd call back when she returned from the London Conference. Then she recorded a similar message for callers to all her numbers.

Alonzo's thoughtful generosity showed when he called the night before and offered to drive the "Boss" and her "Numero Uno" researcher to the airport. His humor continued all the way to the terminal.

"Did Electra give you a pre-trip assignment?"

"I had to prepare a sight-seeing list."

"Well, you better avoid London Bridges if they start falling down because I won't be there to dig you out."

Renee fought back laughing for too long by thinking up a worthy reply.

"My list is so long we might never get there."

"What's your favorite?"

"Make a guess."

Time ran out and Renee wouldn't tell unless he promised pick them up when returning. He did, so she said,

"It's the London Tube, or Underground. I'll tell you all about it when we get back."

Renee became positively chatty during the seven-hour flight when she described the city's world-renown sights on her list. Electra had a suggestion.

"We need to choose the ones we can handle in one day, so let's pick some of your favorites and make the Tube our last stop."

"OK, and do you know the Tube's the world's first underground train? Construction started in about 1830?"

"I didn't, but now I do. What else can you tell me abou it?"

"It's made up of eleven different lines all connected, and it's got over 230 stations. On the map I looked at, each line has a different color and fun-sounding name, like Bakerloo or Picadilly. And the station names come from some landmarks or buildings nearby, like Saint Paul's or Notting Hill Gate. I bet we can get a map at the hotel."

"I'm certain we can because it has a Tube entrance. What else have you learned about it?"

"Well it's deep, and in World War II during the Blitz bombing, about a hundred-and-twenty-five-thousand people used it as an air raid shelter. And since then, it's bigger, more modern, computer-controlled, and ridden by about a million people each day."

"And we'll be two more on Saturday. I'm counting on you to get us a map so we know how to get in and out…"

Electra planned to keep Renee by her side during the conference; she wanted her to see and hear as much as she could, so she sat them near the front of the auditorium for the keynote speaker's welcoming remarks, which blindsided her when he said,

"And among our security software practitioners attending our conference is someone you might have seen or heard on the Telly during NASA's Mars Mission, Electra Kirchner. If she's in the audience, I would like her to stand."

Though inwardly uncomfortable, she played Alisha's extrovert game, bringing Renee with her. When one of the officials spotted her, he rushed for a spontaneous interview.

"Welcome, Ms. Kirchner, to our conference. May I ask who is with you?"

"My number one research assistant, Renee."

"And what are your intentions?"

"To learn about the latest advances in security software, the best implementation protocols, and what future releases will protect us from."

"You've come to the right place. And you, young lady, will you and Ms. Kirchner make time to enjoy some of London's tourist attractions?"

"Uh, I want to ride the Tube, which should be easy because our hotel has a connection."

"Aha, you must be staying at the Zedwell. Well enjoy all you can, and thank you for talking with me."

Electra tried to blend in with the attendees, but she couldn't for the first day because she and Renee made a distinctive pair. However, she did for the remainder of the conference because fame is fleeting and novelty always wears off, especially for this audience.

Saturday brought the start of Renee's sightseeing tour that began at nine a.m. Electra had already given her high marks for her tour mapping method.

It would begin at Picadilly Station and stay on its line, visiting Renee's picks along it and then doubling back for another line to repeat her procedure. Electra made the opening remarks soon after Renee guided them to the Underground entrance.

"London weathercasters say climate change is making the place warmer in the spring and damper too. We'll have to do more riding than walking. I'm so glad you picked sights that the Tube makes so easy to see."

Spring conspired with Saturday weather to make Renee's schedule work even better. Early spring traditionally has fewer tourists, and today's rain discouraged those in town, which meant Electra and Renee had faster access to coveted tourist spots. By mid-afternoon, having already visited Westminster Abbey, Charing Cross, and Oxford Circus, they were on their way to London Bridge when the train they were riding began behaving erratically. Electra saw it all from her front-row seat in the first car.

The train slowed down and sped up, and the lights started flickering. Then the car went dark, and the train slammed its brakes between stations, coming to a jarring stop and flapping its doors open and closed. The train then sped in reverse, racing through one station and then repeating the performance.

Electra used both arms to clutch Renee and a support pole to keep from getting thrown into the aisle or bounced out of the car. The back-and-forth action continued enough times for a terrifying thought to flash in her lightning brain.

Has our train been hijacked? Are Cyberterrorists in charge of the entire Tube?

No more thoughts came. Electra's instincts took over as soon as she saw the lights of another train bound for an immanent collision into where she and Renee were clinging.

She ran like a SWAT teamer to a flapping door, trying to stay vertical while still wrapping Renee in her arms; she timed the leap to safety and made it as her car zoomed full speed into the station. Enough luck was with her; rain and dampness cushioned her crash landing on the marble floor, but she slid headfirst into a pillar just after she heard the frightening sound of the front cars colliding.

Electra's world went black for an unknown number of seconds until Renee pulled her up. The duo staggered through the twisted remains of cars littering the smoke-filled station. Renee found an exit and they ran to street-level safety. Electra flagged down a cab as soon as they got there; she and Renee escaped to the shelter of their hotel.

Neither Electra nor Renee suffered serious damage during the crash, and they told no one they had been in the Tube collision, which all the Telly channels hyped that night.

Renee liked all the announcers; she thought their distinctive accents sounded smart.

Electra picked one on Saturday's late evening news that had a half-hour special report given by an anchor whose words enthralled both of them.

"Even though some passengers on cars closest to impact suffered grave injuries, how fortunate only two trains suffered from what might have been caused by a control computer's software malfunction, or possibly from human error. Officials from the Greater London Authority's TfL told reporters it is too soon to place the blame on man or machine, or whether it might have been simply bad luck or, more ominously, another sign of ongoing terrorism. They also said time might reveal the truth, but then again it might not because today's Cyberworld makes some truths easier to understand, and others harder. Regardless, we shall bring you more facts tomorrow."

Renee's arms and words hugged Electra before going to bed.

"You saved both of us from bad injuries; do you think bad luck or bad men caused the collision? Isn't the security software the conference talked about supposed to keep bad people from becoming Cyberterrorists?"

"It's supposed to, but nothing's perfect. And there's an ongoing arms race in Cyberspace. Cybersecurity companies, like those who attended the conference, are always improving their software.

"But as soon as they do, Cyberterrorists find holes or build trapdoors they use to extort money, corrupt data and software, plant viruses, make fake news, and even blowup hardware. I'm sorry to say the world is not always a kind and gentle place. But you and I are doing our best, so let's not worry about it for the time being. Are you ready to go to bed so we can get up and pack, then catch our flight home?"

"I sure am."

"Good, goodnight, and sleep tight. And when we get to Washington, be ready to tell Alonzo a jolting story."

Electra did likewise until troubling thoughts streamed into her brain. She bolted upright in the middle of the night.

Gads, here's another possible cause for the Tube collision. Is someone or some organization using AI-empowered software to target me? Are they using 3-D surveillance and boots on the ground to hunt me down?

Did I or someone on my team accidentally leak information during our Isilabad attack that could have revealed my London whereabouts? Could there have been hidden chips, body cams, or surveillance hardware in places we forgot to check?

Like where? Maybe in Balil's van? Maybe in him? Maybe in the A-Team's covert location?

I run the risk of adding paranoia to my list of worrisome predispositions if I keep thinking like this. And if I can't stop, I'll need to talk to my singular counselor when I get back to DC. But until then, I'll try to keep those thoughts away from me.

Electra did that through the night, as well as on the next day's flight.

Chapter 27
April 2171

"Storms Forming"

Electra's paranoia dissipated enough not to be a topic for Indira, but she did want Indira's thoughts regarding the Tube collision. Indira started speaking after listening to Electra's imaginative conjectures.

"Yes, what you propose is reasonable but unprovable because we have no data for probability correlation calculations unless we hold another attack that will support a Bayesian analysis or find suspects to interrogate. I recommend neither. You cannot risk another trip to Isilabad."

"So, I guess the best I can do is redouble my contingency planning and always have you or Christi or Renee nearby in case I need more help."

"Correct, and you shouldn't need many contingencies for your upcoming trip to NASA. It is already using my advanced Aphrodite security app."

"I agree; that's why I'm going to bring only Renee. And I already know the agenda when meeting with Britt and Boomer, and if Zoltan shows up, I have a contingency."

"Excellent, but I have something new for you that will modify your agenda. I have completed my analysis of core samples from Mars and the organic scrapings you brought back from the Danakil Depression. I used my DNA Simulation Accelerator software to conclude there is a high probability that the organic fragments found in both came from a carbon-based substrate."

Indira paused for the news to sink in. Electra's expression matched the words that exploded out seconds later.

"Gads, you mean once upon a time there was life on Mars? And if so, it might still be there?"

"Yes, and I have more. Both samples match the DNA segments found in cephalopods better than segments found in humans. The squid research you did several years ago with Jonathan is relevant. So, how might knowing this impact the meeting agenda?"

"I'll play even dumber when they ask me about what I've learned from the Martian core samples. And I can cover this by giving them items that will keep them happy."

"Excellent. Please contact me when you return, and keep working on my high-priority projects until you do."

Indira's avatar vanished from view; Electra stayed at her office to follow through.

She waited a day before calling Renee, which gave her more time to settle into her usual routine as well as keep her obsessive-compulsive predisposition under control. After exchanging greetings, Electra shifted subjects.

"I want to remind you that we'll be flying to Houston on Sunday morning, April 14th, because I got an Email from Britt confirming the schedule. I'll show it to you during the flight. If there's something you'd like to add, we can add it to the Monday morning piece."

"I'll think about it. Is there anything I need to do before we leave?"

Electra's playful tone colored what she said next.

"Of course, there is. Just keep doing what you're doing the way you know best. And please tell China the same. I'll stop by sometime before we leave. See you soon."

Electra's schedule filled so fast she had to replace the meeting with her two researchers with one that would include two of her clone daughters. Eve invited her to have dinner at Nari's holistic café, and it turned out to be the most satisfying one of the year.

Eve and Nari hustled to the counter located just inside the entrance as soon as they spotted her. This would be Electra's first visit to The Youthful You Studio, the innovative business she had financed for them.

Eve conducted a tour of the Holistic Fitness Center area and after that, Nari served dinner at the adjoining Holistic Café. Electra could tell from her daughters' enthusiasm plus the activity in both studio areas that her investment was paying off emotionally as well as financially. Eve hugged her when leaving; Nari promised to have Alonzo join them the next time.

Electra couldn't recall the last time she felt so at ease on a flight, and after showing Renee the NASA schedule, it made the conversation flow even better.

"Is there a topic you'd like Britt to add?"

"You know, everyone talks like the solar system has always looked like it does, but how did it get that way. You know, how did it evolve to what it is?"

"That's a great question we'll let her answer, but let me give you a review of what we talked about a while ago. What do you think I'm referring to?"

Renee questioning look changed moments later.

"It's gotta be how did the Universe evolve. It came before our solar system."

"You're right, and here's enough of a summary to last a long time; everything else is only fanciful high-energy and quantum physics mathematical guesswork.

"The Universe exploded 13.6 billion years ago, like a Big Bang from a point containing all matter. And as the blast expanded, matter in the form of the tiniest particles called quarks began forming protons and electrons, and they started forming hydrogen and deuterium atoms.

"And then all these forms of matter began clumping together into huge groups called galaxies and smaller groups inside called nebula clusters. Gravity caused the clusters, and then it compressed the clusters into proto-stars. As the proto-stars collapsed, gravity caused pressure at the center to start a self-sustaining chain reaction called fission that turns deuterium and tritium into helium, which releases enormous amounts of energy.

"And when this occurs, the proto-star is now called a star, and a series of chain reactions continue inside, eventually creating all the elements the star emits. We call them cosmic rays when they're traveling through space, and gravity causes them to begin clumping together.

"And these clumps became planets and moons and asteroids and comets, anything you can see moving through space. And that's the end of my story. You can ask Britt to pick up where mine ends."

Renee said she would.

Britt ran the 8 a.m. Monday meeting that began without Zoltan, and when she said he and the Director would join sometime later, everyone's mood brightened because the morning session would be pleasant; smiles at the conference room table told her to keep talking.

"Let me highlight the list of topics we'll cover at other meetings this week. Of course, at the top will be what we learned on our Mars Mission.

"And then comes what we can do here on Earth. Then comes the next Mission to Mars. This should be more than enough to get us to Thursday, when Electra and Renee fly back to DC. Any questions?"

Electra asked one for which Britt already knew was coming.

"Renee asked me to explain how our solar system formed. Would you like to give her a brief explanation?"

"I can talk us through it. I won't make or hand out diagrams, but I'll go slow enough for her to jot down what she wants. Renee, please let me know when you're ready."

Renee arranged her pen and notepad, and after glancing at Electra said,

"Commander Starling, I'm all set."

"I think you'll like my explanation. It doesn't need any of that cosmological or quantum mechanical jargon because I use only the force of gravity and Newton's laws to put our solar system together. But first, I'll describe what our 4.6 billion years-old solar system looks like today.

"It consists of eight planets orbiting in about the same plane around our Sun. The inner four inner are called terrestrial planets because they have a rocky surface and molten interior. You know their names, listed from closest to farthest–Mercury, Venus, Earth, and Mars. The outer four are called gas or ice giants–Jupiter, Saturn, Uranus, and Neptune. Six planets have at least one moon, and all have magnetic fields extending from one pole to the other. Those on Venus and Mars are the weakest.

"Our solar system also has three disks containing tiny bits of rocky material and are centered at the sun. The inner one is called the Kuiper Belt, the middle one is the Scattered Disk, and outer one is the Ort Cloud, which extends far beyond Neptune.

"And now, I'm ready to describe the Nebular Cloud Hypothesis for solar system creation. Some event occurred that caused our Sun's nebular cloud to star rotating, and the rotation spun off rotating pieces of itself. These pieces eventually condensed into planets and moons.

"And then, some event on each planet triggered chemical reactions that created water and mineral deposits. And then, some event on Earth triggered more chemical reactions that created carbon compounds that eventually were used in more organic chemical reactions that created life. And that ends my story, but let me mention something about the science that supports it.

"Cosmologists develop the science supporting how the Universe started. Astronomers Astro-Geologists do the same for the solar system, including its planets and moons. And now comes the solar engineering piece. How did all the planets get placed where they are? Any suggestions?"

At first, the question stumped even Electra, but after a minute, she offered some.

"That's a tuffy. I can think of many, and here's the kicker. Unlike for the Universe, which uses fanciful science and math to invent unobservable quark particles and some make-believe unobservable forces, we can actually see all the solar system's planets and moons, and there are only two observable force fields that can cause planets and moons to move–gravitational and electromagnetic. It will take clever engineering to put the planets in motion orbiting the Sun. And that's as far as I'm willing to go. You tell us the rest."

Britt nodded before saying,

"That's my limit. If Renee wants more, I'll let Boomer explain."

Renee looked ready to defend Electra when she said,

"No, that's plenty for me, and I need Electra to go over again what you just did."

"Well then, everyone, including me, deserves a break. Let's go get some snacks."

Boomer looked the happiest as he and Renee escaped to the cafeteria while Electra and Britt followed at a more conversational pace.

No one but these four attended the afternoon session. Boomer led a roundtable discussion that skirmished with the NASA projects that the next three days would explore further.

Bringing the Director and three engineers with, Zoltan took control of the second day's meetings before Britt had said one word. Electra listened attentively for the entire day, setting an example for Renee, but her mind wandered midway through the afternoon. The pattern repeated itself for the third and fourth, but Zoltan brought in different engineers each day. Electra's mind started wandering sooner and further at each meeting. She became so bored by early Thursday afternoon that she started talking to Alisha while tuning out whoever was speaking, and Alisha's fun-loving wits perked her up.

"Honestly, Electra, I could never sit through so many dull discussions. These propellor heads show so many numbers in their equation-loaded handouts they must be approaching the first order of infinity."

"I have to agree. My brain would be seizing up if I didn't have you to get me through. I'll be so happy when Zoltan gives his wrap-up. Maybe you can do something to help me celebrate."

"If you let me, I'll do a moon-walk on the conference table, or maybe couch dance in front of Zoltan to see if he ever looks at anything other than NASA or DOD stuff, but I know you need to maintain your unblemished professional image, so I'll find something afterward that fits our personal world. See you later."

Electra snapped back to reality when Zoltan stood to make his closing remarks.

"We have a plethora of projects lined up to get our second Mars Mission off the ground. They're all important, but among those near the top, Kirchner has to upgrade the Aphrodite control software for the Astro-Androids that will be on the next flight, and she'll assist Starling complete core sample analysis for signs of Martian life. And she'll have to coordinate additional clinicals for the immune system boost drug that her partners have developed."

Zoltan scanned his worn-out audience while pausing to add more importance to his pronouncements before droning on.

"And we've got projects that will contribute to ameliorating climate change. Doing that will keep storms from forming. We will adapt the Aphrodite software for UAV control and ocean floor surveillance, and we will improve atmospheric monitoring via upgraded Aphrodite software for satellite as well as air and underwater drone transmission and control that will assist our undersea explorers, our next generation of robots and Aquanauts, who will hunt for life-creating hydrothermal vents and test our ocean floor mining equipment. There will be no need to harvest rare earths and other materials from asteroids or neighboring planets, for the ocean floor is our metaphorical goldmine.

"And finally, we brainstormed projects for our next target after Mars, which will be Venus. We want to build a manned space station orbiting Venus that will support a Venetian colony floating like a cluster of enormous dirigibles in its atmosphere. We have plenty of projects for Starling and Gowon to coordinate, so let's get to it. Meeting adjourned."

Electra used her return flight to dodge any post-meeting mingling. She and Renee hustled to the airport, and three hours later, when the plane reached cruising altitude, she filed the week's meetings away and answered whatever questions Renee had before talking to Alisha the rest of the way home.

How nice Alisha is always with me. I'm never alone, and she always gives me a different point of view for looking at whatever awaits in Cyber or 3-D space. And I'll ask for Indira's point of view in a day or two. If I get stuck in any storms forming, she'll know what to do.

Chapter 28
May 2171

"West Wing Has Fallen"

Although Electra had plenty of NASA issues to think about when she awoke the next morning, she lacked her usual enthusiasm for diving into projects, so she questioned herself instead.

I must still be feeling the effects of all those boring meetings I had to force myself to sit through. Yesterday afternoon was the worst. Zoltan's wrap-up is still stressing me out.

Perhaps that's why I woke up with headache and tired, twitchy legs unwilling to go for a run. I've got so much to do on the projects he's stressing and so little enthusiasm for starting. And I don't trust him. Britt and Boomer feel the same way. He's hiding something but they haven't discovered what it is. Well, something will eventually happen that'll reveal it.

Lying in bed won't make me feel any better. I'll force myself to run, but I'll cut the distance in half.

Electra felt better afterward but not good enough to work on projects, so she contacted Indira, who spoke as soon as her avatar appeared.

"There's no need for you to recap the meeting. I observed from the Cyberspace shadows. You must move beyond the notion that Zoltan controls the work you do. Your lightning brain is in control."

"But I'm losing interest in all the rational thinking and mathematical rigor required. I'll need you to keep doing all the hard work so I can keep NASA happy."

"Of course, I will. And why don't you find other pursuits that will reignite your enthusiasm? Not today, mind you, but during the coming weeks. Let your Alisha alter ego do more in the creative realm."

"I will, and I thank you for your counseling. I always feel better after our sessions."

"I am always here. Now, go make the most of today."

Indira's avatar departed.

Electra felt good enough to visit her researchers the next morning. Renee didn't need her help, so she spent most of the time listening to China describe the problems.

"Even after months of searching for the remotest Kinsler-Bigger Bro link, I have nothing. And ever since the Senate dropped the threat of impeaching him, media coverage that would help me has dried up."

"I've found nothing either, so put it on the back burner and focus on other issues. What's happening on the NAIA initiative?"

"Feather and Congressman Chaska are making headway. I talk to him every week. And he's a valuable contact for hearing about Capitol Hill concerns before they're leaked to the media."

"What are the latest?"

"Congress won't add anything to its list of Kinslinger Administration's domestic failures, but it will for his mishandling of international affairs. Many on the Hill say he falls down when trying to stand up to China. They're worried about China's rearming North Korea and putting more military bases on the artificial islands it's building in the South China Sea.

"And they're afraid that even the new chairman of the Joint Chiefs of Staff will have trouble keeping the military in Kinslinger's corner."

"Well, I'll add them to my list. Please let me know as soon as you hear other rumors. And as an incentive for you and Renee to keep working, I'll take you out to lunch if today's OK."

China replied,

"It's more than OK. Today I can say TGIF."

Electra returned to her office afterward and did her best to restart working, and she did so for the remainder of the day. China and Renee did likewise.

General Goodman never said TGIF because he treated every day the same. But he knew this Friday would be singular. He was about to launch a late-night special meeting at the Pentagon attended by only the Joint Chiefs of Staff and one other person, Zoltan Sultani.

Standing at the head of the conference table, Horatio's impressive stature commanded attention, as did his words.

"Each of you has ordered key personnel to await your call as soon we know the strike has achieved its objectives. Zoltan, tell us about the strike."

He spoke while sitting at the foot of the table.

"My DOD technicians have just confirmed the SPG satellite is fully charged and operational. I will order the strike when you give the command."

"Everyone, synchronize watches and sit with me as the clock marches to strike time."

The General sat and waited for his countdown to begin.

The incessant chiming of her cell phone roused Electra from a troubled sleep, but she snapped to attention when her eyes began to focus.

Gads, it's 2 a.m. Why is China calling?

"China, it's Electra. Why are you calling?"

"Turn on the news and call me back."

"OK, but give me time to absorb it. Bye."

Electra hurried to her workstation and then turned on her computer and nearby big-screen TV, switching stations until finding a 24/7 news channel. What she began seeing and hearing froze her.

"As the video footage shows, the West Wing of the Whitehouse is ablaze. Fire trucks and crew are struggling to keep the flames from spreading. We do not know who inside may have been injured because we have been unable to contact anyone who might know. Please stay tuned."

Electra did that and more by calling China, who answered after the first ring.

"You and Renee get dressed. I'm coming over."

Electra's headache had faded by the time she charged into her house. Renee and China were waiting just inside the front door for Electra to say something.

"We'll drive to the White House and see for ourselves. Let's go."

Electra parked as close as the police and White House Security would allow, then pushed through a gathering crowd to get to the fence. Electra spoke only to herself.

It's for real and looks like it's getting worse. We'll learn more by watching the news updates. I'll drop China off at the house and then take Renee to my office.

Then she said the same to her researchers before pushing back to her SUV and driving away.

Electra's headache came back, but she ignored it, concentrating instead on Renee and turning on her workstation computer and nearby TV.

They sat in front while Electra invoked Indira's GUI.

Indira waited for Electra to talk.

"I'm sure you know what just happened. No word yet on Kinslinger. What do you think?"

Indira didn't have to answer. The news anchor gave it.

"It has now been confirmed that President Kinslinger is dead, but nothing's been said regarding the cause… hold on… let me connect you to a feed coming in from the Pentagon."

Another window opened. Electra's brain started racing when she saw the new speaker.

"My name is Zoltan Sultani. Unknown terrorists have just attacked the United States by blowing up the West Wing. President Kinslinger perished in the fire.

"This attack puts our nation on a war footing, best handled by the Military. Until further notice, the Joint Chiefs are in control."

Zoltan's screen disappeared, leaving only that of the baffled anchor.

Electra turned off the TV and faced Renee, ready to say something but she couldn't. Words froze in her throat; her trance-like stare showed she could neither see nor hear.

Electra struggled to stand, but her knees buckled, and she collapsed. Renee caught her and then screamed,

"Electra, what's wrong? What should I do?"

Commanding words came from Indira.

"Renee, Electra needs your help. Place her carefully on the carpet, then settle down, sit still, and listen to me…"

THE END

www.ingramcontent.com/pod-product-compliance
Lightning Source LLC
Chambersburg PA
CBHW030814210726
48290CB00002B/575